CIARÁN McMENAMIN

Ciarán McMenamin was born in Enniskillen, County Fermanagh, in 1975. A graduate of the RSAMD, he has worked for the past twenty years as an actor in film, television and theatre. His acclaimed first novel, *Skintown*, was a WHSmith Fresh talent pick. He lives between London and County Sligo.

ALSO BY CIARÁN McMENAMIN

Skintown

CIARÁN McMENAMIN

The Sunken Road

VINTAGE

1 3 5 7 9 10 8 6 4 2

Vintage is part of the Penguin Random House group of companies
whose addresses can be found at global.penguinrandomhouse.com

Copyright © Ciarán McMenamin

First published in Vintage in 2022
First published in hardback by Harvill Secker in 2021

penguin.co.uk/vintage

A CIP catalogue record for this book is available from the British Library

ISBN 9781529112221

Printed and bound in Great Britain by Clays Ltd, Elcograf S.p.A.

The authorised representative in the EEA is Penguin Random House Ireland,
Morrison Chambers, 32 Nassau Street, Dublin D02 YH68

Penguin Random House is committed to a sustainable future
for our business, our readers and our planet. This book is
made from Forest Stewardship Council® certified paper.

For Áine and Róisin

The Sunken Road

His rum is still in his mug between his feet. Francie steps forward, picks it up and hands it to him.

'I want a clear head when I go over.'

'That's the last thing you want.'

'No, Francie, I—'

'Drink it.'

He pulls him off the wall and slams the mug into his teeth, cutting his lips.

'Drink it!'

Francie shifts his grip to Archie's throat and squeezes until his mouth opens. The rum scalds its way around his tongue and along his gullet and then it is over. The others have turned their backs on the moment. The cup is hurled into the mud and Francie crouches, shaking. When he can breathe again he stretches out and grabs Archie behind the knee. Archie reaches down and raps his knuckles on the top of Francie's tin hat, then leaves his hand there so that its weight lets his mate know that they're good.

A new sound cuts through the din, and men spring to their feet and fix bayonets. It takes several seconds for them to realise that it is the sound of silence. They stare at one another and at the sky for clues, then the emptiness fills with a huge explosion and the ground ripples and someone shouts that the big mine under Hawthorn Ridge has blown, and they are rushing at last into the front trench as a bugle stutters and farts and sergeants howl and a whistle shrieks them up and over the top.

They eat in silence. Annie can't remember the last time they ate in anything else. She rearranges two cabbage leaves until they vaguely resemble the African sub-continent and ponders what a load of old bollocks that is. It's not silence, is it? Silence is silent. This is just no words. No words to hide the sound of a practically toothless fifty-year-old woman sucking her way through thick-cut slices of salty bacon. She rises before the single spud she managed to stomach can beat her to it. The guilt will follow, as she washes the dishes then waits by the fire for the kettle to boil, so she can wet the tea. *She's still your mother. You won't always have teeth yourself.* As it floods her she panics at the predictability of their patterns, ingrained over two years since her father died and took all the words with him. 'Eating in silence' my arse.

When she has climbed the ladder and settled on the corner of the barn roof, she lights her final cigarette of the day and stares west across the farm to the dregs of the sunset over the distant coast. On wet nights she used to sit below, in the corner of the loft, listening to the rain on the tin roof, but she hasn't ventured there for some time because she can't bear to see the scrapes she made in the wall when she still bothered to count the days off after the boys had left for the war, nearly six years ago. She counts her chores for the following day now instead; the tedious nightly ritual of putting

3

her boring daily schedule in order. Who shall I feed first? The pigs or the chickens, the donkeys or the cows? At least they talk to her, the animals; at least they acknowledge it when she feeds them. She stubs the cigarette on the metal roof and stands. It's been long enough. The old woman will be in bed now, and she can sit alone in the kitchen instead of sitting in that unbearable silence.

CHAPTER ONE

County Fermanagh, Northern Ireland

May 1922

It is still dark when they come. The industrial thrum of their engine reaches for miles through the morning, but by the time their wheels have caught up with the tune, Francie Leonard is gone. When he leapt fully dressed from the bed, it occurred to him that he had known they were coming. As he vaulted the gate and took off through the fields he knew that he would never be back.

By the time two constables kick the door from its hinges, their quarry lies sweating on a hillside over the farm. Their words get lost amid the drone of an atonal livestock choir but he can still follow their progress as they systematically destroy the two-acre small-holding below. A dull bellow from the Shorthorn bull is silenced by a single rifle shot, then the old Greyhound sow screeches as she struggles along the length of a steel bayonet. The intricate jigsaw of drystone walls that his father built by harnessing the raw power of a son's adolescence is shouldered and kicked back down into the dirt. He hears nothing at all from inside the house until the inspector boots his mother from her bed and stands over her, screaming while her piss runs in rivers over the lovingly scrubbed flagstone floor.

'Where's Francis, Bridget? Where's Francis? Where the fuck is Francie?'

*

Rage carries him back to the bottom of the hill before self-preservation drives him left along the riverbank away from the farm. Five hundred yards downstream, he picks up a familiar scent and follows the finger of tobacco smoke until he finds them lounging on the humpback bridge. He drops and watches the slumped shoulders of the British soldiers, kicked too early from their beds to help Irish policemen catch their number-one quarry. A Crossley Tender armoured car blocks the escape route of anyone basic enough to take flight along a road full of soldiers. On his belly along the bank, he crawls through briars and the sweet stench of wild garlic. He rolls under a hanging rock, a pool short of the old bridge. Three dung-brown uniforms bask above him in the early-morning sunlight. He takes the Mauser automatic pistol from his waistband and places it to his right, the red number nine on the handle vivid among the grey stones and the dirt.

Sitting ducks they are. Fucking peacocks perched cocky, bang in the middle of a bridge like that. Fresh off the boat these lads must be. No one suns himself on the skyline if he's ever tasted Kerry or France. Ten cartridges in the Mauser's box magazine. He will be up there finishing them off before they even know they've been shot. He listens to them gossip as he watches small fish take tiny brown flies from the surface of the water. Northern, definitely: Manchester, maybe, not enough phlegm to be Scouse. Momentarily he is transported back to the trenches.

He is, after all, lying in shite listening to Englishmen talking it. A green mayfly dun hatches through the surface filament and struggles to take flight as it is carried beyond him downstream. He follows its voyage and as it passes a large rock there is the faintest of swirls and it is sucked down into the belly of a much bigger fish. *I see you, sir. I'll be back for you another day, Mr Trout.*

The armoured lorry from his mother's farm roars on to the bridge above and the black ink of the B-Specials' uniforms pours from the back. Local Protestants, armed to the teeth by the fledgling Northern Irish state. Since the truce with the British in the South, his IRA column has been fighting these 'Special' police constables all along the new border between the two Irelands.

A voice yelling, his own name spilling over the side of the bridge. There is something comforting in the familiar edges of the Belfast accent as it bounces off hazel and birch and spits in at him under the rock. District Inspector Peter Crozier grabs hold of a constable with his right hand, hauling himself up on to the wall of the bridge. As he calls out again to the man whom he knows is listening, the left sleeve of his tunic flaps impotently by his side, missing the ballast of the arm that he forgot to bring home from Belgium.

'You're not in Kerry any more, Francie! You're in Northern Ireland now and when we catch you, I'm going to skin you alive myself.'

He can't return to check on his mother as they will be waiting for him at the farm. When their engines fade he doubles back and climbs slowly through steep woodland. He leaves the safety of the trees and holes up in a copse by the edge of a bog. Not fifty yards away is the very ditch where it all began. With his back tight into the base of the thickest hazel clump, he stares down the barrel of the only approach and relives the day when the Great War first came to Drumskinny.

He was hefting fresh-cut sods up out of a deep bed and Archie Johnston was stacking them to dry in a line along the lip. As the spade retreated for a fresh load Archie grabbed its shaft beneath the L-shaped blade and near pulled his friend up into the heather beside him.

'We should go, Francie; for the love of God, we should go.'

When the women brought the dinner from the farms below and the men sat eating among clouds of September's drunken daddy-long-legs, Archie gripped the throat of his cause and near drowned it in his tea.

'The Belgians, Francie; what about the poor Belgians?'

'Fuck the poor Belgians.'

'They're raping nuns and crucifying innocents on the doors of the barns!'

'Who told you that?'

'It's in the bloody papers!'

Francie eased his penknife's point into the skin of a blister and watched the fluid race away from the fresh welt that the spade handle had left in the middle of his palm.

'The bloody papers belong to the bloody bastards who want you to bloody bleed.'

In the evening as he stripped naked and left half the bog in the washing barrel at the back of the house, his mother came at him from the other side of the fence.

'If the Protestants need to get involved that's their business, son, but this is no war of ours.'

Everyone had accepted by then that his father was dying in the room upstairs yet no one had dared voice it. Francie knew nothing of medicine but as he watched his mother being consumed by the inevitable, he wondered if the disease took its name from its effects on the sick or on the people that it left behind.

'You can't go, Francie. You can't leave me and your sisters to work the farm ourselves.'

In the pub the following Saturday, Archie held court in the middle of the floor, fired by the thought of glory and plied with bottles of stout from those comfortable in the weight of the years that would keep them safe at home.

'You've been like brothers since the day you met!'

'Sure you could never let him go on his own, Francie!'

'Someone has to teach those bastards a lesson and there's no better boys than yourselves.'

Belfast's religious pus had never fully seeped through to this quiet corner of Ulster, where religion was avoided inside the only pub. But the boil of Irish Home Rule had risen rapidly to a head in recent years. There were now opposing volunteer armies in the North and the South, the former determined to stay British, the latter determined to throw Britain into the sea. It seemed everyone had decided that the best way to further their individual causes was to march off to war together on the continent. Geography had never been his strong point, but Francie was pretty certain that killing Germans, in France, would have fuck all bearing on whether Ireland stayed British or not.

As he smoked through his hangover with the other God-weary rebels at the back door of the chapel that Sunday morning, the voices sang a very different psalm from the one in the pub.

'The 36th Ulster Division, Francie? Sure, you'd be the only Catholic in it.'

'Head south and join Redmond's "Home Rule" Division; at least they think they're fighting to free Ireland.'

'Don't take the King's shilling, son. Let Archie and his Orange friends make their own beds.'

The bog slopes gently from both sides and there is cover enough from scrub brush and stacked turf to crawl slowly through its middle towards Hegarty's Public House, whose roof slumps at the bottom of the valley. Away to his right lie the foothills of the Rotten Mountain and off to his left, the expanse of Lough Erne splashes the feet of the British Garrison in Enniskillen at one end and the newly formed border with the Irish Free State at the other.

If he can break through the line that hunts him he can cross the border into County Donegal and join the rest of his column, who have been scattered into the South after skirmishes with Specials in Tyrone. He should have known better than to risk his first visit home in over six years but it had been eating away at him since they were sent north to heat things up along the border so that no one in London forgot that it shouldn't be there.

At the bottom of the bog, he scales the left-hand hillside at a crouch and looks down over a steep drop on to the pub where he spent too much of his youth. The Crossley Tender and the lorry from the bridge are pulled up outside and he can see two sentries keeping an eye on the vehicles. Everyone else is inside, then. Sure it's never too early for a drink, especially if you're a soldier or a policeman. The roof of his mouth dries over and he sucks hard on his palate to create a semblance of flow before his throat closes over. Jesus, what would he give for a pint? It's been six years since he stood down there with a drink in his hand.

When the troops have had their fill, the natives will appear and swill for Ireland under the guise of hearing what all the fuss was about. Charlie Wallace the dairy farmer and Barney Edwards the farrier. Jimmy Donegan the dancing man and Patsy Dolan the eternal drunk. Six years ago they had all champed at the bit to get him packed off to war and now at least one of them had busted a substantial gut to get squealing to the Pigs that the big IRA man was back on home soil. Not even a second night under his mother's roof before the door came tumbling in. No one is to be trusted since the bile has poured by the bucketful from this newly cut gash of a border.

He pictures the inside of the old place. The tobacco-stained glorification of Waterloo's bloodbath on the wall inside the door and the crooked Victorian fireplace on the left with the stumpy stools where you could thaw out your shins from the winter. The yellow and black storm clouds in your glass as it thickens and darkens and draws you in for that first sacred mouthful of cream.

He sucks hard on his palate again. He developed the habit under bombardment near Thiepval, wolfing down air and filth and smoke. Begging a God he had always denied for one blessed sip of anything.

The rum ration in the 36th Division was liberal compared to some of the English divisions and many of Ulster's God-fearing Protestants never touched a drop, so there was plenty to go around for those who needed it. The greatest motivator in the British Empire. Most would never even have gotten over the top without the Royal Navy's finest. It was supplemented by brandy and wine and cheap champagne from the *estaminets* when they were back in reserve.

He assumed that the drinking would end with the horrors but when he arrived back in Belfast to work in the sectarian crucible of the shipyards, he could barely stay sober at all. 'The Machine', the other riveters called him, for he worked in silence at speed with barely a break all day. At night he drank himself into the coma required to keep the nightmares from the backs of his eyes. They knew in the yard that he was Catholic, but they also knew that he had fought well in the trenches with the 36th. They saw the scars on his back and arms and those who worked beside him often caught a glimpse of his dead friends when the sparks from the furnace lit up his eyes.

He pushes onwards, skirting the pub. Anger will follow hard on the heels of the booze, and Catholic farms may well be torched before nightfall. The schoolhouse where he learnt to read sits behind the chapel not far up the road. As he lies hiding behind the graveyard wall the lessons of his childhood bounce around inside him and he can smell the turf they carried up the hill every morning, first smoking then taking in the stove at the back of the classroom. There was barely a day that he wasn't greeted after lessons by the fool sitting on the wall. The wide uncomplicated smile slung between his big red clown's ears.

It was the river that had brought them together, two boys from different schools with only a year and a couple of miles of road between them. Francie knew someone was watching him one Saturday morning as he fished in the big turn hole beyond the bridge. He said nothing for the first hour or so as he collected decent-sized stones into a pile beside his fishing pole. His cork disappeared under the water then and once he had landed a trout and dispatched it with two bangs on the back of head with one of his stones, he stood and started to hurl the rest of them into the bushes across the river.

'Come out! Come out to fuck and show yourself.'

He heard a squeal as a rock found its mark and then out came Archie waving his arms over his head.

'Ceasefire! Ceasefire!'

'What are you watching people for?'

'I want to know how you do it.'

'Do what?'

'Catch the fish.'

'Well, come over and ask me then instead of hiding in the bushes, you lunatic.'

Francie had the expertise but Archie had wheels: a heavy old postman's bicycle that his father had brought him home from the market. They became inseparable as they travelled further and further afield on the hunt for bigger and bigger fish. The first time he didn't show after school, Francie ignored it and wandered home with his sisters and their jibes about being stupid enough to lose your own shadow. The second day he lost his temper with the girls, annoyed that their jokes were hitting a nerve, and on the third he ran all the way to the Johnston farm and hammered on the door until Archie's sister opened it.

She stared intently at the wild-eyed boy from the other school, sweating on the doorstep before her. Nine, maybe ten, no more than a year or two younger than herself, but from another world entirely. Once she felt she had the measure of him she spoke.

'So you're the fisherman?'

'Where is he?'

When she brought Francie back out of Archie's damp little bedroom she made tea and explained that sometimes there was nothing they could do about his wheezing and that he often found it difficult to breathe. At least now he knew why he always had to do all the pedalling, while his mate sat on the bar talking endless shite about the Charge of the Light Brigade or Captain bloody Cook or the heroic deeds of the English longbow men at the battle of fucking Agincourt. He picked on Archie less then, the need for supremacy in their friendship replaced by something much truer to the sense of the word, and if anyone as much as mentioned the ears of his funny-looking little friend they felt the knotted fist of his protection in the corner of their mouth.

Back at the pub an engine farts and coughs itself into life and his schooldays are suddenly over. He sprints from the graveyard and jumps into the sheugh that carries excess water along the side of the road. If he goes to ground nearby, they may assume by morning that he has left the area. He remembers from his mother's letters that his sisters are married locally, but he knows nothing of their husbands' politics and their homes would be an obvious target for Crozier. The water soaks through the worn leather of his old boots and the iced shock of it sharpens his mind. After a few hundred yards he slides himself up and out on his belly then takes off through the rushes like a dog-hunted hare.

*

13

Wood on metal wakes him shortly after dawn. Through the barn slats, he watches a girl feed chickens from a battered enamel bucket under her arm. Her dark hair whips about her face and she stops and turns into the breeze so that it can blow the sleep from her eyes. The pair of cows who kept him warm overnight rise gently and show no signs of being put out by his continued presence.

He climbs further into the hayloft and sits surveying the yard below. The girl reappears and stares towards the rising sun before moving off to another chore somewhere else on the farm. He must eat, and soon, before breaking for the border. But first he must ensure that the Mauser's mechanism is clean and dry. He takes the weapon apart and lays each piece carefully between his legs. As he cleans the gun he counts its victims, a force of habit turned morbid ritual. He always used to finish the list of names before the task but it has been brutal up north lately and the Mauser is back on his belt long before the roll-call has ended.

Those two coppers in Belfast had it coming, though he wished the second hadn't offered his back. The two off-duty constables at the side of that pub in Tyrone. The informer in Derry who'd shopped seven men. The four Specials in the lorry they'd riddled in Omagh. Surely at least one of them was his? The tremor starts in his right shoulder, shooting painful signals into the bottom left of his back.

This was the first time he had laid eyes on him since the day he materialised in the shipyard in Belfast in 1919. The well-heeled Union man spreading paranoia and hatred amongst the workforce. Ensuring a raise for the Protestants and that the subhuman Catholic was flushed out of the working environment. 'Protestant jobs for Protestant heroes,' cried the big matinee idol from the Somme. Their eyes had met as Crozier inspected the hull of a half-finished battlecruiser with the owners of the yard. In that moment the puffed-up Union rep disappeared and the terrified soldier from no man's land returned, his body stiff in his soiled uniform, paralysed among the expensive tweed suits of his betters.

Francie walked straight out of the shipyard, and was drinking pints of porter in the city within the hour. No need to wait for Crozier's embarrassment to fuel his lynching. Two days later he befriended a Yank called Sean Molloy in a bar on the Ormeau Road.

Molloy had travelled to Britain at the outbreak of war, and joined the London Irish Rifles 'for the hell of it'. Instead of returning to Boston after the armistice, he had taken a detour, determined to explore the land of his ancestors; but he had never made it past the bars and bottles of Belfast. When Francie met him, he was drunk and telling no one in particular that he had seen more action than the entire US fucking army put together.

They both knew nothing but war, and they had both grown to hate the army that had taught them everything they knew. Molloy for the scores of lives he had witnessed wasted, and Francie more specifically for one pointless death. A week of solid drinking further and they accepted that without military discipline of some description they would be dead within the month. So in the morning they packed up their hangovers and headed south to join the Irish Republican Army and its struggle to liberate Ireland from Great Britain.

Her first footstep at the top of the ladder betrays her. He is on his feet with the gun trained on the girl from the yard before she can take another. Her hazel eyes show shock but no fear and when he shoves the gun back in his trousers defiance fills her and she walks towards him. He raises both hands and opens his fingers to show that he means no harm. She stops in front of him, drops her bucket and punches him as hard as she can in the left eye. He tastes the metal in his blood when she hits his mouth with a second and when he doesn't attempt to protect himself she cries out in anger, unleashing blow after blow into his chest. She grabs him by the shirt front, twists her leg behind his and pushes him back on to the floor, crashing on top of him. She sits back on his thighs staring down at him then she leans forward pressing her mouth on to his, and when she breaks again the blood from his lips is smeared across her cheeks and nose. He reaches up to touch her face but she intercepts his hand with hers and brings her other one down hard in his face again.

'Six years, Francie. Six years I've waited for you!'

His eyes are already swelling from the blows as he looks up into those of his best friend's sister.

'You made me swear to you, Annie.'

She lifts her arm again but then lowers it slowly as his words sink in.

'You made me swear never to come home without Archie.'

CHAPTER TWO

Hédauville, France

October 1915

They only know he is German from his left boot. The colour of his breeches is indecipherable having been interred in the mud for so long, but there is no doubting the quality and style of the long pull-on boot that stretches up and over his calf and fair tickles the back of his knee. His right calf lies somewhere else along with his right foot and his right boot. His tunic and head have been dropped neatly at another station by the shrapnel from the British shell that fetched him, or perhaps by the blast from the German one that had resurrected him that very morning and left him lying in the mud at the feet of his foes.

A baker's dozen of them rings the deceased in a tight yet respectful circle. It is their first German and their first dead body, so time is taken to drink him in and there is reverence in their whispers, for they couldn't bear the dead man to feel the shame of his cold stiff nakedness.

Lieutenant Gallagher materialises one foot from where the head should have rested and after taking stock of the shock on their faces he barks for volunteers to rebury the body at once. The circle splits and hands raw from endless digging ferret down itchy tunnels of serge.

Windy Patterson and Archie Johnston are the slowest to tear their eyes from the decomposition and they find their fingers full of shovel before pockets can be considered an option. Francie Leonard and Jack Elliot exchange glances and then reluctantly saunter back to give their friends a dig out.

The four have been inseparable since they met in a pub the day they signed on for the King's shilling at a recruiting fair in Ballyshannon. Archie and Francie came as a pair and the other two, from different parts of Donegal, had recognised the bond between the Fermanagh men and began to form one of their own.

When they had woken in the grounds of an abbey the morning after the day they met, they stripped buck naked and submerged themselves in the medieval well, baptising their friendship and dousing the flames of the whiskey blaze that still raged through their bodies.

Now, in the bite of late October, they sweat freely as they dig the grave that will restore some dignity to the departed. When it is fully opened Francie and Jack slide a shovel blade each under the torso and half carry, half scrape the dead man back down into the soil from whence he came. Lieutenant Gallagher, a tough but fair Donegal man that they have grown fond of, draws them around him and announces that there will be plenty more of that sort of thing to deal with and that they need to get their heads and stomachs in the game.

Afterwards, in the billet, even Windy Patterson has little to offer as they prepare to march in formation to the gas-testing trench that has been sunk behind the schoolhouse in the village. Unlike the rest, Patterson purportedly popped his death cherry in some style the day after their arrival at the front. His discovery of some 'twelve to fifteen' Canadians 'blown to smithereens' when they left the front line to go on leave to England caused quite the furore. For a full afternoon, he had fielded questions on the subject and the crux of the case came down to how he had extracted the information from the men about their destination when they were, to all intents and purposes, already dead. Windy Patterson felt no responsibility to provide any further facts. When a jury of his fellow soldiers proclaimed him a liar as they lay down for the night, he announced to the world that he didn't give a flying fuck what anyone thought apart from his own dear mother who was unlikely to be joining them in France any time soon.

Windy's grandest fables were often prefaced with the legend, 'Now listen, lads, I wouldn't tell you a lie.' During their training weeks in Seaford, when even a return from the latrines was accompanied by the triumphant tale of a rabid Sussex girl manhandling him dexterously in a bush, the boys came to accept that the gangly red-haired fisherman lived exclusively in the parallel universe of his own imagination. So, on the slog to the gas-testing trench, when his voice is heard singing, 'They are using real gas for the drill, Mary Jane,' no one pays Windy Patterson the blindest bit of attention.

As they stand in line awaiting their turn to descend into the chamber, doubt begins to creep like chlorine under the glorified flour-bags they wear on their heads. Ten feet down into the earth then another thirty forwards under a corrugated roof through pitch darkness and a cloud of whatever chemical is testing the fallibility of their new gas helmets. For Archie, it is the contraption that is testing him. He flails after the man in front and tries to keep panic from awakening the grip that his chest likes to hold over his lungs. He pulls the bag at the crown to lift the useless circular windows back to his eyes but he has to be careful not to raise it too far for fear of exposing his throat and allowing the vapours in around his mouth. He trips on the steep steps at the far end and near buries his head up the arse of the man in front. At the top, he kicks through the smoke blanket and falls gratefully out into the world. The world, however, remains obscured by the mask so he can't identify the owner of the hands that tear him to his feet or the wearer of the boot that propels him into the pliant line of soldiers waiting dumbly for the route march to follow.

They will wear their masks for two miles to become accustomed to the particular brand of suffocation this new piece of kit has to offer. To the accompaniment of shouts and kicks from three NCOs, B Company, 11th Battalion Royal Inniskilling Fusiliers of the 36th Ulster Division, minus the four men who had collapsed in the gas-testing trench, stumble off into the unknown.

Despite disorientation and an increasing inability to breathe, Archie feels comforted by the knowledge that this march at least has a specific purpose. He has been totting up the yards in his legs since they began their training, and has calculated that he has endured enough pointless miles to have walked to France from Ireland in the first place. They have marched everywhere and anywhere but never for good reason. Up and down the Finner strand in Donegal they marched, as the Atlantic spewed on the sand and the moon pouted in the leather uppers of their well-polished boots. Around the headland they marched and along the coast to Bally-shannon. Onwards then to Rossnowlagh beach before turning back and double-timing it for home where they would re-polish the boots and shine the buttons tarnished by the salt from the sea and the sweat that had soaked through their stiff new tunics.

Apart from the mileage, Archie Johnston had revelled in his training. The uniformity and pride of the drill, awaiting one's turn on an ancient rifle until the new ones arrived and the ghost stories from different townlands whispered over the waves at night under wet canvas. For the first time in his life he jumped from sleep every morning. He was full of energy, finally in the place where he was meant to be. Chores on the farm were things to be suffered but here he couldn't do enough for himself, or for anyone else. In the first week of training Lieutenant Gallagher twice had to stop him from going in to the field kitchen after dinner to help scrub the pots as there were people already designated to do it. From England onwards Francie resorted more and more to cynicism but Archie let it wash over him as disembarkation drew closer because he knew that it was their destiny to liberate the people of Europe.

It had all been plain sailing until Crozier arrived from Belfast. His experience in the Boer War had made him an invaluable officer in Kitchener's new model army, but he had been demoted from captain for drinking on duty and sent west to train farmers for their war with the Kaiser. On a warm autumnal morning, Staff Sergeant Peter Crozier pulled into Finner Camp on the back of a Maudslay lorry with a face like a bulldog's arse.

Inside his gas mask, Archie recites Crozier's introductory speech for the hundredth time as he remembers the moon at Finner Camp on a still night and how it would burn a silver corridor on to the surface of the sea all the way to America.

'You country boys will learn the hard way; you will learn the fucking Belfast way!'

A black cloud obscures all memory of the Irish coastline and his chest tightens and his knees buckle. He stumbles then goes down but strong hands lift him and he knows who owns them this time as they grab for his to stop him tearing the mask from his face.

'I can't breathe, Francie; I can't breathe.'

'We're nearly there, Arch. Calm your mind and your body will follow.'

It took Crozier one day to expose Francie's little secret. The memory ignites and he pushes down into his legs then forward beside the solid trunk of his best friend. They'd made a pact back home in Drumskinny. They would protect each other's secrets at all costs, though Francie laughed until he wept saying, 'Some fuckin secrets! A soldier who can't breathe properly and the only Catholic in the 36th.'

He wasn't, though. There were plenty of others scattered among the thousands of men in the Ulster Division and the closer they came to facing the Germans the less anyone cared about religion. Anyone, that is, except Staff Sergeant Crozier. On his first night in camp, he called senior members of the Orange lodges together and asked them straight out if they knew any Catholics in their sections. Someone suggested that they had never met a Protestant 'Leonard' before let alone a 'Francis' and sure it was mentioned that the lad didn't partake in much singing when it came to God and Ulster and the Battle of the Boyne. Francie was the only papist in Crozier's platoon and as far as he was concerned that made him more dangerous than any Hun.

The drill sergeant's yells puncture mask and memory and two hundred shattered bodies collapse to the ground. Archie rips the cloth horror from his face and Francie laughs manically above him.

'You did it; you always do it, you always fuckin get there.'

The severed heads of Windy and Jack float through the sky then their arms appear and Archie is lifted and pulled to them by the front of his jacket.

'We're drinking tonight, my son, and Estelle will be waiting, just for you.'

'Tomorrow we go into the line so there'll be no more marching for the Archie boy.'

CHAPTER THREE

County Fermanagh, Northern Ireland

May 1922

He hadn't wanted her around at first but it became apparent quickly that he would have very little say in the matter. She appeared one evening in her mother's kitchen as the boys took bread and tea and announced that she would be joining them on Saturday morning on their expedition to raid Castle Archdale's orchards. When Francie protested that it was a long way away and the three of them couldn't possibly travel on one bike, she simply answered that she would bring one of her own.

'Would that suffice, Francis?'

'Where will you get one? And don't call me Francis. Only my mother calls me Francis.'

'But that is your name, isn't it? I see Father Sweeney often on a bicycle and I believe he leaves it at the back of the chapel.'

'Father Sweeney is a mad old bastard who will never lend his bike to a girl!'

'Well, Francis, perhaps it's best if he doesn't know I have taken it.'

Francie thought no more about it for the rest of the week but sure enough when he and Archie free-wheeled to the bottom of the Johnstons' lane on Saturday morning, there she was straddling the crossbar of the priest's big black bicycle. Archie howled with laughter and Francie protested that he simply didn't want to go raiding with a girl but deep down he wanted to steal apples with her more than anyone he had ever met.

Wherever the boys roamed after that she was there, driving them onwards through briar and bog. The brains of the operation, his mother had called her.

'That girl has more between her ears than the pair of you put together.'

Her name was Anne back then, Anne Jane Johnston. As the three of them sat in the shade of the bridge with their feet in the water on a scorching June day she announced that as she was now twelve years old she didn't want to be Anne Jane any more.

'What do you mean?'

'Well, you were christened Archibald and you changed it to Archie and he was christened Francis and he changed it Francie so why should I be any different?'

'What do you want to be called, then?'

'Well, Francie, formerly known as Francis, I would like to be Annie, formerly known as Anne.'

'I think it suits you very well; wouldn't you agree, Archie, formerly known as Archibald?'

'I certainly fuckin would.'

That day in the blistering heat, Annie was born and though it was never discussed and neither fella cared, she was unequivocally the leader of the gang.

They were both working full time on their fathers' farms the winter he first kissed her. Archie had a year left yet at school and they had begun to spend more and more time together without him. Much to his father's irritation, Francie was an expert at finding reasons to leave his own farm and help Annie on hers. In turn she was often a welcome sight in his mother's kitchen taking a turn on the butter churn or butchering a chicken in the run by the back door, a task neither of his sisters could stomach.

On a bitterly cold evening Francie was running Annie home on the bar of the bike. At the foot of the bray between their farms he lost control of the front wheel and the pair of them ended up in the ditch at the side of the road. Once he had pulled her to her feet and established that all of her limbs were still working he instinctively kept hold of her and pulled her gently into him. She didn't resist, laying her head on his chest, and when she lifted it again he moved to put his mouth on hers but she started to laugh from embarrassment and pushed him away.

Spurned, he turned and lifted the bike, for fear his eyes might fill. He was about to throw his leg over the saddle when she spun him from behind and her lips were on his and their tongues met for the first time, then suddenly he was on the bike again, cycling home alone with a grin splitting his face from one side to the next because he knew that everything had changed for ever.

They did their best to keep it to themselves, careful not to upset the balance and leave Archie outside in the cold. It was as though Francie and Annie's love did no damage by itself but voicing it, actually acknowledging it out loud, would burst the bubble. Neither of them ever discussed it with their friend and brother for fear that the very conversation would be the moment that their childhoods ended. At work in the fields and in the smoky lungs of the pub, Archie always seemed appropriately to disappear when the other men ribbed Francie about his girl. Through training at Finner and at Seaford in Sussex they both answered negatively the endless questions about girls back at home; even though Archie knew and Francie knew that Archie knew, they couldn't admit it as it had always been the three of them together.

*

On the back of the cart he takes short shallow breaths so as not to choke on the stench of the damp hay that covers him. His neighbour has no idea that a fugitive is buried behind him so he will show no nerves if they are stopped by a patrol. Alone in the barn he had dozed and twitched through the whole of the previous day. When the darkness arrived so did Annie, but when she had given him food she left and he lay awake in the straw imagining her warmth in the bed inside. At dawn when the sun came through the cracks in the walls he woke to find her standing watching him.

'Did you shoot the pregnant woman in County Clare?'

The world turned pitch black then and the muscles in his abdomen spasmed and locked. He could barely hear his own words over the high-pitched buzzing in his head when eventually he managed to answer her.

'Where did you hear that?'

'The one-armed police officer you were in France with told it to the pub.'

'Did he now?'

'Said you shot a man you had served with, in the back of the head.'

'He was killed in Cork; I was never there.'

'Did you shoot the woman, Francie?'

'I shot her husband. He was a bad bastard of a copper and he had it coming.'

What he could never explain was that in order to kill Inspector Drake his bullets had to pass through his wife Milly, who had lain on top of her husband in a desperate attempt to protect him. Nine bullets from several guns entered various parts of her body, some of them Francie's – and probably the ones that mattered knowing the steadiness of his shooting compared to the others who had let loose all around him.

He had thought nothing of the dead woman in the week that followed the ambush but then the pregnancy rumour found them hiding up in the mountains. There was no way of verifying it and the men satisfied themselves that it was a lie put about to demonise their patriotic efforts. But for months after hearing it he lay every night, following the journey of a bullet as it left his gun and entered the stomach of Milly Drake before passing through her unborn child en route to the chest of its father.

Crozier's lie about shooting Major Peacock in the head angered him. Hadn't he enough to blacken his name with? Maybe they really believed he had been active in Cork. He had heard about the Major's execution and those of the other spies and informers and he was glad the chiefs of staff in Dublin had never sent him there.

He had risen quickly thanks to his military expertise and a calm head under fire. Any doubts among the men about trusting a northerner who had fought in France with the 36th were put to bed by his willingness to kill and ask no questions. Dublin needed men in the field who could drill farmers and teach them how to shoot, and who better than a fellow farmer who had been shooting people in France and Belgium for the last three years? Himself and the Yank Molloy helped to raise units in Clare and Mayo before they were moved on to Kerry. Major Peacock had fought well in France and had been fair to the men under his command, but he had come to Cork after the war and when the Irish conflict evolved he had masked up at night and led parties in lifting and executing suspected IRA volunteers.

Under the hay Francie bites into his tongue and rips at his palms with his nails to stop himself from crossing the Channel. He will visit that hell when he sleeps; there is no need to lie there now, not even for the memory of the Major. He would have had Peacock shot had it been his decision to make. He is glad that fate never had the opportunity to force his hand. It is much easier to kill a man if you are looking into his eyes for the first time.

On the outskirts of Ederney, he slides from the back of the cart and waits in the ditch at the side of the road.

There is no sign of any police as he wanders through the village trying to avoid the eyes of the crowd gathering for market day. It is easy to find the information he needs from the gossip all around him.

'The Specials are out in force along the border and Republicans have taken Pettigo and Belleek.'

He listens to an old face and a fresher one that he remembers from the Gaelic football pitch, as they argue over the identity of the Irish forces.

'The soldiers in Pettigo are from Michael Collins' official Free State Army.'

'Listen, y'oul bollocks, it's the IRA have invaded from the South and captured the whole of Belleek.'

They are probably both right. His own unit had been on the way to Belleek to raid the police barracks for weapons when he left them for his mother's farm nearby. He knew that there were Free State troops in the area as well as IRA men. My God, what a mess. It felt like only yesterday that they were all fighting the British together, one united entity with a common goal and foe. When Michael Collins and Arthur Griffiths came home to Dublin from London with the Anglo-Irish Treaty still burning holes in their pockets Francie had known right away that it wasn't for him. He hadn't been fighting for three-quarters of Ireland, and the quarter to be left behind was the one of his birth. An Ireland partially free but that would still swear an oath to the King was not the one he'd been killing for. The independence movement was torn down the middle. The Yank Molloy was a Collins man through and through and he had lost all reason and punched Francie in a pub in Killarney for scoffing at the treaty. In the morning when they woke in the same bed with the same hangover, the American wept with remorse and they had shaken hands and accepted that their journey together was over.

Two weeks later Francie left Kerry in a column of men unofficially sent north to take the war to the security forces of that new state. Despite his official line that the war was over, Michael Collins understood the value of keeping the anti-treaty Republicans in the ranks believing he hadn't given up on the North and sure it never did any harm to keep London reminded that the Paddies still had their guns. As director of intelligence for the IRA, Collins was one of the most wanted men in the Empire. For years the British had chased his shadow around Dublin not even knowing what he looked like and now he had sat in London, staring at their Prime Minister across a table.

In the market he is surrounded by faces ripe with the potential for recognition. Most of the Specials who hunt him are local men, some of whom he may even have shared a trench with for the best part of three years. Crozier, in his new role as Specials inspector, must have raced from Belfast to Fermanagh when word broke that his number-one target had resurfaced.

Before Francie had left this morning he asked Annie if he could speak with her mother about Archie but she had flatly refused.

'She will go to her grave happier if she never sees you again.'

'Just a few minutes.'

'In her eyes, you've betrayed Archie and everything that he ever fought for.'

He had nothing to say. Years of rehearsed sentences, but all of them trapped in his chest.

The Specials lorry roared then from the bottom of her lane. Crozier had discovered where Archie's farm was and figured it might well be somewhere an old comrade would seek refuge. Francie reached out for her but she brushed him away and turned towards the house and he took off again, racing for the neighbour's cart that she had assured him was market-bound that very morning.

He picks a Dennis lorry full of cattle bound for Castlederg in County Tyrone. His arrival among the animals will cause a stir so he coincides his entrance with the lorry's engine starting and pulls himself into the back of the vehicle as it begins to move away. The cows writhe and empty their bowels but they quickly relax and he crouches behind the driver's cab, his head wedged between the black-and-white haunches of a cow and the shite-caked shoulder of a young bull. Friesian cattle, no less. A rarity in Ireland and an arm-and-a-leg commodity. These will be on their way to a rich dairy farmer somewhere in the Derg Valley. Despite the burning in his knees and thighs, he stays down in the corner away from the tailgate for fear of being spotted. After an arduous climb, he hops off at the top of Scraghy Hill and jogs downhill through a dense growth of young ash trees. At the bottom sits Killeter village, where he can pick up the river and follow it to its mouth on Lough Derg. There he will find the village of Pettigo and his boys, if the rumours are true.

At the foot of the hill, he stays two trees deep while skirting the small cluster of grey buildings tossed around a bridge. When he is far enough from the final house he breaks cover and heads for the river. He will follow it west, its course as good as a road on a map as it snakes and races through the burnt brown bogland.

Beneath a roaring gulley, he strips to the waist and slides into the icy water, numbing body and brain and releasing the caked dung from his trousers and boots. Under the waterfall the torrent batters his head and shoulders, forcing him to the bottom where he holds his breath until the fog clears and his thoughts become focused. He can hear her voice in his head again. For years he had grasped for it but all trace of her had been eradicated the moment he lost Archie. When the guns stopped in Belgium the shock of the silence was louder than any barrage. His head filled with nothing and he became confused and terrified and at times lost all sense of balance and struggled to walk. When he was spoken to gently the voices exploded in his ears and when he first heard birds sing with no war din beneath them it was like he was hearing birds singing for the first time and he panicked and the world spun, tipping sideways, and he lay in a Belgian field for hours. All memory of noise had been blown from his brain and he would have to learn sounds all over again. There was peace at least in the shipyards as the crash of industry had blocked out the roar of the silence. Gradually he filled in the blanks again but he could never remember what Annie's voice had sounded like. Not without facing her and hearing it again. Now, six years since the last time, his worst fears have been realised. He can hear her voice at last but it's telling him that she never wants to see him again.

Back on the bank, he watches for the salmon who await the flood that will allow them over the fall to their spawning beds upstream. Tight against the far bank there is a boil on the surface then a fish leaves the water and crashes back down again in bored frustration. He can tell by the purple sheen to its flanks that it has been in fresh water for at least a couple of weeks. From the Atlantic Ocean at Derry, through the River Foyle into the River Mourne, then onwards upstream to this pool here on the River Derg.

Archie and he had poached these salmon. All the way from Drumskinny, their arses taking turns to eat the bar of the bicycle before hunting for the fresh-run silver fish who had covered even more miles than they had to be there. Not a mile ahead of him lay the scene of Archie's greatest triumph. He had pulled the blade of his billhook through a thirty-pound Springer on a baking-hot day when the first flood of a dry season had run off rapidly from the night before. The fish's great tail had given it away. Archie spied it protruding from the water on the lee side of a rock and he abandoned his boots and waded towards it. He came at the large stone from downstream then ripped the curved blade through the water with both hands and all of his strength, spearing the salmon clean through its back just above the tail. In its death throes the huge fish ripped three times from bank to bank but the wee man never let go of the handle as raw Atlantic power pulled him between rocks and dragged him twice beneath the water. When finally Archie slithered up into the grass, dragging the huge fish behind him, Francie had near drowned in his laughter.

The memory has him smiling for the first time in an age. As he pulls his shirt on he plays with the foreign feeling in his face, allowing it to move from left to right across his mouth before permitting it to spread from top to bottom. By the time he is fully dressed he is laughing out loud. Archie struggling to hold the huge fish over his head as he whooped in triumph, clumps of black hair stuck to his face and his dark brown eyes never more bright and alive.

He sits facing the pool so he can keep an eye out for more salmon and begins to take the Mauser apart. He had taken the gun from a Scotsman that he killed in Galway, who had taken it from a German he had killed in Belgium; a burly Glaswegian Black and Tan inspector with an overbearing ginger moustache. The Tans had been on the rampage locally. Men who were brutalized in the trenches, then armed by the British government and let loose on the civilian population of Ireland. His presence in the police barracks that night had been an unexpected bonus as he was at the top of the IRA's list of suspects for a spate of reprisal-killings in the area.

The barracks was an old stately home near a crossroads, converted for the purpose by the Royal Irish Constabulary. Charlie Larkin and Seamus Enright, the best shots in the column, lay behind the gateposts at the bottom of the driveway keeping the bottle-green uniforms pinned inside with a pair of Mauser rifles. The building was set into the base of a shallow hill so the rear escape route was easily covered by a handful of shotgun men, allowing the main body of the IRA flying-column to get to work on the roof.

The slates were blown off in patches with home-made gelignite bombs made sticky with well-tested clay. Some fell back to earth, blowing in the windows at the front of the house, but the ones that held blew ragged sores into the hard, black slate skin so that the paraffin could soak into the wooden rafters below. A pump had been commandeered from a creamery in the village and it had arced thick jets of paraffin up on to the exposed beams before jamming completely, to the despair of the watching IRA men. The pub beside the barracks where the landlord and his family were held was raided for bottles, and glass and oil projectiles were hurled up on to the roof. Ladders appeared and Francie, Jack Neeson and Yank Molloy took centre stage on the roof of the barracks. Molloy and Francie fired at will between their feet at the unseen policemen below fighting desperately to prevent the spread of the flames. Neeson, who had been a grenadier in the trenches, lobbed bottle after bottle straight into the two biggest holes left by the explosives. A loud whoosh and a petrifying roar from within announced its coming as the fire took hold of the bones of the structure. An orange ball shot upwards through the jagged holes into the night sky and Jack Neeson, drenched in paraffin from the bottles, shot up with it.

It was the fall that eventually killed him, though had he avoided the broken spine he would have spent the rest of his few days in bed in agony, such was the degree of the burning. They rolled him around on the ground and beat him with coats to extinguish the flames, unaware of the crippling damage they were inflicting to his already shattered frame. Francie and the fair-haired Yank Molloy were trying to make him comfortable on the floor behind the bar when the word came through that the surrender was imminent.

Out from the barracks shat the Peelers, clinging to the tails of a stained white shirt tied to a rifle. A sergeant from County Limerick and three constables, two of whom the local volunteers identified from their days at school together. As the roof squealed and prepared to give in, the Limerick man admitted that there was indeed still one more man inside the barracks. Many times they called in to the Black and Tan inspector to come out and give himself up, but to no avail. As the chimney stack on the left of the building crashed through the timbers and buried itself in the floor, an arm appeared from a downstairs window and the inspector's Mauser automatic sent three badly aimed bullets out to greet his visitors. When the bulk of the roof finally gave up the ghost and fell to earth he came out all right, but he came out swearing and he came out shooting. Two rounds from the gateposts met him on the pathway, lifting him into the air and setting him down like a bag of spuds ten yards from the front of the house. One bullet had entered neatly through the bottom of his stomach and left a whiskey-glass-sized hole in his back en route to the door of the house. The second had successfully negotiated a pathway from his ribcage up into the ball socket of his right shoulder.

Francie and Molloy stalked him cautiously, unsure if he still had the pistol under his control. When they stood over him he spat blood up at them twice and tried in vain to lift the gun with his useless right arm. Francie took it from him and pinned the arm to the ground with his boot. The Scot howled from the pain of it.

'Where are you from, Inspector?'

'Fuck you, Paddy.'

The Yank lit a cigarette and stuck the safe end in the watery blood on the inspector's bottom lip as Francie took in the array of field decorations pinned to the chest of his tunic.

'France or Belgium?'

'Bit of both.'

'Me 'n' all.'

'Well, there's a thing.'

'Are you responsible for the murders in this parish last Tuesday night?'

'Which murders would they be, now? We've had quite a few.'

'Did you partake in the murders of two teenage boys carried out by masked men in the village on Tuesday night?'

'I didn't see any masks. Perhaps I was blinded by the boot polish that was running into my eyes.'

His breath quickened defiantly then slowed completely as the stomach wound sucked him into the ground.

'Where did you take your Mauser?'

'A *hauptmann* in Ypres. Had to finish him with my shovel. Proper soldiers, the Huns – not like you cowardly bastards.'

Francie dispatched the Tan with the man's own pistol. Two shots to the chest, though the kick from the Mauser caught him off guard the first time and the bullet blew some of the throat away. He watched for a moment as life withdrew through the mess, then he ended it with the second pull. When they had examined the arms haul from the barracks and divvied it up for distribution the next morning, Francie still had the Mauser hanging from his belt and he took comfort from its considerable weight.

A loud splash breaks his concentration as he puts the last pieces of the gun back together. He looks up to see the ripples where the salmon fell back into the water and as he rams the magazine back in place the barrel of a gun is jammed painfully into the base of his skull. He knows instantly that it's a gun because experience has taught him that a gun is the only thing worth shoving into the back of a head. He tosses the Mauser on the ground and raises his arms

35

slowly until they are both in the air by his ears. He can tell from its width on the nape of his neck that it's a double-barrelled shotgun and so he takes a gamble on its owner being a farmer rather than a constable.

'Have I wandered on to your land?'

The piece is cocked, a sound he has heard a thousand times, though never so close to his brain.

'I'll be gone, I just needed to wash.'

A boot between blades and he crashes on to his face in the gravel. He lies still, awaiting instruction, but when eventually he hears a match struck and smells tobacco he rolls slowly on to his back to meet his taker.

'The big IRA man, eh? Captured by a girl.'

She sits smoking her cigarette, the shotgun jammed between her knees. She looks different than she did on the farm, the skirts replaced by britches, her hair ripped back out of the way.

'Maybe the police should hire some women. Bit of female intuition and this mess would be cleared up in no time.'

She stands and tosses him the shotgun.

'You're going to need that. There's a storm coming for you, boy.'

He bends and lifts the Mauser, shoving it in his belt.

'What did Crozier want?'

'To know if you'd been there. He told my mother that you're a traitor to her son and to all the men who died in France and that he won't rest until you hang. Told us they have a line of men closing the entire border and that no rats will be sneaking back down into the Irish Free State. When they left I followed you to town and saw you climb into the lorry.'

He lifts the shotgun and makes the distance. When he moves for her mouth her hand comes up and covers his. The other hand puts the cigarette back between her lips then she moves off towards the hill.

'We need to get back to those trees for Orion.'

'Who the fuck's Orion?'

'My horse, Francis. You didn't think I ran all that way now, did you?'

Her plan is simple. Risk the exposure of the roads in exchange for their speed and literally gallop across the border before the ring can be closed.

'Why did you come?'

'I'll help you across the border for old time's sake. Then you're on your own.'

Under Annie's steady rein the big chestnut stallion canters into the village of Killeter. The single street is completely deserted. Halfway along two curious donkeys wander into their path, forcing Orion to trot around. When Francie scouted the place earlier, these animals had an owner and his senses flare as they approach the dwellings at the edge of town. He studies the houses, sensing that something is wrong, then realises that despite it being a bright afternoon all the curtains in the windows are closed. The shotgun is wedged between his stomach and the small of her back so he pulls the Mauser and rams it into the horse's side and they take off at a gallop for the bridge. He empties the magazine at two Specials guarding its foot and taken by surprise they dive into the river as Orion cuts left on to the crossing and disappears like a Howitzer shell towards the hills of Donegal.

CHAPTER FOUR

Forceville, France

November 1915

Six men hang off anchor ropes as gas cylinders stuff the huge silk sausage, raising it into the air above where the boys lie smoking. The steel umbilical cord that keeps the observation balloon connected to the world is paid out from a drum on the back of a Thornycroft lorry. The basket bobs on the grass then steadies as two Signals officers clamber in. They have parachutes strapped to their backs and binoculars and a glass frame holding a map and an assortment of complicated measuring devices that only Windy Patterson claims to understand.

'Instruments for measurement and observation.'

'That's the height of your insight, Windy?'

'Simplified for present company, Jack.'

'Sherlock Holmes will be out of a fucking job.'

The four boys toss their cigarette butts and stand as the colossal banger shrinks in the big blue pan above them. The two men suspended beneath it disappear completely to the naked eye and the onlookers rue the lack of a telescope or some field glasses of their own. All along the front, identical balloons gaze down on the war but this one is theirs and they follow its progress with pride as it moves up and away.

When the wire snaps they can't differentiate between the sharp crack and the random artillery percussions that they are still growing accustomed to. The balloon's ascent appears no more rapid from a distance and it is only the shouts from the crew at the lorry that alerts them to the unfolding disaster. Men panic and run in circles as nature intervenes, blowing the balloon north towards the village. Onwards over the supply dumps and beyond the railway sidings it flies, to the training areas and the horse pens, before crossing the lines of British support and communication trenches. When it reaches their front line it holds for a minute on the breeze like it knows instinctively to proceed no further but then the wind changes again and no man's land is spanned in seconds. As it sails into range over the German trenches the rifles and machine guns of the Boche unload into the defenceless cloud. As quickly as it started the shooting stops and the silence is louder than a hundred Maxims. Fifty feet below the balloon two small white lilies blossom and the men from both armies watch the Signals officers glide gracefully back down to earth and out of the war.

'Will they shoot them as spies?'

'Course not; POWs they are now.'

'Fair play to them.'

'Is right, Archie; I don't think I would have had the balls to jump.'

'The Germans; fair play to the Germans for not shooting at the parachutes.'

They consider themselves early but have been beaten to their usual table in the corner of the *estaminet* by a clatter of boisterous Antipodeans. If the decibels are to be trusted, these soldiers have been sampling the local produce for quite some time. They leave four tables between themselves and Down Under but before their drinks appear they are surrounded by weather-beaten faces from the furthermost pink bits on the map.

'You lot English, mate?'

'Irish, mate.'

'We've been up front with your lot, Dubliners from the 16th.'

'We're Ulster men, from the 36th.'

'You're the mob that think you're bloody British!'

'We are bloody British and bloody proud of it!'

'Well, those Dubliners can fight; they're as tough as fuckin nails, mate!'

Archie bangs the table.

'Gerry won't know what's hit him when the Ulsters come into the line tomorrow.'

'All right, mate, keep your bloody hair on.'

The bottles of warm champagne and cloudy cider arrive wrapped in the wiry arms of Madame Bussiere. Her pale blue eyes watch greedy boys from above the bone-sharp ridges of her cheekbones but whatever conclusions are reached they are seldom given voice to. On several occasions, Archie has marvelled as she banished men from her bar with the slightest ripple of maternal disappointment in those big sad eyes.

'The wine's weak as piss, Paddy, but if you chuck it in with the cider you'll get where you need to go.'

'I'm not a Paddy, pal.'

'You sound like one, mate.'

'At least I'm not a convict.'

'I'm not a fuckin convict.'

'You look like one, mate!'

'You lot from New Zealand?'

'Asking an Aussie if he's a Kiwi's like asking a Mick if he's English.'

'Or like asking an Ulsterman if he's a Mick.'

'Now we're fuckin getting somewhere!'

*

Madame Bussiere has three dark-haired daughters and a sullen son who help her manage the affair. Windy and Jack exclusively cast the two older sisters in their sordid fantasies but it is the youngest, Estelle, who feeds Archie from the palm of her hand. Their father watches from an ebony frame above the bar, the blue serge of his French uniform turned black in the process of capture. He has a splendid Victorian moustache and the severe stave in his brow reminds the soldiers to keep their hands off his girls when they're under his roof. They have heard rumours that he faced the Hun through the mud of Verdun but no one has the heart to ask his family if he is still alive.

The poky bar is crammed to bursting when she finally makes her entrance. Archie's back stiffens and he ignores their sniggers as his gaze follows her around the room. Once last week she caught his eye and held it but he didn't know if she was admonishing him or inviting him to say hello so he just kept staring until she vanished. As the bottles empty, the volume swells and the air is filled by a tone-deaf multinational choir. Three of the Australians have stayed at the table with the Ulster men. The bulk of the clientele are from the 36th Division and the Australian 4th with a smattering of English sprinkled throughout to remind everyone who they will be dying for.

Jack Elliot, a fair-haired sheep farmer from Ireland, and Corporal Lynch, a fair-haired sheep farmer from Australia, are having a heated debate on nationality while the rest mix their drinks and goad them onwards. Lynch is a thirty-something whose face has been beaten much older. The lines burnt into it by the Tasmanian sun are packed tight with French mud, leaving the impression of a thespian made up for his Lear. The cider is tart and the champagne is heinous, and stirred together the concoction could clean their rifles, but the end takes precedence over the means and they steel themselves and put it away. Archie barely hears the others as he watches Estelle gliding between the tables. The more of the potion he drinks the further from the floor she appears to glide.

'But you're Irish and you're fighting for the country that occupies your own!'

'We're British and we're fighting to prove our loyalty.'

'Listen to yourself, mate; to an Englishman you're as Irish as they come.'

'Why is an Australian fighting for England?'

'My ancestors were English.'

'Your name's Lynch, mate.'

'Me father's side were Irish but me mother's side were English and I fuckin love me mother.'

'Francie's not British.'

Jack puts his drink down and rolls his eyes at Archie, whose brain sprints to catch up with his tongue, then they all turn to Francie, who smiles sheepishly, wanting nothing to do with this line of enquiry.

'Sorry, Archie?'

'Francie doesn't think he's British and he isn't here to prove his loyalty.'

They stare at Francie, waiting for him to explain why he is in France, until Corporal Lynch intervenes.

'Of course he is, kid, we all are; we're here to prove our loyalty to our mates, now drink your bloody grog.'

'I think he's had enough; one eye's gone to the shop and the other's coming back with the change.'

They take turns singing the songs of their homelands and emotions swing from pride to loneliness then from homesick back to happy never to see the fucking place again. In a lull in the entertainment, Estelle and one of her sisters appear and start dumping all the empty bottles from their table into a milk churn. To a man, they hit their feet, clearing space for the girls at their work, except for Windy Patterson who grabs Estelle by the elbow and starts pointing and slurring in Archie's direction.

'He's mad in the head for you, Estelle; will you just sit with him for a minute?'

She smiles nervously then pulls her arm away, looking at her sister for support.

'Just for a wee minute, like; can't you see the way he stares at you?'

Archie's chest constricts and he knows that before he can defend himself the breath will already have left him. A searing burn ignites under his collar and when her eyes follow Windy's finger up into his scalded face he pushes back into the throng of men, scattering stools and soldiers. He turns and kicks for the night, the sounds of men's laughter forming an allegiance behind him to chase him from the room. Shoulder first through the next knot of bodies, he makes it to the door and barrels his way through it. Outside the darkness is complete and fresh air refuels the booze until the world spins out of control. Breathless and dizzy, he blunders his way across the yard then trips and falls, banging his head against the wall of an outhouse. He reaches upwards for the structure then straightens his legs and pushes his face into the cold wet stone. A patch of moss tickles his nose and the smell of it is old and damp, like behind the schoolhouse where he ate the bread and jam his mother gave him every single morning. He peels away and pukes all over his feet.

Francie finds him curled in a ball a few feet from where he left his dinner.

'You all right? He meant well, Arch.'

'He'd do better to keep his bloody mouth shut.'

'Come back inside, the craic's good. No one even noticed you leave.'

Archie retches again then manages to sit up and Francie perches beside him.

'Remember the first time we got drunk, Arch?'

'You don't forget breaking into the house of God to steal his altar wine.'

'We just borrowed it.'

'And never put it back.'

'Pretty hard to put back when we puked it all over the back wall of the schoolhouse.'

'Took me three hours to get home that night. I had to crawl up the lane at the end. Didn't want to go through the kitchen so I knocked Annie's window until she let me in. Christ, she nearly killed me.'

'She was jealous we hadn't saved her some wine.'

'She took the rap in the morning. Told my mother it was her fault I was sick for she made me eat a load of raw gooseberries for a dare.'

'Let's go back in.'

'Christ, I ran away from her, Francie. I fuckin ran away.'

'Come on, it's grand; we told her you were bursting for a shite.'

They hear nothing of the shell's journey due to its steep trajectory. It explodes a hundred yards short, hurling handfuls of shrapnel into the buildings all around them. The second falls a similar distance away but more to the right and they are up and gone before a third can leave more than the contents of Archie's stomach on the ground.

When they burst back into the *estaminet* everyone is standing to silent attention. Madame Bussiere breaks the spell, shouting and gesticulating to her brood, and they are gone into the dark, racing for the safety of the wine cellar. The men listen to the sporadic pattern of the Boche ordnance as it hunts randomly for targets. Nine maybe ten more explosions, then it is over.

Corporal Lynch leaps on to his stool, raising a toast to the Kaiser and all of his blind bastard children, and laughter fills the void. They slake and sing again and Archie feels stronger; the shelling has pushed his flight on to the back pages of the evening.

Windy Patterson and a cockney called Williamson appear behind the counter lobbing bottles out into the crowd. Estelle and her brother return and howl French expletives at this intolerable escalation. When their mother materialises and announces that the evening is over Lynch nods to a pair of his coves who sneak behind her with the pins already plucked from their Mills bombs. They hurl the grenades out into the night and when the dull thuds erupt, Madame and her offspring are out the door again and racing for the cellar.

For the next two hours, they create their own Hun bombardment with a box of grenades liberated for the purpose from the Australian billet. Two or three bombs every ten minutes keeps the Frenchies snuggled tightly between the barrels of last autumn's labour. When every drop in the *estaminet* has been drunk Corporal Lynch and Francie Leonard stand at the doorway saluting the paralytic soldiers as they file past, placing the money from their pockets into a discarded British battle-bowler. When they are the only two remaining Francie and Lynch return to the bar and respectfully place the overflowing helmet as an offering on the altar beneath the sobering picture of Madam Bussiere's husband.

CHAPTER FIVE

County Fermanagh, Northern Ireland

May 1922

A mile out of Killeter she accepts that no one is giving chase. Behind her on the horse Francie's dead weight drags her from side to side until she pulls up and asks him what's wrong.

'My back's done from years of sleeping rough. It's all right for you, you're in a saddle.'

'You're like a bloody log strapped on behind me.'

'I'm sorry.'

'Just relax, we need to move with the horse.'

She feels him give in to her body, then. His arms fluid around her waist as he holds the shotgun across her thighs and tries his best to melt into her back. She allows herself to lean into him a little and eventually they find the sweet spot where their bodies move in tandem with the animal's. A row of poplars stand sentry along their left for a stretch and when the sky opens up again the trees have been replaced by a speedy little shallow stream running along the side of the road.

Francie lies with his face in the water, making nearly as much noise as the horse. On her belly beside him she drinks a little then scoops water on to the back of her neck to cool herself down. When they stand they are close and she wonders if he will try with the kissing again. He won't get anywhere, again. You can't show up unannounced in someone's barn with a gun and a reputation Jack the Ripper would be proud of and think you can just kiss away six fucking years. She looks at his mouth, surprised by how much it has changed over the years, then realises it's because his lips are cut and swollen from her punches.

'I'm sorry.'

'For what?'

'I shouldn't have hit you.'

'Wouldn't have expected anything else.'

'Am I that bad?'

'Well, it wouldn't be the first time, would it?'

She smiles at the memory, then heads for the horse so that he can't see her reliving it.

Archie's twelfth birthday was approaching. She was fourteen and Francie the unlucky number between them when her father announced that for his boy's big day the three of them could go to the market in Kesh together. He needed a new creamery can and when they had paid for that they could spend the change on sweets. It was only three miles to the village and they decided to walk and take turns carrying the can on the way home. The plan came to her in bed the night before as she lay thinking about Kesh village, because Kesh held something of great interest to Annie Johnston: a railway station, with a line to the coast.

For as long she could remember she had been obsessed with the ocean. It was the beating heart of many of the books she read, bringing people together or tearing them apart. The world was a just a myriad of people in different places and only the sea could decide whether they would find each other in the end or not, so how could she even begin to understand the nature of anything if she hadn't even seen the bloody thing? When her father had brought her home a copy of *Robinson Crusoe* it instilled in her such a sense of panic and claustrophobia that she couldn't pick up another book for weeks. She was Robinson Crusoe now, imprisoned on her tiny island by an endless sea of green fields and shit-brown bog. At night she'd pull her knees into her chest and imagine herself adrift on a raft, oblivious to whatever lay beyond the black water that filled up her bedroom. When daylight's fingers touched her face she'd leap into the morning swearing blindly to herself and to God and to anyone else who was listening that Annie Johnston would be getting the hell out of Drumskinny.

As they set off after a special birthday breakfast of soft-boiled duck eggs and soda bread, she informed the boys how the day would unfold. Archie wasn't sure and complained that they would get a hammering from Father for spending his creamery-can money on train tickets and it was his birthday after all so maybe he should decide but Francie lit up at the idea of seeing the Atlantic and quickly convinced him that now that the possibility had been presented to them they simply couldn't turn down the biggest adventure of their lives.

They barely spoke on the train, three noses glued to the window as the huge machine pulsed and screeched and spat them the twenty-five miles to the coast. The tide was in when they reached Bundoran and they ran all the way to the stone pier at the far end of the beach and stood on it for hours, shrieking with delight and terror when a bigger wave rose up over its end. Annie counted the waves until she had determined a pattern, explaining to the boys that every seventh one was the big swell, then they dared themselves forward wave by wave until the seventh reached for them and they sprinted backwards away from its grasp. When they had exhausted themselves they wandered into town and spent the rest of her father's money on huge ham sandwiches and bags of toffees and walked the streets watching the great and good of the world going about their holidays. Not until the train was nearly back in Kesh did anyone raise the small issue of the money or the complete and utter lack of anything vaguely resembling a brand-new

48

creamery can. Archie got himself into such a panic that he would surely bring on one of his fits until Annie stood and presented the final part of her plan.

They would be 'robbed' on the way home from Kesh, perhaps somewhere near Francie's schoolhouse where the Rooneys, a family of ill repute, lived. Then, as long as everyone manned up and stuck to the story, no one would be any the wiser. It was some hours later as they trudged past the schoolhouse that she stopped and announced phase two of operation fake robbery. One of the boys would punch the other repeatedly so that it looked like he had been beaten up whilst heroically holding on to the creamery can. Archie protested that he should have to neither punch anyone nor be punched on his fuckin birthday so she asked Francie if he had the balls to take a few slaps from a girl.

Her first blow glanced off his cheek and when he sniggered she snapped and punched him full in the eye then socked him again square in the mouth before he could open it to protest. When all was said and done and the interrogation was over it was undoubtedly Francie's injuries that carried the day. Her father grilled them like a judge at the kitchen table but he never got past the fact that the boy had clearly taken a hiding. Annie played a blinder, vividly describing events that never happened and teenage boys who didn't exist, but then she had her father wrapped so tightly round her wee finger anyway that he would never have doubted a word that his little lady said. Completely in the clear and on a high from finally seeing the ocean, she had an entire week then to laugh at Francie, as his eye turned from black to blue and then onwards from green to a rather sickly yellow.

Three miles later and one short of the border, she finds herself speeding towards the back of a lorry. Francie shouts in her ear and she slows Orion to a trot to buy time for him to make the call. It doesn't look like a police vehicle, though it's hard to tell as she knows the Specials have been commandeering anything locally that they can fit bodies into. Her choices are limited if she leaves the road. Directly to the left are some shallow hills that offer cover but to their right and further ahead on both sides lies open bogland that would neither hide them nor take the weight of the horse.

The lorry slows so as not to spook the animal when it passes. Francie has dropped his arms from around her waist and is trying his best to hide the shotgun behind her back. When they're two hundred yards out the lorry pulls its nose slightly to the side to offer more room for their passage and the change in angle exposes a row of peaked caps above the tailgate. Two men in black jump down and as their weapons are passed out Francie yanks her left arm, and she is jerking the horse's head around and they veer off the road, Francie shooting behind her head. The cracks from his pistol are deafening as she feels the horse panic beneath her then shoot towards the foothills.

How could they have been so stupid? While she has been worrying about who was behind them they've galloped into the lorry that dropped the guards at the bridge before rushing on to man the border crossing. She doesn't turn but pictures them kneeling in a line to steady their arms. When the volley sings, she hears bullets come alive all around them. Francie grips her waist, trying to shield her body with his own. Orion drops his head as rounds zip past his ears then he stumbles at the bottom of the hill and they begin to fall. Francie throws the shotgun and grabs the saddle but as its knees buckle the animal roars and he is up again and strong and they are gone behind the hill.

When they reach the summit of the second hillock Francie turns to see their pursuers beginning to descend the first. The distance makes shooting pointless but the word is out, and he knows the word will soon spread into a fully coordinated manhunt.

They can't return to the road and the only way to get to the border now is to cross an expanse of high ground stretching for many miles. Whatever comes their way Francie is going to miss the shotgun.

They dismount to cross a wide stretch of bogland between them and the next rise. It has been dug in places, the turf stacked and ready for the cart, but closer to the rise it is uncultivated and difficult to navigate. Wet peat guzzles on Orion's legs and the exhausted animal begins to slow them down. They climb again then trudge a plateau to a scrubby treeline which they exit on to a steep, well-worn lane. Half a painstaking hour later Annie announces that the horse needs to rest. Francie scouts ahead to ascertain the lie of the land and when he returns he can see that she has been crying. Orion has collapsed and lies covered in a thick white lather of sweat. When he has coaxed the horse slowly back on to its feet he finds the bullet hole just behind the right shoulder. There is no exit wound and he knows that Orion's race is run.

They take it very slowly for the next few hundred yards until she points to some mature oak trees planted a couple of fields' width from the path. Beneath the protective umbrella of branches, they settle the horse amongst the walls of an old farmstead. The roof is long gone but the structure remains sound and they sit in the dwelling room by the stone fireplace while the horse lies dying in the room next door where farm animals slept for generations. When Francie takes the Mauser from his belt and sets it on the hearth for easy access Annie crosses to him and picks it up.

'Show me.'

He watches her eyes to see if the story will change and when he is sure that it won't he flicks the safety off and shrugs. Annie plays with the weight of the gun in her hand then walks through the doorway and shoots the horse twice, once in the heart and once in the head. She returns with her saddlebags and tosses him the bread and cheese she packed this morning and they sit on the ground and eat in silence. She tries to hold his eyes but he glances at her briefly then stares off through the open doorway instead.

'Killing people for years but shocked at someone putting a poor animal out of its misery?'

'You know nothing about killing.'

'I'm sure you'll teach me.'

She watches to see if he'll take the bait but he stays calm and that angers her.

'Why the hell did you join the IRA?'

'Because I hate the British army.'

'You were in the British army?'

'Then I guess I'm fully qualified to hate it.'

It's his turn to stare at her now.

'Why did you come after me, Annie?'

'I don't know yet. But I'll be sure to let you know before you hang.'

Beyond the abandoned dwelling, they find more. A scattered chain of shattered homes guiding them up the hillside. He'd seen them all over Ireland. Entire settlements where everyone left on the same day for the same coffin ship. After they had ambushed and shot Inspector Drake and his wife in County Clare they had spent the night in a famine village in the stony wasteland of the Burren, knowing that they were now the hunted. The sadness of the place was palpable. No one slept that night and barely a word was spoken as each sat with the history of his own.

Nearly half of the column had family who had left during the famine for America. Molloy's maternal grandparents had met in the hold, bound for New York. They had given each other something to live for while dozens died of disease all around them. Francie listened patiently that night as the Yank clambered along the branches of his entire family tree, then as the first hints of grey started to spill into the corners of the sky, Molloy offered something up that he had told never told another. He had left America and run off to the war because he had been caught sleeping with his brother's wife.

'He's five years older than me and she two more older than he. They met when I was thirteen. So she was there, as I grew from a kid to a man, like an older sister but not, so those other feelings, the ones that cloud a man's mind, would always get in the way. It happened first when I had just turned twenty. My brother worked in Washington and New York a lot and in his frequent absences we kept on going for two full years until I came down from his bed one morning and found him waiting for me at the dining-room table with a revolver where his coffee should be. I don't know how long he had known for, but it must have been some time for his anger had already faded into something worse. He could barely look at me as he told me to leave and never to come back or he would have no choice left but to kill me. I don't believe to this day that he would have had it in him but then he hit me with the real threat. He told me that if I didn't return he would spare our mother the sordid details. And so I was exiled, Francie. It would take a poor son to hang around until his mother found out who he really was.'

At dawn they shared a cigarette for breakfast and moved out to meet the soldiers.

The British had taken defensive positions in the night and they opened up with Lewis guns when the first man came into range. At that point, they could have easily disappeared back up into the rocks but instead, they charged, driven downhill by the ghosts of the village. Two men died and four were captured. They didn't know if they had killed any British. Only those who witnessed Crown corpses first hand and the recipients of the telegrams in Whitehall knew for certain how many troops were ever lost. Claim, claim and counter-claim. They could never have killed them all, anyway. It was a matter of keeping the threat alive until London got bored with the hassle. The expense of keeping an army in Ireland was the key to it leaving, not individual violent deaths in the middle of nowhere.

Annie walks a short distance ahead and he is watching the slender line of her back and admiring how her body moves perfectly as one entity when she drops to her hunkers and waves him down. The ground has flattened into a small plateau two hundred yards across and they must cover this to continue up the opposing hill. At the top of this, the figure of a man is clearly outlined on the darkening skyline. He watches them as they get to their feet and stare back. The clothing is civilian but in this crucible of civil unrest and guerrilla warfare that means nothing. There are no sheep on the hills so he is unlikely to be a farmer, yet if it was an ambush or a local loyal to the Crown, why would he have shown himself?

They climb halfway up the rise to their left and move forward along its gut rather than expose themselves on its ridge or face the open terrain of the plateau. When they arrive at the spot where the figure had stood he has vanished into the dusk. The land continues at this level for some distance and they push on through rush-covered terrain that will never dry come even July. By the time they reach the next ascent it is the moon that illuminates their silence. Francie picks three oak trees growing close together in a row in front of some ruins. There are viable escape routes should they be attacked from any side and the walls will offer shelter from bullet or breeze. When the last of the bread and cheese is finished she gets up and walks into the darkness. He collects kindling and sticks around the old site and sets a fire between the walls then sits and cleans the Mauser methodically in the light from the fire.

As he works in silence he gives in to a feeling that's been building in him all day. Something he hasn't felt for a long, long time. A feeling of fear not for himself but for someone else. She could have been killed earlier. She could be killed in the morning. What have you done dragging her into this? You're a bollocks, Leonard. A selfish bloody bollocks.

He stands and stares through the doorway but there is no sign of her returning. In the morning you must tell her. You must man up and send her home.

With her back pressed into the furthest of the oak trees she lets his question poke her repeatedly while she tries to locate an honest answer. Why did you come? Why did you come? A hundred reasons or maybe one. I've already lost Archie and no matter who you've become isn't it easier to help you than to read about your funeral in the paper? And how dare you ask me the bloody questions? Why did you stop writing to me? Why didn't you come home? You detested your father's Republican politics yet now you're 'fighting to free Ireland'? She has worked herself into a silent rage. She should be over there screaming these questions at him but it's too early yet. She needs to know that he won't get up in the middle of the night and run away from the answers.

There is a barely discernible change in the air above her head and a white streak cuts through the night from high right to low left, landing on the ground in front of her. She doesn't breathe as she watches the big bird of prey until it senses her and turns to stare back. The round shape of the face is clearly visible as it takes her in, though it is too dark to make out the eyes. They watch each other for a few seconds and then with one pull on its impressive wingspan the bird is gone and she is left sitting with her final answer to Francie's question. Why did you come? I came because I was bored.

'There's a fire; come and stay warm.'

He is standing over her and he puts his hand out and she takes it, rising to her feet.

'There was an owl, swooped not ten feet in front of my face.'

'Their hour.'

'Not seen one for years.'

'The nesting pair at the Dolans' gone?'

'When Charlie and Jamesie passed their nephew tore down the barn.'

'Both?'

'Jamesie with the drink then Charlie with the broken heart.'

'They were twins, right?'

'Just brothers.'

They curl around opposite sides of the fire and watch the flames chew through the last of the wood.

'I was with your mother when your father died.'

He is wide awake, his heart moving through his chest into his throat.

'She took it well, had time to prepare.'

He wills words to come, to thank her.

'Your sisters were a great comfort to her. I stayed the three days of the wake and helped with the tea.'

He opens his mouth, desperate to say anything, to acknowledge the cards she has put on the table.

'Anyway, I thought you might like to know.'

He rises on an elbow to let the breath past his chest down into his body.

'Did you see the oul cunt before he went?'

She bites her lips but it bursts through anyway, spreading across the embers where it catches in him and they are sharing their first laugh for six years.

'I did but he couldn't speak, hadn't for months.'

'Thank fuck for small mercies.'

The second wave is deeper and when it has receded part of the wall that has been built between them has been washed away.

CHAPTER SIX

Hédauville, France

November 1915

Crozier wakes them with his feet. They take a couple of boots each as he moves by but when he comes across Francie he carries on kicking.

'Get up, you drunken bastards, get up!'

When he tries to rise, Francie is shoved backwards and hammered again and again.

'I said get up!'

He catches a foot en route to his chest and hauls himself upwards leaving Crozier on his back in the filthy straw. The sergeant is up in an instant, his nose fighting Francie's for a place in his face.

'You struck a superior.'

'I struck no one.'

'Court martial for striking an officer.'

'You're not an officer.'

A hundred statues refuse to breathe – not a buttock nor a moustache twitches.

'You smell of drink, Leonard.'

'Off-duty last night, Sergeant.'

'We go into the line tonight and you've been drinking?'

'Off-duty last night, Sergeant.'

'You a fuckin parrot? A papist parrot, boys, that's what we've got ourselves here.'

The laughter comes but it's forced and frightened. Jack steps forward and opens his mouth but nothing comes out.

'What is your problem, Elliot?'

'We all had a drink last night, sir.'

'We all?'

'Yes, Sergeant.'

'There are one hundred men in this billet, Elliot; are you going to stand there and tell me that every single one of them took drink last night?'

'No, Sergeant.'

'Why not, Elliot?'

'That wouldn't be true, Sergeant.'

'So you're a liar, Elliot.'

'No, Sergeant.'

'Then you're confused, is that it?'

'No, Sergeant.'

'Maybe you're still drunk, Elliot; are you drunk on duty, Private?'

'No, Sergeant.'

'A liar and a fuckin parrot.'

He steps back into Francie's face and studies it closely.

'This is what happens when you let Catholics into the British army, boys. Drunkenness, laziness. A right filthy mess.'

He kicks Francie's kit, scattering it across the stable block. Francie exhales loudly and rocks back on his hips, his right shoulder dropping for the punch. Archie recognises the body language from their days fighting with boys from other towns and he knows that his friend has finally snapped. He barges past Crozier, creating a barrier between the two men.

'Leave it now; it's not worth it, Francie.'

Archie holds Francie's eyes until the mist begins to burn off and then it is over. Crozier walks to the side and addresses them both.

'How very touching. Field punishment, both of you, as soon as we come out of the line. If you make it out of the line.'

During training he had punished Francie often in the dunes behind Finner strand. Crozier had a favourite slope for the purpose and his reasons for choosing it were twofold. It might have been shorter than some of its neighbours but there was none steeper on the west coast of Ireland. Its gradient could finish a man after one ascent in full kit, never mind the double figures Crozier demanded. His second reason was the view. The summit offered the perfect window on to the mouth of the Erne where it flowed into the Atlantic and as the men sweated years off their lives trying to reach him Crozier sat staring out to sea imagining the life he could have made for himself beyond the horizon if he had only listened to his brother.

'Why run away to America, George, that's what they do? We have the docks and the shipyards.' His brother said that just because he'd been a soldier didn't mean he had to live the rest of his life at war, but what did George know? Christ, how he wished he had gone; kept his mouth shut for once and looked out for himself rather than Ulster. He could have swapped the shipyard for one in New York or been an officer in their army with his experience from Africa. But he didn't go because he believed in the Union and Ulster and if necessary he would die protecting what he believed in from those Papist bastards down in Dublin. So he had stayed, and now at the bitter reality of forty he was preparing for his second war while behind his back Britain made promises to Dublin and Papists were joining his beloved army because they'd been promised Home Rule when it ended.

He was careful when he punished his men. He always brought a subordinate who would testify to its efficiency and he would never put a man on the dune alone and risk being accused of prejudice. He brought them in twos and threes for the slightest misdemeanours and if he wanted specifically to get to an individual, a friend was dragged along on something trumped up. The necessity of his actions wasn't questioned. He was whipping farmers into fighters and his superiors never doubted his motivations as the reality of France drew nearer.

Only once had Crozier broken his own rules. Returning from a thirsty day's leave he had ordered Francie from the mess tent as the sun set and marched him alone to the shoreline. At the foot of the slope, the accused asked what he had done wrong but the reply, rasped back through a whiskey fog, was simply that he would never do anything right. Crozier's legs were too unsteady to carry him to the top for the performance so he stood at the bottom as the rising tide lapped around his ankles, howling his orders like a man possessed. By the time Francie completed his fourth descent the sea was above his sergeant's knees. Exhausted, he tripped at the bottom and rolled into the water where Crozier lunged for his collars, submerging him completely before beating and yelling him back to the foot of the climb. The sheer force of his rage left the older man spent and he sat in the waves while they slapped around his chest. The fifth ascent was impossible. The sand held Francie fast, sucking the air from his lungs as acid raged through the muscles in his back and legs. He sank to his knees but Crozier's orders resurrected him and he pushed onwards as the coarse brine-drenched trousers grated the skin from the inside of his thighs. When he could go no further he collapsed sideways into the sand where he lay at a precarious angle looking up at the evening's first stars. He waited for the volley but no more screams came from below. Crozier had either returned to the pub or drowned in the surf where he sat.

A seagull appeared above and as he watched it get closer it swooped towards him and landed nearby. It squawked at him twice then cocked its head so that they could watch each other from the same angle. When it hopped closer he foresaw it taking flight with his eyeball in its beak, so he summoned a shout but all that came from his mouth was sand. When the bird started towards him at speed he pushed downwards with all his remaining strength, freeing himself from the grip of the dune, then rolled back to its bottom and came to rest in the sea beside Crozier who sat submerged to his chin, staring beyond the horizon towards America.

CHAPTER SEVEN

County Fermanagh

May 1922

Francie comes to and sits bolt upright between the walls of the farmhouse. His groin and thighs are drenched in sweat and at first he thinks he has soiled himself in the dream state. Embarrassed, he looks to her but she is nowhere to be seen. He wades out into the morning but the sunlight can't burn through the mental fog. Sitting by the wall he closes his eyes and his temples throb in time to the low drone high above in the clouds. Synapses spark and he explodes to his feet and is up into the belly of the nearest oak tree. Branch by branch he hauls himself skywards. Halfway to the top he sees light bouncing off metal above. On a strong bough he secures himself with his legs and pulls the branches apart with his hands. The red, white and blue roundels are clearly visible on the wings of the Avro biplane as it makes its second pass over the farm. As it disappears from sight the change in the engine note tells him that it will come around again. He moves position and something else catches his eye below. Annie has come out of the bushes and is standing in open ground, her hand shielding her eyes as she stares at the heavens.

'Go back, go fuckin back!'

He slides earthwards, ripping skin from wrist and shin, then the ground hits like bullets through each ankle.

'Annie, lie down, lie down on the ground.'

She can't hear him over the roar and as the plane dives for a proper look she sprints towards the walls where they slept. He stays where he is until it's gone. Better they don't see them both, though the damage is probably done. They run from the farmhouse to the treeline at the base of the hill and lie in the shade until their chests stop burning.

'Can they really see much from up there?'

'Everything, they can see everything.'

Hazels cover the rise to its summit and they stuff their pockets with nuts as they climb. A steep descent and a short bog later and they are on to the lower slopes of a much tougher climb. Exposed now to any binoculars below, they move in spurts from one rock formation to the next. At a small stream coming through the limestone they gorge on mossy water and raw nuts. Again steadily upwards stopping only when lungs sear. She hears it first and pulls him on to his knees beside her. He watches her search for the sound again then rises to go.

'Listen!'

'It's your imagination.'

As he moves off she slaps him hard in the stomach and yanks his arm until he meets her on the ground.

'Jesus Chr—'

She slams her hand over his mouth.

'Just shut up and listen, Francis.'

He is enjoying her ferocity when the rumble greets him. She lets her face say it before crawling into a gap between two large rocks. He watches the sky trying to decipher the aeroplane's direction then shoves himself into the shadows beside her.

'Don't tell me I'm imagining things.'

'Don't call me Francis.'

The plane circles the mountain and each time its racket recedes they climb in sprints to their next hiding place. The further they rise the more acute the gradient and their progress slows as the countryside spreads out beneath them. Tight against a parched trickle of a waterfall they stare up into the belly of the beast as it flies over their heads and glides downhill towards the green and brown patchwork quilt of the valley below. Halfway between themselves and the bottom the pilot wiggles his wings in a nod to someone on the ground. Francie focuses on the slopes beneath where the signal happened until he catches flashes of sunlight bouncing off metal. Probably Specials but it could be British soldiers. District Inspector Crozier has clearly convinced someone that the prize is worth it if the RAF are playing ball.

They push on until a few hundred yards from the summit he turns and signals for her to stop.

'If they take us you're my prisoner.'

'Crozier saw me at our farm.'

'I went back; I took you hostage and stole your horse.'

She studies his face then her eyes rest on something over his shoulder and she whispers.

'Francie ...'

He turns to find the man they saw yesterday standing not fifty feet away waist deep in a clump of gorse.

'You'll tear your clothes in there, mate.'

The man says nothing. Francie's chest and shoulder tighten and he breathes into the joint to release it for the draw. The man's cap is pushed back on his head in a boyish fashion and the caked lines on his forehead are clear even from this distance. His suit is filthy and ragged and Francie knows that this man has rarely left the mountain. Got to be sixty if he's a day.

'You live up here?'

Silence. He doesn't even move his head. Francie points back down the hillside.

'*Saighdiúirí Briotanacha.*'

The Irish works. The old man comes out of the bushes and walks towards them, stopping close enough for them to gag on the years of stale sweat trapped in his clothing. His shirt collar is black with dirt yet done up proudly with the tie that is tucked neatly behind his hole-ridden waistcoat. A man so proud of his Sunday best he hasn't taken it off for twenty years. He points in the same direction that Francie had.

'*Briotanacha?*'

'*Sin é.*'

The old man looks at the two of them in turn then back down the side of the mountain; he spits on the ground and shakes his head slowly.

'*Briotanacha.*'

With the smallest twitch of the head, he signals them to follow him and he takes off with surprising speed back into the gorse.

She follows them along an old sheep rut that cuts downhill in acute twists and turns, coming out between huge rocks into a natural basin in the hillside. There is a small lake in its middle and they wind their way around this towards a series of derelict homesteads similar to those that they slept in last night. The dwellings are without roofs, bar one in the corner of the settlement furthest away from the water. The old man heads for this and pushes through the door, waving them inside.

It is difficult for Annie to adjust to the darkness. Even though it is afternoon the windows are so small and so filthy that barely any daylight reaches inside. The contents are rudimentary, to say the least. A wooden chair set by what is more of a bench than a table and a second over by the hearth where the cooking is done. The chimney breast is black from the open fire in this badly ventilated room and the ceiling bulges in the middle, looking likely to come down at any moment. The owner takes his seat by the hearth and starts to move pots and a griddle out of the way so that he can set a fire. When the turf is sending a dark pungent smoke out into the room he produces a pipe from inside his jacket and takes to banging it violently on the leg of his chair. Happy that it's clear he cuts a plug of sticky dark tobacco with a penknife and proceeds to pump more fumes at them. Annie begins to cough uncontrollably, which their host finds hilarious and his belly laugh follows her outside after she has made her excuses. She stands in the ruins next door with her eyes closed, searching for the aeroplane's engine, and when she is sure she won't find it she relieves herself then heads for the lough to wash the day from her back and the smoke from her eyes.

When she's done she returns and sits on the floor by the fire. The man finishes his pipe, places the griddle in front of the flames and flattens potato cakes on the metal rungs for the cooking. The smell reminds Annie that she hasn't taken hot food since leaving her mother's and her stomach tightens, forcing bile and hazelnuts upwards into her throat. She thanks the man, telling him that she is grateful for his hospitality and friendship. There is no reply. She isn't even sure if her words were understood and Francie hasn't enough Irish to attempt it. Annie repeats her name, pointing to herself then at the old man, to try to decipher his, but she receives only a cheeky grin in return. An ancient black kettle is lifted off the heat and he pours them tea thick and black enough to improve the roads in the valley below.

The only other thing in the room bar the chairs and bench are stacks of old newspapers. Annie gets up and begins to leaf through the issues on top. Intrigued, she digs deeper and deeper into one of the tallest piles.

'These papers go back for ever, look, 1883, "A Meeting of the Irish Home Rule League".'

She laughs as she opens window after window on time.

'*Irish Times,* 1875. "Captain Boyton's swim. American Captain Paul Boyton crosses the English Channel in twenty-four hours." There is a *News Letter* here from 1832, Francie; where the hell did he get them all?'

He rises from the floor and joins her at the treasure trove.

'Visitors, people returning up the mountain with supplies.'

'"Agrarian outrage in Kerry"; "War with the Boer"; "Mr Parnell in America"; "Famine in the West".'

One hundred years of printed history. The old man leaves the fire and joins them. Annie puts the paper she is holding back on the pile.

'I'm so sorry, I should have asked.'

That smile again, deep and warm and genuine. There is a smaller pile on the floor in the corner and he starts to sift through it, passing her up specific newspapers.

'These must be his favourites.'

'April 1912; "*Titanic* sinks with great loss of life".'

He shows her some more and she engages, intrigued, but then he hands her one that wipes the smile from her face. She runs her eyes over the yellowing front of the *Belfast News Letter* then drops it gently on top of the pile and wanders back to the fire.

Francie lifts it and reads the headline:

2 July 1916. BATTLE OF THE SOMME. ULSTER DIVISION. ALL STILL GOING WELL.

They had over five thousand casualties by 2 July. Two thousand of them dead. He lifts his eyes from the paper and finds those of the old-timer watching him. The smile has gone and in the brief moment when their eyes meet Francie gets the strange sense that somehow this man knows he was there. The older man takes the paper from him and puts it back on the pile before covering it with another. As he moves back to the fire to turn the potato cakes he rests his hand gently on Francie's shoulder for the merest of seconds.

An hour before sunset Francie heads out to learn how close the hunters have crept. He stays off the sheep track but follows it to where they met their host that afternoon. From here he cuts uphill, stalking the summit then the upper slopes on the far side. There is neither sight nor sound of anyone. He doesn't like it. An entire search party shouldn't be hard to find. There is no way they marched up to the top of the hill then marched back down again. It is dark when he makes it back to the cottage by the lake. Annie is asleep in a blanket on the floor by the newspapers. The old one smokes by his fireside and barely acknowledges him as he enters. Francie pulls the second seat up and places the kettle back in the embers. It is instantly lifted off again by his host and placed on the floor between them. He disappears into the room where he sleeps and comes back with a green bottle, a chipped glass and a blue and white enamel mug. He places the bottle and the vessels on the hearth and gestures for Francie to choose his weapon. The younger man picks up the glass to the delight of his audience, who roars with laughter then snatches it from him.

Whatever is in his mug it's not what the bottle was manufactured for. The clear spirit is potent enough to strip the smoke stains from the ceiling and to purge the years of filth from the oul fella's collar. Hardened though he is from years of drink, Francie winces his way through the first cupful. They remain in silence yet are completely at ease. The bottle is half full when they take into it, and empty before very long. The older man's smile dances across the room to the newspapers and he produces another full bottle from somewhere between the outbreak of the Franco-Prussian War and the conclusion of the Russian Revolution. Francie has sampled plenty of *poitín* on his travels through Ireland but this stuff is in a different league. By the third helping the bottom half of his face has frozen and he has lost the commission of his tongue. By the end of the fourth, he can't decipher whether his arse is on the seat or hovering just slightly above it. When they have finished the fifth the oul boy opens the door and points at the moon and they leave Annie sleeping and fly off together to the side of the lake.

Francie sits by the water's edge while his partner hovers a little way off, singing mournfully to himself in Irish. The tune has a crippling beauty to it that pushes Francie on to his back where he lies and wishes more than anything that he understood the lyrics. The woman in Galway who had housed and fed him for a month while he drilled new recruits comes back to him again. Her filthy scowl when she learnt he had no Irish, then her refusal to cook for two full days upon hearing he had fought for the British.

'You don't speak the language of your country, yet you took up arms for the oppressor who stopped you from learning it?'

He had fought a constant battle to be accepted through his years in the South. There were plenty of volunteers who had served in France but his Ulster accent and senior rank would always stand against him.

'Coming down here on your high horse from the Black North to tell us what to do?'

There was little point in explaining that he only went to war because his friend was determined to and he was in love with the friend's sister and had promised to look after him because he had asthma and a tendency to fuck things up just by looking at them, and he shouldn't, in fact, be anywhere near an army, never mind a bloody gun, even though it's the only thing he had ever wanted since he first started reading shite romantic novels about war as a boy. There was little point either in explaining that he wasn't alone.

Twenty thousand National Volunteers had left and fought in the trenches and many turned their guns on the British again once they came home. Even Tom 'the legend' Barry down in Cork and Michael Collins' own shadow, Emmet Dalton of the Dublin Brigade, had done their bit for Blighty and been forgiven. But Francie was an Ulster man so once a Brit, always a Brit. He searches for Archie up above in the stars. She has barely mentioned your name, kid. Yet you're always here. The boy who brought us together, who will always keep us apart.

2 July 1916. All still going well.

Why did it take so long to filter back? Every single person on the other side of the Channel knew what the hell was going on. Finding no answers in the constellations, he shuts his eyes and moves backwards in time across a continent. Curled up in a muddy hole he listens to the various inflections of Empire dancing past him along the supply trench towards the front. Glaswegian and Geordie, Cork man and Welsh. Canadian, Indian, Australian, cockney and Dub. The closer up-and-over comes the quieter they become. The good-luck charms of their accents evaporating with the morning mist. When they are heard again they will all sound the same. There is a uniformity to men's voices when they choke on their own blood while begging for their mother's tit. A million shells from thousands of guns for hundreds of hours.

'Not a rat'll have survived under that, boys; we'll be drinking in his third line by lunch, boys!'

It was planned for five days then up-and-over, but the weather changed the minds of the generals and the delay drowned the men in a sea of doubt. Half mad and trapped in filth, they waited, thousands together yet each alone, each knowing deep down in the arsehole of his heart that the Germans lay waiting too.

Archie shakes him by the collars to wake him for his watch. He grabs his friend by the wrists and hauls himself into the night but when he finds his feet he is standing by a small lake on a mountain-side with an old man in his Sunday best.

Back at the fireside, they keep drinking. Cold salted potatoes are raked from a saucepan with filthy fingers. As they digest their meal, a prolonged howl echoes across the lough and Francie is on his feet by the door with the Mauser in his hand. It comes again. High-pitched, almost human, a tortured child, then down through the register into the diaphragm of something much older. He laughs at himself and returns to the fire. You've had a few too many, Francie boy, getting spooked by the nightlife, son. The third time and the old man is up off his seat skipping towards the door. He puts his face and hands flat against it for a second then steps back and watches the latch, clearly disturbed.

'*Bean-sidhe.*'

It is the first word the old man has spoken since the hillside when they first met. Francie has encountered these superstitions in every corner of Ireland, pagan myth still strong amongst the country folk.

'No banshee. Foxes, fucking.'

He guides his comrade in drink back to his seat and pours them each a large distraction.

'No banshee, just booze.'

As they put paid to the second half of the second bottle it takes a while for the oul fella to stop staring at the door. In the corners of Francie's eyes parts of the room move at different speeds. A heat finger claws his spine and if he doesn't stare directly into the fire it changes colour, coming towards his feet in a molten green-and-purple river. As the warmth in his back spans his thighs and dances around his balls he gives in to the liquor for liquor always knows best. He downs the contents of his mug and stares at the old man, studying the landscape of his face. The cracks on the forehead are

71

vanishing gradually as dirt runs away in the streams of sweat sprung by the heat from the fire. The smaller lines around the eyes and mouth begin to soften too and when the banshee cries again a younger man stands and beams down at Francie and he knows that he has seen the smile before as he floats from his seat to greet it. They are standing so close that he smells booze on breath then he's grabbing the jacket and shirt and pulling him in for the hug and the sweat is much staler than alcohol and the stubble is coarse on his cheek as he grinds it into his own.

'It's yourself, then, is it? You took your time.'

'I'll wake her, will I Francie? I'll wake her and we can tell her how I really died.'

It's the man not the morning that wakes him. He has been asleep on the floor behind Annie, his tongue stuck to the back of his eyeballs, his body syphoning hers for heat. He remembers neither the decision to sleep nor the transition to his current position. There is a high-pitched whine in his ears and when he opens his lids nothing happens. You've done it this time; you've actually drunk yourself fucking blind. He swears at the old man and closes his eyes again. There are horses somewhere nearby. At least two of them whinnying in his immediate vicinity. The old man's boot bounces off his arse and he is up to teach the oul fucker a lesson when he sees the panic in the face. An intricate military mime including marching and shooting gets lost in the fug of the hangover, but when the soldiers begin to shout outside the penny finally drops. Out through the half-door at the back of the house, his hand over Annie's mouth then along the wall to the gable end. When the old man has checked beyond he bundles them around the corner and starts to rummage by the edge of a turf stack. A rope loop then a trapdoor lifting and they are kicked into the foundations of the cottage.

There is a narrow strip of light at ground level at the far end and they crawl towards it. When he makes the distance Francie lies flat and lets Annie roll over him so that she can have her face closest to the only air source.

Their hideout is no more than three feet high and five wide so they lie down, pulling knees to chests. This wasn't dug for keeping animals in. The beasts would suffocate down here in hours. Catholic clergy more likely. A priest hole from the persecution times. If he could get the old one to speak he would soon find out if there is a mass rock nearby. On his side, in the dark, he fights to control the panic that floods every cell. You have been here before. Holed up like a rat while the terriers circle above. When the adrenalin levels begin to settle, the hangover returns and sweat runs off his back by the pint. He shifts a little so that he can pull the Mauser and hold it in his right hand. His left hand reaches for her and he squeezes her fingers gently in a repetitive pulse. The gun is no use down here. If the trapdoor opens and he pulls the trigger they will simply count to ten then lob a grenade down between them.

Voices shout all around as the buildings are searched, then directly above there is a loud crashing as the door is kicked off the hinges. Don't these arseholes ever just knock?

'What's your name?'

The accent is local. The Specials are in town.

'Have you seen a man and a girl on the mountain?'

'Fuckin answer him when he talks to you.'

The oul fella's silence is greeted with a fist in the guts. Beneath the house, they hear the dull thud of him hitting the floorboards followed by a fit of coughing. Horses whinny again, only this time they are directly above. How the hell did they get horses up here? There must be another route up the border side that isn't as boggy or steep.

'This is the only one we've found, sir.'

'What does he know?'

'Won't speak; can't maybe.'

'Course he can; Fenians never shut the fuck up. Bring him outside, he smells like he could use a dip in the lough.'

'Yes, Inspector Crozier.'

With Francie between her and the only way out, Annie begins to suffocate beside the small ventilation hole. She closes her eyes and tries to regulate her breathing but she feels entombed and the only thing for it is to keep them open and focused on the outside. The feet of the constables pass back and forward through her narrow field of vision. Directly in front, she can see the rushes at the edge of the lake and when the horses arrive she can tell that one is black and one chestnut and that the riders who dismount wear very impressive boots. When they have finished their business inside the cottage a much less remarkable pair is dragged out behind them. She sees his back hit the floor between their heels and then hands on both sides grab and lift until his raggedy legs are pulled rigid between the smart uniformed ones that hold him up.

'Who has been visiting you all the way up here, Granda?'

His silence weighs heavy on her lids but she fights the panic and keeps watching.

'Fetch my whip.'

She crushes Francie's hand until she imagines the knuckles of his fingers bursting through the skin.

'Take his jacket off.'

Francie's body twitches then tenses and she knows that he is holding himself from rushing outside.

'Have you seen a man and a girl on the mountain?'

Crozier's voice is as calm as the day is long and he waits for an answer before a single crack announces the whip's arrival in the flesh of the old man.

'There's a bottle on your hearth with a glass and a mug beside it. Both are still wet from the drinking. So, either you had a guest or you kept swapping seats to keep yourself company, is that it?'

Another note from the bullwhip.

'Musical fucking chairs, was it?'

A flurry of lashes crushes the old man to his knees before a prolonged howl lowers him backwards into the dirt directly in front of Annie. Boots rain into his stomach and crotch before he is hauled back on to his feet and into the face of Crozier.

'Your vocal cords work, then. I'm only going to ask you once more. Where are the man and the girl?'

He opens his mouth but the only sound offered is a dry retching as he hawks his guts down his front.

'Gentlemen, what's the only thing better than a village with one Catholic in it?'

The report from the heavy Webley revolver bounces through the ventilation hole off the hard ground, punching Annie in the eardrums. Her voice slips out a little but gets lost in the shock wave that follows the firing of a gun.

'A village with no Catholics in it.'

The old man's body has been blown several feet backwards and he lies staring up at the sky over the cottage where he has lived since his mother gave birth to him in the back room. He sighs loudly as his life begins to piss from the large exit wound blown open underneath his shoulder blade. As he exhales for a second time his head rolls to the side and his eyes come to rest on Annie's. They watch each other as the oul fella tries to remember who the pretty girl is and what the fuck she is doing under his house. Slowly a smile creeps from his eyes, heading around the ridges of his nose and into the corners of his mouth before he dies.

CHAPTER EIGHT

Beaumont-Hamel, France

November 1915

They are brought into the line at dusk. As the sun retreats they advance through a bombed-out village where nothing remains intact. Horses and mules decompose on the roadsides and as they are smothered by fouled air they know that there are human carcasses hidden amongst the beasts. Broken buildings rise from the shadows like rotten teeth stencilled on the darkening sky, then abruptly there are only mud walls and blackness above as they descend into the third line of support.

Archie focuses on Windy's outline as they stumble further into the intestines of the world. In the moonlight, the taller man's helmet is silhouetted amongst the stars but closer to the front the defences deepen and he sees neither his friend nor the strangers sleeping in holes in the walls who curse and snore as they pass. They are joining the Royal Hampshires in the line, the Englishmen tasked with spoon-feeding the Inniskillings through their maiden ordeal in the trenches. There is a bottleneck at an elbow in the second line and they meet the retreating troops whom they will replace. Pressed into chalk and clay, Archie's belly still brushes each passing soldier and his stomach turns at the putrid stench of men who have held the line for six nights. Not a word of greeting is uttered; each Englishman focused on escaping his own personal hell, each Ulster man wondering what form his will take.

As they move into the fighting trench star-shells burst over no man's land and fingers of light poke into the cracks in the earth, momentarily illuminating the fear in their eyes. Lieutenant Gallagher passes with a counterpart from the Hampshires and a series of whispers and gestures disperses troops to various sections of the line.

They take turns during the night standing sentry with a chaperone. Archie is promoted to the firing step at 3 a.m. after hours of twisting and turning in a furrow barely big enough for himself never mind him and Francie. His guide is a Welsh miner named Harris who joined the Hampshires during a trip to Southampton's carnal district, as he had no intention of suffocating with his mining compatriots in their subterranean duel with the Germans beneath the front line.

'I've been underground waiting for the roof to come in for years, boy. I'll take my chances up here where I might at least get a look at the bastard who takes me.'

When they had first arrived, the Ulsters spent days at the mouths of these tunnels clearing the tonnes of chalk and clay excavated by the moles deep beneath their feet.

Archie stares through the sniper's loop, searching the narrow strip of land between themselves and the Saxons who hold the line opposite.

'I can't make anything out, Harris; sure I could see better than this underground.'

Every lump and shadow is something or nothing and when he searches for anything again it has retreated into the corners of his imagination.

'Use your ears, boy; your eyes will learn to follow.'

When a Very light captures the world momentarily in a blaze of phosphor his face is through the loop, eager to give names to the shadows. Harris grabs him by the scruff and rips him sideways, slamming him into the chalk wall.

'Keep your head away from the gap when the flare goes up. His snipers always know where we are.'

Their section of no man's land is roughly fifty feet across. In certain parts it is as narrow as thirty and where a sap juts out at right angles from their trench, the belligerents can be as cosy to one another as fifteen feet. Back in the hole with Francie they whisper and wonder their way through the remaining hours of darkness. When they try to sleep it is Annie who whispers to Francie as the memorised sections of her last letter repeat themselves in a loop.

I've entered the pony race at Drumquin fair next week. That gobshite Barney Edwards the farrier lodged a complaint saying girls should be banned from entering as they have the unfair advantage of being lighter on the animal. I told him to consider his own weight and withdraw as he'd break the poor animal's back. It's bad enough missing Archie but I am lost without you. How dare you both bugger off and leave me with no fun to live for? I don't think your father has long. I ache for us to be alone again.

He focuses on the old man. Somewhere deep there is the glimmer of a fond memory, a face that he looked up to when it looked down on him. But it is only a glimmer. As soon as Francie was deemed old enough for punching he took more than his fair share. He won't be fucking mourning.

Beside him Archie has no hope of sleeping either. He has never felt so alert and alive. His senses are tightly tuned and his body feels hard and supple and ready to bounce into anything. He presses his cheek into the cold earth and imagines the face of a German mirroring his own, pushed into the clay, not the width of a football pitch away. After so many months of waiting Archie Johnston is ecstatic to be part of the war.

Stand-to before dawn brings everyone to the firing step with bayonets fixed, the new boys taut, fearing imminent assault, but the Hampshires loose in the knowledge that Jerry needs his breakfast too. A shout traverses the line with the whoosh of Stokes mortars hard on its heels. As the shells fly towards German heads Lieutenant Gallagher and Sergeant Crozier encourage their men to release, and with heads half protruding the 11th Inniskillings blindly empty their first volley of the war into the mud and the barbed wire beyond.

With the hornet's nest well and truly kicked the fire step is abandoned for what little cover the scrapes and dugouts can provide from the reciprocation that will follow. When it comes it comes hard. Two *Minenwerfer* shells explode just behind their section and a machine gun kisses the lip of the trench where their tin hats have just been. It is over as quickly as it began, the Saxons eager to return to their black bread and coffee.

The remainder of the day brings little activity: movement is restricted during daylight. Work parties are organised to refill sandbags and repair duckboards and the walls of trenches damaged by rain and shell-fall. The boys still chew on a mortar mix of biscuit, bully beef and cold tea when a corporal comes sprinting with the news that Jack and Francie have been summoned to the command bunker. They aren't invited down into the warmth of the structure, and as they stand at attention by its entrance the smell of frying bacon wafting from its womb has them drooling for home. A full hour later, when the officers have finished their meal, Crozier appears through the hanging blanket and announces that they have been chosen for latrine duty.

A slit trench has been dug into the forward wall joining it to a deep hole where a whizzbang fell short. The men must advance here in order to perform their ablutions. It is a dangerous place to linger as the increased activity makes it a likely target for enemy artillery. Two privates from Winchester, overjoyed at being relieved, furnish them with shovels and a bag of quicklime. They explain that the right-hand side of the latrine is collapsing and needs shoring up then they beat a hasty retreat. Towards the end of the entrance channel, a rancid wave slaps Francie and Jack and they grip each other, doubled over, struggling to keep hold of their breakfasts. The lime must be scattered liberally and it is only when their first shovelfuls hit the bed of faeces that they see the rats. Jack loses his battle and vomits energetically.

'It's only shite and rats, for Christ's sake, Jackie.'

Jack points without looking to the right-hand side of the latrine and when Francie follows the gesture he finds the arm sticking from the partially collapsed wall. He yells murder at the rodents, their prize now discovered, and throws shovel after shovel of lime in their direction until the bag is empty and they have disappeared into their own clandestine system of underground tunnels.

'Dirty bastards; Jesus, the dirty bastards.'

'Did you see the size of thon huge one? It was as big as a cat!'

As they await the hot food that nightfall promises, the ex-miner Harris explains to them that the brown rats grow so large from gorging on the livers of the corpses in no man's land.

'The black ones don't get as big but they'll still chew through your belly if you're left lying out there too long.'

When the rations arrive, suspended between two men in a steaming bucket, the stew of nondescript meat with peas and beans has fairly lost its appeal. Dinner is followed by an unexpected delivery of mail and a rumour that the rum ration that refused to materialise at breakfast is on its way via the supply trenches. There's a letter for Windy from his mother and Francie and Archie smile at Annie's neat hand before stuffing theirs into pockets where they will remain until her stories can illuminate the dawn. By the time the rum party has found their corner, its ranks have been swelled by a clump of officers. Lieutenant Gallagher introduces Captain Jackson from the Hampshires, a well-fed cheerful man in his forties who announces that he will be needing volunteers for the Inniskillings' first trench-raiding party tonight. Archie's arm shoots into the silence, followed by that of a man called Newton from Donegal town. Francie glares at Archie then steps forward and fires his own arm skyward as Sergeant Crozier appears from behind the two officers to appraise the volunteers. Crozier stares at Francie for a second then turns to the other two whose hands went up first.

'Johnston and Newton, take your rifles and make your way to the command bunker. You'll receive double rum rations and orders when you get there.'

Lieutenant Gallagher thanks the volunteers, explaining that they won't take more than two men from any one squad, then the officers move on towards the next knot of men. As Crozier steps in behind them Francie jumps forward blocking his path.

'Please, Sergeant, I volunteered.'

'Eventually. I'm not letting a raiding party face the Hun with a rat in its ranks. Your boyfriend can fend for himself.'

The smile is small but it lives on his lips and he savours its taste before moving off in pursuit of his betters.

A reconnaissance patrol twenty strong will sneak across no man's land to see what can be gleaned from German nocturnal activity. If the opportunity arises they will bring back a prisoner for interrogation. Fourteen of the Inniskillings and six experienced Hampshires assemble below a section of wire prepared for their exit the previous night. There is to be only one bayonet man, who will take the lead if they enter the German trench. Fixed bayonets are cumbersome in no man's land, and have a habit of catching the moonlight. A

Hampshire called Archer is picked for the task and curses as he fixes steel, enraged to be sent on a raid the night before leaving the line. Sergeant Thompson, a Hampshire raid veteran, will lead, accompanied by Crozier and an English Lance-Corporal called Watkins, who distributes Mills bombs and trench clubs amongst the silent troops. Archie is offered the handle of an entrenching tool with a large hexagonal iron nut wrapped around one end above embedded steel spikes but he declines, preferring to have both hands free for the use of his rifle.

'Rifle's no good up-close, son; have your spade or a good knife at the ready.'

He discards equipment as instructed, puts the pair of egg-shaped Mills bombs in his pockets then pulls the chin strap of his helmet so tight that the blood must surely stop feeding his brain. They haul themselves from the trench one by one and leak through the hole in the wire. The darkness is impenetrable and at first Archie feels safer out here than he did dug into the earth. As they inch away from their line, though, every scratch of cloth on soil or bump of metal on stone screeches in the night and he feels as exposed as the day he was born.

The hairs on his body freeze to attention as he snakes along on his belly, desperate to stay with the heels of the man in front while trying to keep the banging of his rifle from giving them all up. Instantaneously his sense of direction vanishes and he doesn't know if they are crawling directly towards the German line or veering diagonally left to the largest shell hole as instructed. He slithers up and over the legs of the man ahead and receives a sharp kick in the stomach to tell him that they have stopped. He rolls and stares at the stars, wondering why they have stopped without any cover. A pop is heard and when the flare bursts overhead he stares at it and is completely blinded. When darkness returns he is kicked in the shoulder and they undulate onward, his skull filled with a molten bright-white glare. The surface is ridged and holed from the endless shelling and every dip holds a pool of stagnant water or a quagmire of stinking mud. The bile of the Earth rising from its stomach to cling to his uniform, and by the time he rolls sideways into the big shell hole Archie is soaked to the skin.

Francie and Windy stand watch. They've heard nothing since the others slipped through the wire. Jack joins them, too fidgety to sit alone in the dark, and the trio hold a silent vigil by the loophole. Lieutenant Gallagher has stopped by twice for news and both times appeared nervous when none was forthcoming. They will know for certain when it comes. If they use stealth there will be shooting and shouting and if they bomb first all hell will come back in the other direction.

Francie fingers the envelope that has burnt a hole in his pocket since its arrival. He could crouch in his funk hole for a match-lit look but it feels wrong to read her words when her brother is not safe beside him. Why the fuck did he volunteer? A series of flares this time in a variety of colours. Are they ours or theirs? Must be theirs if they are bursting directly overhead. Green, purple and white flashes suspend the world briefly in an eerie glow. Again the whoosh and the envelope is out for the coming glare so that at least he can see where she has written his name. When the darkness smothers them once more she whispers urgently in his ear.

You let him go alone?

What was I supposed to do?

For the love of God, Francie, go out and bring him back!

The dull whump of grenade detonations and the three friends instinctively grab for each other's tunics, knowing that it is finally on. Silence follows the blasts then the desperate single howl of a dying animal is drowned in a cacophony of shooting.

*

83

Archie pulls the pin from the second grenade and hurls it towards the din of his first. He should have counted to three before releasing it but his imagination ran riot, presenting his shattered body parts in a blood-soaked stack at the bottom of the crater. The second clap feels bigger than the first but it could be from another's bomb as there are four of them in the shell hole providing cover for the raiders. Seven now or is it six explosions then a shout rises and he knows that the boys are up and into it from the position they have crept into just twenty yards short of the German front trench. He drags his rifle to the lip of the hole but Newton the Donegal man grabs him by the arm.

'No shooting; you'll hit ours on their way back.'

Tight beside one another, they paint pictures of a fight that can only be heard, then Newton again pushing him away, for if a shell comes in it will take them both. The sky bursts bright white and Archie finds the other two lying away to his left. When the night returns he hears boots approach and difficult breathing then a clatter of rifle fire and a machine gun opens up on the tangle of men who fall gratefully into the hole all around him.

Sergeant Thompson orders covering fire and instructs Crozier to make for home with half their number, but as they leave he realises that he doesn't have the prisoner.

'Watkins and Irwin had him, Sarge, but they're not fuckin here yet.'

Flare after flare arcs through the night and the machine gun hammers at the rim of their shell hole. The next patch of darkness brings three more men over the ridge and down into cover. They return fire in the direction of the German line without presenting their heads to the machine gun. Archie slides downhill into the crater to reload and finds himself lying beside the German prisoner, who has his right ear buried in the mud and Watkins' revolver barrel buried in his left. He looks familiar, the Hun, with his floppy black fringe stuck to his forehead with sweat. Can't be much older than himself. Archie stares into his eyes and the boy looks back, utterly terrified, and as the light dies again he remembers and he wants to tell the fella that he is the absolute duck egg of a boy McCusker who sat behind him in school, only there is no point because they don't speak the same language.

There are nine of them in the shell hole and Thompson orders a two-wave retreat during the next pair of blackouts. Archie and Newton along with Thompson, Watkins and the prisoner will go first. As soon as it is dark again the sergeant grunts an order and Archie bursts over the top. The German machine gun hacks at their backs and they hit the mud only yards from where they started. When the dazzle returns Archie sees Watkins struggling with the prisoner and Thompson lying motionless on his back just behind them. Newton rises and breaks for the British line but he is cut down immediately. Archie drags himself on his stomach to Watkins and grabs the German tightly from behind around the knees. The three of them lie in this awkward embrace. The only sound between machine-gun bursts is the bleating of the German, who writhes sporadically. He cries out in fear but Archie doesn't understand the guttural words. He understands Watkins perfectly, however, as he explains to the German that if he doesn't shut his filthy mouth he will strangle the cunt stone dead. When the boy ignores him and calls out again he is answered by the sickening thud of a hammer being embedded in meat. When the next flare ignites Archie rises just enough to see Watkins bringing his trench club into the boy's head for the second time. The third blow opens the skull completely and as the flare dies slowly there is enough light left for Archie to accept that despite what he was told by the Welsh miner Harris, the colour of a German's brain does not match that of his uniform.

CHAPTER NINE

County Fermanagh, Northern Ireland

May 1922

She doesn't know how many hours they've spent underground but when they emerge the sun has transformed the little lough from grey to blue and the blood beside the cottage has dried into the earth staining it black. The Specials took the body with them. Crozier announced that the old man would give a better performance tied to his horse when they got to the bottom of the mountain. He will be listed as the latest addition to the burgeoning kill list of one Francis Leonard. The big IRA hero who kidnapped a girl then shot her horse in front of her eyes before slaughtering an old man for a bottle of home-made whiskey.

'Propaganda, lads; nothing in war is more important than propaganda.'

Twice she had tried to crawl over Francie to escape from the tomb and twice he had held her back.

'They're watching.'

The stale booze on his breath in the tiny space had smacked her on the nose. When they dozed fitfully she covered his mouth each time he cried out. In sleep Archie was mentioned twice and many others whose names meant nothing to her. Names from France, perhaps, or names from other parts of Ireland where the killing had continued. It was the first time he'd spoken her brother's name since the morning in the loft of her mother's barn. Neither of them seems capable of raising him.

She was shocked that in their predicament Francie had stayed up all night drinking. When eventually he had come to her under the blanket he had stumbled then trod on her ankle and she knew that he was drunk. As she strips naked and slides into the lough to rinse the underworld from her skin, she knows that it is more drink he is looking for as he tears the cottage apart room by room.

It is late afternoon when they begin their descent. The potato cakes are a distant memory and the hunger, as well as the horror, keeps them quiet. Undercover when the terrain allows then hard and fast through open spaces. From cairn to copse they inch their way downhill towards the new line drawn between the two Irelands. It is Annie who can bear the silence no longer, desperate to distract herself from the old man's smile sliding off his face into the dirt.

'Where exactly is this border?'

'It's pretty unclear.'

'So how do we know when we have crossed it?'

'We don't.'

'How do the Specials know when not to cross it?'

'They won't.'

'So they stop?'

'I wouldn't.'

'What exactly is the plan here, soldier boy?'

'We head for Pettigo. It's definitely in the Irish Free State; last I heard, anyway.'

The land flattens somewhat and they push through a band of oak and chestnut to find themselves staring on to a farmyard below.

'Stay here and nurse your hangover; I'll go and find us some food.'

'I don't have a hangover.'

'Of course you don't, Francis, and I'm the Queen of Sheba.'

Amongst the cows, in the byre, she catches her breath and begins to feel an inch like Annie for the first time in three days. She laughs at the realisation that here, on her knees amongst the piss and shit of the herd, she actually feels at home. All of her big chat about school and the town or the city one day. A teacher maybe, or at the very least having your own farm with Francie where someone else could sit in the middle of the shit for you. Francie changed everything. Even Drumskinny was bearable as long as she was with Francie Leonard. 'Where's all your big chat now, little lady?' It's what her father had called her from the day when barely two years old she toddled out of the kitchen and straight into the pig pen. The big sow had taken it upon herself to protect the child from the rest of her brethren. Some maternal instinct for the small perhaps but when her father finally found her the mummy pig had positioned herself across the corner of the pen, trapping the child safely away from enquiring snouts.

'Would you look at the little lady, eh, the queen of the pigs?'

Her mother was for butchering the sow the following month but her father would hear nothing of it.

'That pig is that little lady's angel.'

It was never said with anything other than love in his voice and he adapted its tone throughout the years to suit her dreams as they grew in tandem with her arms and legs.

'You'll have whatever you set your heart on, little lady.'

Her father had less patience with little Archie, though he loved him too in that man way where it's never allowed to be shown. Quirky clumsy Archie Johnston was not cut out to be the heir to her father's kingdom, a few acres of boggy land on a hillside in the middle of County Nowhere. Land barely fit for spuds never mind anything that would have made them any money. It was his empire, none the less, and his life went into the soil and when his only son poured his into a hole somewhere on the Western Front the little lady was left to take up the reins. So she tucked her dreams up in bed so that she could sow the spuds and milk the herd and feed the chickens and stack the turf and fodder the cows and lie alone every night waiting for the only man who knew she was there.

Her father had recognised the light that shone between her and Francie. He knew long before they did the shadows it would cast as they grew. Whether her mother acknowledged it or not she chose to fight it when they became old enough for it to matter.

'You can't marry a Catholic, Annie, so get it out of your head.'

'But it's Francie, Ma, and he doesn't believe in God.'

'For the love of Christ, Jim, would you tell her?'

But her father never would. He'd leave the room or ignore his wife and put his head in the paper but he would never condemn his daughter's heart.

'The little lady will do as she pleases, Ellen; she always has.'

When her mother stormed from the kitchen in exasperation he would wink conspiratorially at his daughter and enough had been said. And this is how it went until the war came knocking. Her brother and her boy just got up and left. When the big brass death penny arrived home instead of Archie, her father couldn't support her dreams any more. He needed her to keep the farm on the correct side of the divide now. His own health deteriorated with the death of his son, and her mother made hay with the guilt.

'You can't now and that is the end of it. You'd be giving the land that four generations of your ancestors lived on to the Catholics.'

'Francie doesn't believe in that.'

'Well, what does he believe in? He betrayed his own to fight for the British.'

The cancer took her father in less than three months. It could well have been in him for years, as the doctor put it, but it was the shock of Archie's death that raced it through him. In the end, it was Francie himself who sealed her fate. For, despite all of his promises and letters from the front and all of her arguments and protestations to her mother, Francie never came back for her.

She finds a bucket and selects a heavy-looking heifer. Milking is overdue and the herd look fit to burst. Relieved to shed some of its load, the animal takes to her hands making barely any sound. The eggs are harder to come by. The overnight lay will have been picked at first light and the chickens protest loudly as she hunts through the hay on her hands and knees. At the far end of the run, she finds five freckled surprises hidden in tight near a corner.

On the edge of the wooded slope, they crack holes and suck straight from the shells then let warm milk shock their cold empty stomachs. They cut along the fringe of the trees until the farm is safely behind them then edge out into the open. Below them across a wide bog lies a large expanse of water. Francie points to his left where she can just make out the mouth of the river on the lough shore.

'Lough Derg. That's the top of the river we crossed back in the village. It forms the border along here so I think we might already have crossed.'

'How far is Pettigo?'

'Couple of miles beyond the lough. If we circle it to the right we should stay in the Free State.'

They hunker amongst fern. Francie scours the landscape while Annie becomes captivated by the beauty of the scene below her. A light mizzle begins to fall, that almost imperceptible rain that seems to soak you through quicker than any downpour. She puts her hands to her brow, shielding her eyes and framing the lough below as a great artist would. The colours in her painting are all variations of grey and yet there is nothing remotely dull or boring about the sky coming down to meet the water on the horizon and she is aware in the moment that she is seeing this lough exactly as anyone who has stood here in the last thousand years has seen it because nothing before her has ever changed.

They are already soaked through as they stand and begin to move slowly through the uncultivated bogland. Only a few hundred yards into it they stop and stare at each other as a familiar drone returns. Prostrate in the open there is nothing they can do as the machine soars down the hillside above the treetops. The pilot turns so quickly that Francie knows immediately they've been spotted. He grabs Annie by the arm and they are off towards the granite-coloured water. The first pass is head-on and the flat terrain enables the pilot to fly as close to the ground as he would dare. They dive into heather as he roars by, only feet above them. The squelch of wet turf drains their legs as they force themselves forward, knowing that the turning plane will soon be racing for their backs. She stumbles beside him but then is up and away and as the engine roar closes he pulls out the Mauser and turns to face it. Firing on an aeroplane with a sidearm is futile but he knows that its machine gun is about to mow them down so it is all that he can do. He empties a full magazine at the plane as it approaches then it is gone past him and it is only when he is running again that he realises that it never fired back. Reconnaissance plane, no gun mounted. His shooting and the roar of the diving engine will have alerted any troops nearby. The plane banks steeply and prepares for another pass from a different angle. He is trying to tire them out. They won't have a yard left in them if they make it to the shore. Annie has made good ground out in front. They are about halfway between the trees and the lough. As he twists his head again to check on the bastard his legs disappear beneath him into a bog hole. Gripped to the waist he throws the Mauser into dry heather and tries to pull himself free. The harder he struggles the tighter the grip and as he shouts out for Annie she appears above him and pulls on his wrists with all of her remaining strength. When they are back on their feet and moving again they realise that the roar is receding into the distance.

'Gone?'

'To let them know we're here.'

By the mouth of the river, they lie exhausted until their legs stop shaking. Now that they are discovered Francie reasons they should double back along the river as the shore of Lough Derg is completely exposed. Among the rushes, they crawl towards a bridge a few hundred yards upstream. Almost immediately the river bends sharply to the left and they sprint, crouched to the rushes on the other side of the oxbow. Concealed again, they are about to push for the bridge when they hear voices. Francie pulls the Mauser but he has lost its remaining clips from his jacket in the bog hole. Toothless, he tosses Annie the weapon and signals for her to stay where she is as he slides into the river. He submerges himself inch by inch so as to make no splash. Once it has breached his clothes the cold focuses his mind and soothes his battered body. Every joint smoulders after their two-day cross-country hack. He drifts along the bank, hidden by the overhang. In front, he catches glimpses of their black uniforms between himself and the bridge. He needs to get beyond them so that he can draw them away from Annie. The closer he gets the more disorientated he becomes as it seems that the Specials are also standing in the water. Around another bend and he sees them clearly at last. Two priests in soutanes pulling a net into a boat in the middle of the river. The water begins to shallow here and by the time they see him he is wading towards them like an apparition from the depths.

'A bit of fishing is it, fathers?'

They stare in shock as he hauls himself over the side of the boat and lies in a heap among their gillnet and the half a dozen salmon who have been trapped in it. The men of God stare, confused at the intruder who smiles back up at them from the middle of their harvest.

'You're for feeding the five thousand, then?'

'Who are you?'

'I'm the fella that aeroplane's looking for. So, you give me and my friend a wee lift and we'll say fuck all about the poaching, padres.'

CHAPTER TEN

Thiepval, Somme, France

1 July 1916

Archie watches Windy Patterson lighting one cigarette off another for the tenth time in an hour. He checks his watch to find that it is still nearly 6 a.m. His watch has said 5.55 for ever. Maybe it has stopped?

'What time is it, Windy?'

'Five fifty-five; six minutes after the last time you asked me at five forty-fucking-nine.'

Beside Windy, Francie stands then crouches, intermittently trying to take some pressure off legs that have had little sleep for days. Beyond him, the Sampson brothers from Enniskillen have been taking turns to pray out loud to each other since dawn broke. Archie studies Francie for signs he will snap. His line is that he has no problem with a man and his God as long as the man doesn't bloody ram it down everyone else's throats.

Directly opposite Francie, Jack Elliot leans on the chalk wall with his Brodie helmet in his hands as he twists and twirls it through three hundred and sixty degrees twice then puts it back on top of his head. He checks the mechanism of his rifle for dirt and when he is satisfied for at least the thirtieth time that it is clean, his hands return to his head for the helmet. This routine has been playing on a loop now for the best part of an hour and it is clearly driving Francie to fucking distraction.

Above them the trees still vaguely resemble trees. This is not the case for all of Thiepval Wood, stripped by months of incoming and outgoing, but here behind the front line where they wait to advance, you can imagine the forest as it used to be if you can block out the roar of the bombardment. At night the sky is painted by the German guns and you can follow the shells in your mind as they whistle down towards you. If one explodes in the trees the roar is more terrific than its earthbound counterparts. Among the branches, an eruption of yellows, blues and oranges and a shade of almost green that Archie is sure has yet to be named. The tree itself becomes the weapon then, showering the trenches in large branches and a hailstorm of deadly splinters.

Earlier this morning the Germans dropped tear-gas shells. The cloud made its way along the man-made maze in the earth and soldiers who didn't get masks on quickly enough stumbled blindly in circles, their faces streaming. Days before they had carried four large poison-gas canisters forward themselves to a pair of saps in the front line opposite the formidable Schwaben Redoubt. But when the gas was released on to no man's land the wind changed direction, blowing it back into the wood where it killed four of the Ulster men sent to deploy it. The Sampson brothers had taken it as an omen. He who corrupts the lungs of his enemy with vile poison does not deserve to have God on his side. The Schwaben Redoubt, with its deep bunker systems, pillboxes and machine-gun nests, would have to be taken by hand. It was ever thus. In precisely half an hour they will stumble forward and try. Firstly into the front-line trench vacated by their comrades from the 9th and 10th battalions, then over the top in a second wave.

Archie stares at Francie's boots and tries to remember the configuration of German lines. For days back at Clairfaye farm they had assaulted a dummy trench system constructed with the assistance of thousands of aerial photographs. Their task today is to cross a steep stretch of no man's land with a sunken road running through it from left to right, then consolidate the vital Crucifix trench junction on the slopes of the Schwaben Redoubt. The Devil's Dwelling Pace, they call it. Held and reinforced by Schwabians from Württemberg for nearly two years. Archie pictures himself in training, weighed down with 70 pounds of gear, running up a hill half as steep as the one he faces today before climbing through ditches with no Germans and no bayonets and no machine guns nor bunkers dug so deep the bombardment probably won't matter, and then he starts to laugh uncontrollably. Francie steps forward but Archie raises his hand to say that he's got this covered then Jack takes his helmet off again and starts to revolve it in his hands and Francie snaps.

'Will you for Christ's sake keep that thing on your head?'

'Sorry, Francie, I'm fidgety.'

'I can see that; you're like an oul woman.'

'Relax, Francie, I'm sorry.'

'Just put the fuckin helmet on your fuckin head and stop playing with your fuckin rifle.'

A shell lands not far behind and they are showered with splinters and lumps of chalk and clay. More crash through the trees followed by shouts of 'stretcher-bearer!' then the sky is full of incoming German rounds as a counter-barrage develops.

'They know we're coming.'

'Shut it, Windy.'

'Why else are they shelling now?'

'Because we've been giving them hell for a fucking week?'

'Well, clearly that has been extremely effective, Jack.'

Jack jumps forward and grabs Windy by the webbing but Francie intervenes before any blows land.

The dull crump of British mortars is followed by the big guns' rapid roaring along the line and the forest shakes then turns on its side in an attempt to slide off the face of the planet. The final hurricane bombardment means it is almost time. Archie's watch reads 6.30. It hadn't changed for ever and now he's lost half an hour of his life in the blink of an eye. He might not be getting many more half-hours. He stares at the sky through the trees as it lights up from the detonations and wonders if shells ever collide in mid-air as they pass each other on the way to their destinations.

Crozier and Lieutenant Gallagher appear around the corner accompanied by a corporal and a private carrying the rum ration in big brown jars.

'Ready, boys?'

'Yes, Captain.'

Gallagher toes a large roll of wire on the ground that will have to be carried across for strengthening any German positions they take.

'Let's just get there double quick. If something is holding you back, ditch it. Rifles, ammunition, water. Anything else is a bonus.'

'Yes, sir.'

Some come forward with tin cups but not all. The Sampson brothers like many churchgoers in the division are teetotal. Unlike fellow-believers, though, the Sampsons take their ration anyway and keep it for their friends. Archie stares at the familiar black initials on the earthenware jar as the sticky liquor pours. SRD. Supply Reserve Depot. Schwaben Redoubt Death.

As the party moves on to the next clump of men, Crozier hangs back for a spit in their ears.

'Let's show them what the Skins are made of, boys. Stay together when it gets rough. Take no prisoners or they'll come at you from behind and at all times keep one eye on the fuckin Rebel.'

He beams at Francie then trots off with his tongue out ready for Gallagher's arse. 'The Rebel' is all Francie has got since the rising in Dublin at Easter. 'The Catholic rebel who went to the wrong war.' The amusement Crozier has taken from it has been a relief. He will often give in to laughing at the Rebel now rather than kicking him. Once the officer has disappeared the non-drinkers offer up their spoils. Frank Sampson religiously gives his rum ration to Windy Patterson, even though he is prone to calling him a scurrilous liar, and his brother Jacob alternates between Archie and Jack. Today is Jack's turn and he throws it back before he has even finished swallowing his own. Frank steps towards Windy with his tin mug raised then hesitates and holds it out to Francie.

'I'm grand, thanks.'

'I'd like you to have it.'

'Why's that, now?'

'Because you're one of us.'

'Thank you, Frank.'

'May God strike me down for swearing, Francie Leonard, but Sergeant Crozier can go and fuck himself.'

Francie nails the rum then falls into his own world against the wall. The Sampsons kneel beside him, resuming their prayer, and he watches them, bemused yet jealous of the strength they take from their fairy tale. Yesterday morning as the rest attended service with the company chaplain, Francie was escorted to an ambulance that had been circling the division collecting its Catholics. A handful of them in the back were driven north to the 29th Division's positions where they joined with Englishmen in hearing mass said by an Irish priest. It had always felt like a performance to Francie, even as a child. It had all the trappings for the creation of illusion. A stage, costumes, a man reportedly on a higher plane than his audience, who were prepared to believe whatever he told them. Yesterday, though, he had taken some comfort from it. He didn't understand why, but there was something in the hypnotic repetition and in the way, despite years of being anywhere but mass, his mouth had opened and the words still poured out.

'*Confiteor Deo omnipotenti, et vobis fratres, quia peccavi nimis cogitationi, verbo, opere et omissione. What I have done and what I have failed to do ...*'

He had numbly mumbled those words a thousand times in the tiny church on the Rotten Mountain but had never once stopped to think about what he was actually saying. His thought gets broken by Archie who has started laughing uncontrollably again. There is a strangled quality to the sound as it leaves him that suggests it could turn to sobs at any minute. His rum is still in his mug between his feet. Francie steps forward, picks it up and hands it to him.

'I want a clear head when I go over.'

'That's the last thing you want.'

'No, Francie, I—'

'Drink it.'

He pulls him off the wall and slams the mug into his teeth, cutting his lips.

'Drink it!'

Francie shifts his grip to Archie's throat and squeezes until his mouth opens. The rum scalds its way around his tongue and along his gullet and then it is over. The others have turned their backs on the moment. The cup is hurled into the mud and Francie crouches, shaking. When he can breathe again he stretches out and grabs Archie behind the knee. Archie reaches down and raps his knuckles on the top of Francie's tin hat, then leaves his hand there so that its weight lets his mate know that they're good.

A new sound cuts through the din, and men spring to their feet and fix bayonets. It takes several seconds for them to realise that it is the sound of silence. They stare at one another and at the sky for clues, then the emptiness fills with a huge explosion and the ground ripples and someone shouts that the big mine under Hawthorn Ridge has blown, and they are rushing at last into the front trench as a bugle stutters and farts and sergeants howl and a whistle shrieks them up and over the top.

CHAPTER ELEVEN

Lough Derg, County Donegal, Irish Free State

June 1922

The priests pull hard, driving the boat from the shelter of the bay into the headwind that whips across the broad surface of the lough. There's a healthy chop to the wave but they quickly establish a rhythm that propels the sleek wooden craft away from shore. They hear the reports of the weapons dancing across the waves before they see the men who pulled the triggers. Crozier, elevated on horseback, draws their eyes to the troops that kneel before him a hundred yards north of the mouth of the river. Huddled in the prow of the boat, Francie knows that they are out of range but the young priest at the stern stands and faces the bullets, his arms raised to the sides to emphasis the cut of his cloth. Francie smiles at this confidence of office then whispers to Annie.

'Crozier wouldn't think twice about shooting a priest.'

When they reach the exposed middle of the expanse she begins to shake uncontrollably and the younger priest pulls old sacks from under his seat and helps her to wrap them around her torso for insulation. He doesn't look old enough to buy a drink. His hair is as dark as Archie's was and the face, alert and intelligent, reminds her of Francie, before he took the boat to France in 1915. The older priest is just that. His back is bent, his hair is white and his hands on the oars look as rough as any man's who has spent his life outside working the land.

The buildings on the island are becoming discernible when the bell reaches them across the water. Its meter is hypnotic and the oarsmen instinctively relax, lengthening their stroke and letting it fall on each toll. The top of the bell tower is clearly defined against the evening sky for the final stretch of the journey. Once the boat is moored at a rickety jetty the old priest disappears with the pilfered salmon and his apprentice leads them uphill into the settlement. The main buildings form a crescent around the bell tower, which sits on top of a mound of rock, a crucifix proud at its summit. Facing this at the end of a clearing is a large stone church. The other structures are substantial and whitewashed and a stone storehouse finishes the collection. Annie has heard often of this place but never thought she would actually see it. St Patrick's Purgatory, Lough Derg. The place where Catholics come to pray for forgiveness. Pray would be putting it mildly. They starve themselves of food and sleep for days on end in the hope of divine influence. 'The Pope's Dream Factory,' her Uncle Ivan had called it. 'The place the fuckers go to beg for miracles from a virgin.'

The young priest introduces himself as Father Michael before taking them to one of the whitewashed houses. They pass through dozens of barefoot people, some mumbling strings of prayer but most offering up a resigned sullen silence. The men wear no hats and the women's shawls are whipped tight around their faces. Inside, Father Michael locates a patchwork quilt for her to wrap herself in and has steaming black tea brought, which scalds her insides. When her body is warm again it still shakes so she lies on the ground and rolls herself up in the quilt. When she closes her eyes she sees two pairs of black riding boots so she opens them again quickly for fear the old man's face will appear. It won't just be the pilgrims who get no sleep tonight, then. Whatever tomorrow brings she knows that she is a different Annie from the one who left home two days ago. The older man returns and she thanks him for his efforts in rowing them here. He nods and smiles before taking Francie away to meet the Prior.

Outside again the young priest insists on giving her the guided tour. He is a nice boy, handsome and kind. The pilgrims shuffle by, stopping for prayer at what he describes as various 'stations'. He watches her take it all in.

'You're not Catholic then, Miss Annie?'

'Are my eyes too close together?'

They share the laugh to the obvious irritation of two women kneeling by a stone at the base of the tower, the upturned soles of their feet raw from exposure.

'Are people barefoot in winter too?'

'It is part of the process, part of their penance.'

'They want forgiveness?'

'So that their souls may be purged from the stain of their sins.'

'I thought they came here to ask for help.'

'That too. They offer penance for their sins or to seek help in their lives. Relief from sickness or from sickness in a loved one. Pilgrims have made their way here from across Europe for hundreds of years. We had people come all the way from Cork last year just to pray for help in getting the British out of Ireland.'

They stifle their laughter as another group of women shamble past and join the two at the rocks below the tower.

'This station marks where the entrance was.'

'To what?'

'The Underworld; Heaven, Hell or Purgatory.'

'Why would the entrance to Heaven or Hell be in the middle of nowhere in Ireland?'

'It was said that the souls of the dead followed the sun west where they would enter the Underworld according to the lives they had lived. You couldn't get further west than this back then.'

She watches the people around her make their way through rocks and mud, their faces drawn in concentrated studies of seriousness.

'I wonder if religion doesn't keep people focused on their problems, Father, rather than setting them free.'

Father Michael looks off towards the white house where they had taken their tea. In the window to the top left two priests stand silently watching him as he converses with this woman below.

'After two years on this island, Miss Annie, I often wonder the same thing myself.'

In a room overlooking the hungry pilgrims, Francie waits for Prior Kinahan to appear. Seated at a grand-looking mahogany desk with a mug of black tea, he studies the backs of the two priests at the window who have been brought in to add some clerical muscle to proceedings. He wonders if they enjoy it. The pain of the people. That is, after all, the point of their existence on the island. Providing an environment most suitable for hardship in all its shapes and forms. Could anyone blame them for taking great pride in their work? The pilgrims must have their money's worth. And oh, what money the pilgrims are worth. *If a man has travelled all this way to feel scourged at the pillar then scourge the bastard we shall!* The bitterness of the black tea cuts through his reverie. Couldn't they have stuck a splash of milk in it? Or a drop of whiskey? Priests love a drop of the good stuff. There's probably a bottle in a drawer on the other side of the desk.

The door to his right opens and the Prior's entrance is preceded by a sickly cloud. Incense, filtered through vestments stale from mothballs and years of sweat. The aroma transports him to a back room in the church of his childhood. For three whole years, he had served our Lord as an altar boy. Father Sweeney was a hard taskmaster, a cruel man trapped in a small parish that suited neither his ego nor his needs. His punches went a long way to teaching the young Francie that despite what anyone told him, this God did not have his best interests at heart. At least for him, the father's frustration had only found form in his fists. Or he might well have followed Donal Hegarty over the side of the crooked bridge.

The Prior takes the seat opposite and when Francie rises he gestures him sat with a finger struggling under the weight of a large gold and ruby ring.

'Don't tell me your name, though I am sure that I know it already.'

'Thank you, Your Grace. For your hospitality and for the help of your priests earlier.'

'They say you chastised them for their fishing techniques?'

'I poached that river myself as a boy and their methods are more humane than mine.'

'We have fished the waters of the lough for centuries. I am sure no one will begrudge the necessity of a few salmon from the river.'

This could go either way. As he has learnt many times over the last three years in Ireland, sparring is standard with the clergy. It simply depended on the personal politics of the priest. Mayo, Clare and Kerry were a mixed bag when it came to men of the cloth and what they thought of the struggle. On the ground, he'd encountered nothing but quiet support or a turning of the head when the situation required it, but from the pulpit, it had been a different matter. It is one thing killing British soldiers but it wasn't easy for God to be seen to support a guerrilla army whose meat and two veg was murdering policemen born and reared in the very communities where they were gunned down.

'So you came over the mountain?'

'I've climbed bigger hills.'

'It's unforgiving when you don't know it, and you had a lady with you.'

'She's tougher than any man.'

'Does she know who she travels with?'

'We've been friends since school.'

'You've come a long way since school.'

The Prior is well lived in, and it has been a life that has wanted for little. His burgundy face glows energetically above the stark black sheen of his costume as though his skin was freshly buffed just before entering the room.

'You can't stay here.'

'We'd be happy to move on first thing in the morning.'

The Prior rocks gently in his seat for a bit then nods his head in agreement.

'If you're caught, we didn't know who you are.'

'Naturally.'

'I can't risk the Specials attacking the island.'

'Aren't we in the South?'

'No one seems capable of locating our new border yet, never mind respecting it.'

'They come across?'

'Frequently, on sectarian rampages. Two girls were shot nearby yesterday. The IRA presence along the border hasn't exactly benefited the Catholic population.'

'We're here to protect them.'

'You're here because you want a fight and you've run out of people down south to fight with.'

'North or South, it's all just Ireland to us, Father.'

'You grew up here, so spare me the ignorance on the intricacies of the North.'

'Do the British trespass?'

'Not yet but they will do. I have heard talk that your friends taking over Pettigo could be the straw that breaks the camel's back.'

'We have every right to be in Pettigo, it's in the Irish Free State.'

'Half of it is and half of it isn't. The river is the border and it runs through the middle of the town.'

The Prior bursts into laughter as he watches Francie try to process the information.

'They drew the border through the middle of a town?'

The Prior's beetroot head looks fit to burst.

'They drew the border through the middle of a country; do you think they care about one little town?'

'They can't just leave the place cut in two.'

'Well, they are going to. People live on one side but work on the other. There are people from both communities living in countries they don't want to live in and no amount of shouting or shooting is going to change that now.'

'Shouting and shooting have brought us this far.'

'And it's far enough. You know the Church's position. You've freed as much of Ireland as you're going to and shed too much blood while you were at it.'

'You don't happen to have anything a bit stronger than tea, do you, Father?'

'This is an island where people come to make a sacrifice. It wouldn't do if the clergy running it were drinking now, would it? Gentlemen?'

The priests at the window turn to face him and he dismisses them with a flick of his ring. When they have closed the door behind them he pulls his chair closer to the desk and leans towards Francie.

'If half the things I've heard are true, your soul needs more than drink.'

'I can assure you, Father, that at least half of them are true.'

The priest stares at Francie for what feels like an age then opens the drawer in his desk and produces a bottle of Midleton whiskey and two glasses.

'Only the best for God's representatives on Earth.'

'You sound bitter. Have you lost your Lord?'

'I never found him.'

The priest half fills both glasses.

'If my shoes had as much blood on them as yours, I'd be hedging my bets.'

'There was one thing I never understood about Christianity, Father.'

'Yes?'

'You teach children that they can do what they like and he will forgive them anyway.'

'That is not a blueprint for a life of evil.'

'But it's pretty confusing, don't you think?'

The priest stares at him again, considering his next line of approach.

'So how has Francie Leonard got himself to where he is tonight?'

'Cause and effect.'

'You've made choices.'

'Didn't God make them for me?'

'God doesn't make the choices but he often presents us with the options.'

'Who presents them the rest of the time?'

'The Devil.'

'Well, that's me fucked then.'

He lifts the glass and inhales. The whiskey smells sweet and clean. Compared to the old man's mountain juice this stuff is the nectar of the gods. It is smooth and creamy in his mouth but still rude enough to burn the sides of his tongue.

'A fine drop.'

'Let me hear your confession.'

'Let you hear all my secrets?'

'Repent, tonight, before it's too late.'

'Do you know something I don't, Father?'

'You might as well leave here absolved of your sins.'

'You see that's the problem. I can't promise you I've finished committing them.'

They stare at each other while the priest pours them more whiskey.

'Go home, Francis. The war is over.'

'I went home a few nights ago and some constables kicked the door down and assaulted my mother.'

'Have you thought about America?'

'Many times, but it's full of Americans.'

The Prior's laugh is belly-deep this time and it is still in him as he rises and walks to the window.

'At least make sure the girl gets home.'

'Maybe I don't want her to go home.'

'Well then, make her a home somewhere else.'

Francie drains his second glass and joins the priest at the window. They watch the people below stumble sluggishly from station to station as the sun sinks into the lough behind the church.

'Twelve years on this island. I wouldn't mind going home myself.'

'I've seen the real entrance to the Underworld, Father.'

The Prior says nothing but turns to face him.

'I closed my eyes and ran straight through it. When I opened them again there were bits of men everywhere and dozens of nearly-dead begging me to finish them off. I hadn't the guts for the finishing so I knelt with a fella from Derry and tried to put his back in for him. I made a right fucking mess of it. I had his intestine caught around my wrist and arm and some of him stuck around the webbing on my tunic and I'm not sure to this day if I ripped bits of him out while trying to put other bits of him back in again. He was dead for a long time before I gave up. Sometimes I can still feel the wet warmth of him, wrapped around my forearm. It's in France, by the way, the entrance. In case you ever want to go there on a pilgrimage.'

The claret colour has drained from the Prior's face. He walks to the desk and lifts the bottle of whiskey. He opens the drawer but then shuts it again and puts the bottle back on the table.

'Keep it under your coat. There's no drinking on the island.'

He walks to the door that he entered through and closes it quietly behind him.

CHAPTER TWELVE

Thiepval, Somme, France

1 July 1916

Archie is halfway along the sap cut out into no man's land when he hears the tap-tap-tap of the first machine gun.

A khaki bottleneck blocks his progress and the fear of one shell taking all and sundry drives him up and over the side on to his belly. Others take similar action then out in the open by the edge of the wood, they rise together in the eye of the storm.

The ground blisters with impacts and he hopscotches around holes, ducking from lumps of earth bigger than his head and the hiss of bits of metal intent on removing it. Up ahead a shell lands behind two men and they shoot skywards like a pair of acrobats bouncing off a trampoline. They land hard, forming strange violent shapes in the dirt as he passes. One has no head and the other is intact bar the leg that he looks confused to have lost in mid-air.

Onwards Archie spins as men crumple or burst all around him. Some rise and stumble forward but most once down stay fallen. To his left on higher ground, Jack keeps up with him, screaming murder from his contorted war-face. In the seconds between shell bursts, the machine gun is always there, a pneumatic finger impatiently hammering on a door.

The rear of the Tyrone wave is visible ahead as they struggle through the barbed wire but they begin to topple sideways like a line of dominoes as the tapping finger finds its range.

Halfway across no man's land men much closer to Archie begin to fall, then others closer still and the air splits beside his right ear then his left as the bullets move past, missing his head before finding a home in a line across Jack's chest. He looks surprised as his arms involuntarily toss his rifle into the air then he is down and gone and Archie knows he will never get up again.

He changes direction but his foot catches and he topples forward, crushing his hands under the rifle. When he tries again he falls in pain and he turns to find Francie holding on to his ankle. An officer appears and shouts at them to get up and move forward until a bullet rips his throat out. His face registers confusion as he runs his fingers through the mess where his windpipe used to be then he topples forward on top of Francie. Between them, they shove the corpse away then Archie rises again and Francie tackles him around the knees.

'Fuckin stay down!'

'We have to move forward.'

'Crawl then; crawl to the Sunken Road.'

The bottom of the road is covered in bodies. Not all of them are dead. Along the far side, a line of men flattens itself in the dirt, wishing it would open and bury them whole. Among the screaming of the wounded, shouts of action traverse the line as soldiers try to paint some order over the mess. Francie spots Windy Patterson and Jacob Sampson to the left and he signals to Archie and they make for the faces they recognise.

'Officers, are there any officers left?'

The question travels the road but finds no answer. A constant dribble of men escape from the madness above and the road is soon filled to bursting. It is a steep-sided farm track that has settled through the landscape for centuries. The side they lie against is ten feet deep and it would be lunacy to leave its cover and push for the

German line. Artillery rounds hone in, one opening a breach in the southern wall before its friend finds the sweet spot and bodies float into the sky before raining their parts down on to the men below. Francie scrabbles around for a discarded canteen and downs half of it then offers Archie the rest. He watches him drink slowly, stopping between each sip to allow his lungs to fill up again. Archie coughs his deep, rasping cough, spilling most of the water before it gets to his lips and Francie knows that even if they make it past the wire to the German line, he won't have enough puff left to fight with his own shadow.

A larger party leaps yelling over the edge and soon Lieutenant Gallagher is up on his feet again firing orders at frozen troops. Behind him, the bare-headed Crozier scrabbles about on his knees behind the captain, pulling helmets off the dead until he finds one that fits. Gallagher draws men around him in a circle and roars orders through the din. They will leave the Sunken Road and sprint to the German wire, then fight their way to the Crucifix trench junction as planned. Two lines, one above the other, lie along the facing wall and wait for the signal. Above their helmets, Crozier's and Gallagher's boots grip the chalk and when the shout comes from the lieutenant they are up and over again.

A shell bursts in front and Francie and Archie hit their stomachs beside a man calmly holding the contents of his in his hands.

They have run into interlocking machine-gun fire from Thiepval village on their right and Beaumont-Hamel on their left. The sight of two men snared in barbed wire tells them they are not far from the German line. The men are stuck fast and yank frantically at their uniforms and webbing before a machine gun arcs past, riddling them both with bullets. Germans appear ahead, moving along the top of a trench from left to right. Archie rises on his knee and starts firing at their moving helmets.

'There they are, Francie! We're almost in their line!'

He stands then immediately throws himself down again as bullets rip all around him, then he is up and off in a crouch towards the wire. Francie checks that no one is watching then just as Archie passes him he takes aim and shoots him point-blank through the left calf.

He shoulders his weapon and hauls his writhing friend to his feet. Archie yells in agony when he tries to put weight on the leg so Francie gets hold of him under both arms and drags him back towards the shelter of the Sunken Road. When he drops Archie at its edge, the smaller man wriggles free and is up on his knees ready to advance again and Francie grabs him round the waist and throws both of them over the side where they roll to the bottom and come to rest on a bed of bodies. Francie untangles himself and crawls back to the foot of the ditch before turning to Archie.

'Stay here and wait for the stretcher-bearers; just fuckin stay here.'

He scales the ditch and is gone back towards the German wire.

CHAPTER THIRTEEN

Lough Derg, County Donegal, Irish Free State

June 1922

Annie can smell alcohol on him when he returns. She knows it's fresh as it has a sweeter smell than this morning's rot. This time he asks her to join him for a drink. They wander the shoreline until they are safe from curious eyes. Among stones stained copper by the rusty water they sit and stare through the dregs of daylight at the moon's reflection on the lough. She has drunk nothing stronger than tea in her life but she takes the bottle when offered.

'How much do I drink?'

'As much as you want.'

'How much do I need?'

'As much as it takes.'

She gasps as the whiskey falls into her gut.

'Like something you'd put down for the rats.'

He tries to take the bottle back but she whips it away for a second assault.

'It might kill you, but it's only going to warm me up.'

'The world is full of things that will kill me; drink just helps me ignore them.'

'You always drank, before anyone tried to kill you.'

'Not so much.'

'You're a Leonard, it's in you.'

'Drink didn't kill my father.'

'It was doing a decent job until tuberculosis showed up.'

She watches him thinking about it with the bottle to his lips then she picks up a stone and hurls it out into the water. They are on an island, he can't wake up and run away from any answers here.

'Why did you come home, Francie?'

He stares at her, acknowledging that this can be put off no longer.

'I needed to know whether I could or not.'

'Did you expect to run around Ireland shooting people for three years then just come home and blend in?'

'Everyone else will.'

'Everyone else isn't from the North, where half their neighbours use their name to frighten their children.'

'The Northern Ireland thing wasn't really part of the plan.'

'Understatement of the fucking decade, Francis.'

When their laughter subsides the silence lengthens and she panics that the moment will be lost.

'Why did you stop writing?'

He has known for two days that the question was coming but it doesn't make the answer any easier.

'Guilt.'

'Jesus, Francie, it wasn't your fault and didn't we need each other to get through the pain?'

'I wasn't myself.'

'I wrote and I wrote, pouring my heart into a hole. Can you imagine what that felt like when nothing came back?'

'I didn't want to come home and move on like he had never existed. He'd have been there every day, watching us over the end of the bed. I thought we could go somewhere else, start all over again. But when I did write, once I was back in Belfast, and you never replied, I knew you couldn't forgive me.'

'You were in Belfast?'

'I wrote you ten times. I wrote and I wrote, pouring my heart into a hole.'

'Don't you dare mock me, Francie Leonard!'

She jumps to her feet too quickly and even after standing still for a few seconds the world keeps on spinning.

'It's a bit hypocritical, don't you think?'

'I didn't get any letters from Belfast, Francie; I swear to God, not a single one.'

He studies her face for the trace of a lie.

'I had my mother check in the village, Annie. Gerry Ormsby the postie told her they had come. He knew my writing from all the letters I sent home from the front. He handed them personally to your mother. When I heard that, I knew you had moved on. A friend, Molloy, was heading south to join the IRA so I went with him as my head was wrecked and I couldn't see any other option.'

The bell on the tower starts to ring and it is inside her skull, banging from one side to the next, and before she can grab hold of her mind someone is calling her name and she turns to see Father Michael waving and Francie stuffing the bottle under his jacket and then they are moving back towards the buildings and the toll in her head stops but is replaced by the same three words being spat out over and over again. The old bitch, the old bitch, the old bitch. The old bitch.

Reunited with the living and the dead they have settled in the corner of a wide room at the back of the church where the pilgrims sit swallowing yawns. Annie has given up on sleep, for every time she shuts her eyes she finds the old man from the mountain smiling at her before he dies. She studies the bleak faces in rows all around her. Their ages vary and she calculates that roughly two-thirds of them are women. Do they really believe this? Will they really leave tomorrow and trudge home in the genuine belief that the sick will be cured?

Throughout her life there has been conflict between her mother's faith and the facts that she sees all around her. It was one of the fundamental reasons she fell for the boy from the other half of her community. Francie didn't think like everyone else. He was the only person she had ever met who refused to go along with the herd. Neither of them believed the marginally different versions of the same lie they were told every Sunday but Francie was willing to say it out loud. She remembers as clear as yesterday the first theological discussion they'd ever had. The three of them were on top of the mountain of hay they'd helped Francie's father and a team of neighbours stack inside his barn that morning. She was lying between the boys peeling an apple with Francie's knife when he let rip about the sermon he'd sat through the Sunday before.

'It's all just a set of rules invented to keep us in line.'

She sat up and listened, carefully cutting the apple into equal segments as Archie took the role of devil's advocate.

'But it's fundamental to us understanding the difference between what's right and what's wrong.'

In bed that night as she imagined what it would feel like if Francie kissed her, his words came to her over and again.

'Are you seriously telling me that without religion we wouldn't know the difference between right and wrong?'

They had held Archie over the side of the hay mountain after that, the pair of them with an ankle each, laughing so hard they nearly dropped him as Francie demanded that he renounce his god and forfeit his share of the apple.

A woman maybe ten years older catches her eye and the smallest of smiles plays out in her mouth. Annie reciprocates but her smile freezes as she sees her future in the tired lines framing the eyes.

Religion and Farming: the two things she has railed against her entire life that have gradually closed in around her as the years slipped by. They seem like sensible options compared with a life on the run with Francie Leonard, but my God could she ever go back now? The rage builds in her again. Your own daughter? Trapped her, all for yourself. And you could never even ask me how my day was when I had cooked your dinner for the seven hundredth night in a row? Did you read my letters or just hide them? My God, did you read them? She is startled by a snore in her ear and she elbows him hard in the ribs. He snaps upright and starts fumbling for his gun and she grabs him by the wrist.

'You're supposed to stay awake.'

'What?'

'It's part of your penance.'

'Hilarious. You should sleep, you'll need energy tomorrow.'

'It was the only chore she insisted on doing every week. The trip to the village for the messages and post. "Sure it keeps me young to get off the farm once a week. I soon won't be fit for the journey at all." She took a lift every week in Harry Hilliard's pony and trap. "It's best I go, Annie, or he'll only have you tortured about marriage." So I let her. Why wouldn't I? If you can't trust your own mother.'

'She never liked me.'

'She did, when we were children. She never forgave you.'

'For not bringing him home?'

'For surviving, when he didn't.'

They are tucked tight together on the bench to protect their whispers from the congregation and when she speaks again he can feel her breath on his face.

'So, now that you know you can't go home, where will you go?'

'I don't know yet.'

'You used to want to see the world.'

'I got as far as France and the food put me off.'

She digs him in the ribs again and when he starts to snigger angry heads turn and glare them quiet.

'You going to spend the rest of your life looking over your shoulder?'

He turns to face her, their noses almost touching, and she can smell the boy she used to lie naked with in the loft of her father's barn.

'I'm done with all of that.'

'Since when?'

'Since now.'

She plays with his answer in her head, debating whether she could ever believe it.

'Have you thought about America?'

'Why does everyone keep asking me that?'

There is movement across from them and Father Michael nods at her and turns away and they stare at each other for a second longer than they would have yesterday then rise and follow him from the church.

In the kitchen where he gave her tea the priest shows them a pile of blankets on the floor. On top of the table is a side of salmon on a platter with some boiled potatoes.

'When you have eaten try to sleep. The Specials are hunting for you on both sides of the border.'

They are halfway through dinner when he returns with a black bundle which he places on the table in front of Francie.

'You should wear this tomorrow when you leave with the others.'

Shortly after dawn they take their seats in the middle of a large open boat and wait for the returning pilgrims to fill in the space all around them. As they pull into the morning breeze Annie is glad of the human insulation. The priest beside her looks uncomfortable in his stiff new soutane and she leaves him to his reflection for fear of laughing in his face in front of his flock. She did point out as he donned the disguise that it didn't cover one of the most sought-after faces in Ireland but he'd proudly announced that he'd never been photographed and that the Crown forces had arrested twelve different men thinking them yours truly over the previous three years.

'The only one who knows what I look like is Crozier.'

She asked him then about the man who wanted him so badly but the reply raised more questions than it answered.

'When someone has seen you at your worst, you don't rest until that memory is erased.'

Released from the island's silence the pilgrims chatter loudly on the boat. The man directly opposite has been staring at them since they first sat down. He nudges the woman beside him and Annie watches as the nudge becomes a whisper. The hessian bag full of Francie's clothes is jammed between her thighs. The gun that she now carries digs intermittently into her back with the rolling of the boat on the water. There was nowhere for him to conceal it in his new role as a man of God. Even though there are no bullets left, the bulk of the weapon in her waistband makes her feel somehow more confident. The man in front can contain himself no longer, and his question is loud enough for those nearby to hear. 'Wasn't Father in secular clothing last night?'

Francie leans forward and places his hand gently on the man's knee.

'Indeed I was. My sister brought me to Lough Derg as I have been suffering a Crisis of Faith since the death of our mother. Grief had clouded my vision but now I can see the path clearly again.'

On dry land Francie corners an oarsman and asks him the route.

'It's the one road all the way.'

'Where's the border from here?'

The man sighs and spits on the ground.

'From here to just outside Pettigo you're in the Free State, but when you get near the village it's confusing. Stick to the Pilgrim Route, it goes straight to the railway station and that's where your boys are.'

It's seven miles to Pettigo and at penitent's pace it will take them all day. The outfit fights Francie's stride and he knows that if the need arises he won't be running very fast in a bloody dress. The young priest insisted that the plan was flawless even though Francie assured them that the outfit meant nothing to Peter Crozier. If anything it might draw him towards them, a black rag to a bull.

Crozier had put little faith in religion at the front. It was the only thing that they'd had in common and Francie had often wondered if this shared note enraged the sergeant. The English troops were more susceptible to doubt when it came to the afterlife, and Francie had enjoyed them for it. Most toed the Christian line but he had met men from Derby, Manchester and London who shared his belief that when it was done it was fucking done. Archie and his comrades from Ulster attended service when it was offered, grasping whatever chance they had to bow to the big man before going over the top. Whenever the padre appeared, though, Crozier could always be found off on his own somewhere writing letters. When in reserve there was the opportunity for mass for the Catholics but Francie never took it. Yet, instead of his apathy uniting them, this lack of belief filled Crozier with a fervent rage. He once found Francie asleep in the billet while the battalion attended a service given by a minister brought over from Belfast. There was mass on offer simultaneously with a priest from the 16th Irish Division and most of the Catholics from the Ulster Division were in attendance. After the obligatory booting awake, Crozier demanded to know why the private wasn't praying to his God.

When faced with the simplicity of the answer Crozier's mind had prolapsed.

'You don't believe in God?'

Over and over again, as the battalion's possessions were kicked halfway home to Ulster.

'So, Private Leonard, a fucking Fenian, knows better than everyone else in his platoon?'

'No, Sergeant.'

'Where is Johnston?'

'At service, Sergeant.'

'Where is Patterson?'

'At service, Sergeant.'

'But you know better?'

'No, Sergeant.'

'You think you can waltz into my army and tell people they're wrong to believe in God?'

He stopped short of physical violence on that occasion. A man wound so tight with rage he was unable to lift his arms. Instead, he trumped up a charge about Drinking in the Line even though they were in reserve. It was forgotten in the confusion as they were moved forward a day later to relieve the Manchesters who had suffered a trench-mortar bombardment for two days and two nights. When they left the line a week later they fell in with some of the same Manchesters in an *estaminet* two miles behind the line. A captain who had been drinking for several days approached the Ulster men asking if anyone knew a Peter Crozier. He couldn't believe his luck.

'So, is he still a black-hearted bastard?'

They didn't put their hands in their pockets for the next two hours as the bottles piled up alongside the sorry history of their staff sergeant major. The captain had trained with, then served alongside, Crozier in South Africa. Crozier had taken the ferry determined to join a proper English regiment in her Majesty's British army. What he hadn't expected, though, was to be treated differently to everyone else. Trying to justify his Britishness to his English brothers in arms while speaking in an Irish accent just didn't cut the mustard.

'To us he was just Irish but ashamed of it, so he was bullied from the start by officers and men alike.'

They had christened him Paddy, his own name lost until he could make it back to Belfast and find it. Paddy Crozier, the general dogsbody of his unit.

In South Africa a major who had Irish staff at home chose Crozier for his bat man, exempting him, to his horror, from almost all front-line fighting. The closest thing to action that Crozier saw for the majority of the Boer War was guard duty when the regiment took their stints at the camps. There were two categories: white camps, where the women and children of white South Africa were dying of disease in their thousands, and black camps, where the indigenous Africans were rounded up behind the wire to die at an even faster rate than their conquerors.

It was in the black camps that Crozier had developed his taste for violence.

'He changed completely when he found people further down the food chain than himself. His frustrations came out as violence towards the blacks. He patrolled at night hoping to bump into anyone outside their tent so that he could fuck them up with this big heavy walking stick he carried.'

The month before the war finished Crozier had kicked a teenager unconscious for refusing to bow his head as he passed. When they disembarked two weeks later, the boy had still not woken. Crozier was to face disciplinary action and a possible court martial but when they returned to England it was conveniently forgotten amidst the public outrage at the now notorious camps. This is how

Archie and Francie found out from a drunken captain in the Manchesters why Sergeant Peter Crozier hated the Irish: because he'd been treated like one.

They shuffle to a halt on the well-worn dirt road then inch on to the grass verge under a row of whitethorn bushes. Francie sits with Annie as the flock of sheep pass, then he stands and waves regally at the farmer who bows slightly to the robes. When they move again the pace increases and it's not long before the roofs of houses are visible in the distance. They follow the river into town and as they approach the first buildings a shot is heard in the distance and everyone stops. There is a reply from closer by then a further two rifle cracks and Francie knows that he is listening to snipers taking potshots at each other. The pilgrims mutter amongst themselves then turn and head back the way they came. Francie grabs the arm of the man who spoke to him on the boat and asks him what he is doing.

'We're hardly walking into the middle of a battle now, are we? There's a storm coming for those fellas, Father.'

Annie catches his eye, acknowledging how strange it was that the man had used her turn of phrase from a few days previous. He takes her gently by the arm and they move against the flow of pilgrims.

The row of tiny terraced houses on each side of them appears to have been hastily deserted. Front doors and windows lie open and clothes and furniture are strewn around on the street, either dropped in retreat by the owners or scattered by careless looters. They are only a hundred yards in when the sound of rifle bolts being slammed home behind them stops them dead in their tracks. Ahead a dozen barrels jut from windows and three IRA men wander from a house into the middle of the road to casually wait for them. Francie checks behind him to find another two blocking their escape then keeps walking towards the men out in front. All three carry Lee-Enfield rifles and have flat caps on their heads. Two wear belted trench coats and the third slouches in a decent-looking grey tweed suit. He scours the faces as they get closer. He knows the man on the left and he smiles warmly as he approaches John-Joe Monaghan, the son of a publican from Westport, County Mayo. The fella can't see beyond the disguise, though, and he lowers his rifle and his eyes in respect as the priest approaches. When Francie is less than twenty feet away there is a loud order from behind the IRA men, who step to the side making room for four Irish Free State soldiers hurrying towards them from the centre of town. Their dark green uniforms are a sharp contrast to the IRA men's casual attire. The only officer among them wears his peaked cap at a precariously jaunty angle and he swaggers towards them, shouting at the top of his voice.

'Father Francis Leonard, as I live and breathe! Perhaps you'll come into town and hear all the men's confessions?'

The American twang sounds alien on a small street in the backwaters of County Donegal. It had sounded wrong in Mayo and Kerry, too, but Francie has never been so glad to hear it. He moves forward, offering Molloy his hand, and the Yank takes it and pulls him off his feet into a bear hug.

CHAPTER FOURTEEN

Thiepval, France

1 July 1916

At the bottom of the ditch, Archie lies on his back and realises two things. Firstly, he is extremely tired. A fatigue greater than anything he has ever known pushes on his chest and pulls on his skin. His second realisation is that being shot is fucking painful. He remembers the moment he was hit but as he tries to focus on the point of entry a tide throbs along his leg into his groin until he is in so much agony he can't remember where he has been shot in the first place. A third realisation comes later. He may even have dozed off for a while because the light is slightly different and he isn't sure if anything is real until his brain engages and the soundscape returns to blow his dreams away.

Tap-tap-tap-tap. Tap-tap-tap-tap.

He listens to the machine guns and is considering how they sound like the Lambeg drums back at home when it hits him. He was shot from behind. He sits and runs his hand over his calf until he finds the tear in his blood-soaked trousers. He puts his finger through the hole in the material and runs it through the congealed blood on his skin until he finds the hole in his leg. He screams as he pushes the finger inside the wound then he searches along his shin until he finds the exit wound. The bullet came out to the left of his shin and a large piece of bone is poking through. He howls in sheer frustration then curses the bastard luck that has plagued his whole life. Only you could set out to attack the Germans but get shot by your own side, Archie Johnson, you blithering fucking idiot. He scans the world around him. Bodies, piles of them, bits of them, sprinkled in with the whole ones. He studies an arm across from him halfway up the bank. It has come away whole and the uniform sleeve is still intact. When he rolls his head to the right he can get the sunlight to bounce off the wedding ring on the third finger and he knows that it is someone's left arm. He stares at the limb for too long and can't decide if the hand keeps raising its thumb at him or if his mind is a cheeky bastard.

He crawls to the skyline, dragging his leg past the offending arm and sticks his head over the top. The German bombardment has lulled to sporadic blasts and he is thinking that now is as good a time as any to try for his own line, when he spots grey uniforms to his right running towards it. The German counter-attack stalls as a group of British come out of the wood to meet them, then he spies khaki uniforms to the rear of the grey, shepherding them across, and arms shoot for the sky and shouts of '*Kamerad, Kamerad!*' reach him and he realises that the grey uniforms are prisoners. He can only assume that the oncoming British realise this too but they open up with intense rifle fire and many rush forward and run the Germans through with bayonets. Someone is yelling, 'Ceasefire, ceasefire!' to no avail, then the shells start raining in again and the British turn and hoof it back into the wood.

He slides again into hell as incoming rounds find the road and bodies are lifted and shuffled and dealt out again in a different order. At the bottom, he curls himself around a shallow shell hole. Archie is not a gambling man but his logic follows that, though entirely feasible on a day like today, the chances of another shell landing in exactly the same spot are minimal. Between a dead man and one with a messy chest wound begging him for water, he gets his canteen off his webbing and downs half of it before giving the rest to the man. He is older, maybe forty, and he thanks Archie before greedily draining it. He announces proudly that he is from Castlederg in County Tyrone, and Archie tells him that he and Francie used to poach salmon from the river there a few miles further upstream and the man explains that he is a bailiff on that river who catches the poachers and they laugh about it until the man dies.

Beneath the howl of shells and industrial tapping, moans leave the men reverberating above the road in a low continuous groan. Over this bass line a higher pitched whine, one continuous buzzing note from a million flies that have settled on a thousand bodies. The production line of wounded never stops, with most of them now spilling back over from the German end. There is a yell above and Archie looks up to see Windy Patterson sliding to the bottom on his arse with one hand in the air like a cowboy. When he hits the bottom Archie calls out to the beanpole, who tramples over dead and alive alike to reach his friend. He flops down opposite Archie, hugs his arms around himself and starts spitting out tactical updates at him like a telegraph machine.

Francie, Lieutenant Gallagher and a bunch of stragglers have made it through the German wire. Everyone else, including Crozier, appears to be dead. The first wave of Derrys and Tyrones have pushed through the second Hun line and are fighting on the Schwaben Redoubt.

When Archie demands to know if any of this is true or just his usual bullshit and why the fuck he isn't fighting with them, Windy unfolds his arms and shows Archie where his left hand used to be. Only then does Archie take in the blood-soaked tunic and the face that is the colour of winter.

He wraps a rifle sling around the arm above the stump and yanks on it as hard as he can, while Windy's screams wake half the dead around them. The leather bites into flesh, which clamps down on vessels slowing the bleeding instantly. They agree that the severity of his wound means that they need to run for the British lines now, whatever the risk. If he dies in the open he dies. If he stays under-cover and waits, he dies.

'Ever heard of a fisherman hauling nets with one arm, Archie?'

'You hated it anyway, now you can steer the boat and shout orders at the rest of them.'

'Are you coming?'

'I can't run.'

'You saved my arm, you can borrow my legs.'

At the top Archie peers through the smoke and dust at the line of trees no more than a hundred yards off. The sap that brought them out this morning is far off to the right. If Windy is to have any chance they must retreat directly across no man's land from here, and quickly. Archie dumps his webbing and they rise and move, holding on to each other like kids in a three-legged race. Before they have made twenty yards the tapping finds them and rifles crack from the village and they are down again in a heap in the dirt. They lie stone-still as bullets dig up the ground all around them, then it's up again and back down into the Sunken Road as quick as three legs can carry them.

At the bottom, Windy Patterson starts to cry. Archie leaves him to it while he gathers water bottles from soldiers who no longer need them.

'We're fucking fucked here, Archie.'

'They'll come for us. What time is it?'

He checks his wrist but his watch is gone and he realises for the first time since going over the top that he has absolutely no concept of time.

'They'll come, after dark.'

'It's July, Archie.'

'So?'

'So, it never gets fucking dark.'

CHAPTER FIFTEEN

Pettigo, County Donegal, Irish Free State

June 1922

Annie sits in the main hall of the railway station watching men with guns establish that they have established very little. She listens intently, trying to fathom the intricacies of the politics as men perched on ammunition crates try to grasp the basics of the geography. Irish forces have taken over the nearby village of Belleek. However, Belleek, thanks to the vagaries of the new border, is no longer in Ireland. The Specials from the North tried to retake it but got run off, leaving a section of their men stranded. Due to the expanse of Lough Erne, the only way to rescue them by road is to come directly through Pettigo, which would mean officially invading the fledgling Irish State. So, the IRA and the Free State Army have put their differences aside to hold the town in the name of Ireland. Only six months ago there was no Free State Army and most of its soldiers were still in the IRA. Annie is relieved that the East and the West have nothing to add because the North and the South are fucking complicated enough.

She listens to all this being relayed to Francie, someone of apparent importance to the men in uniform as well as the ones in civilian clothes. They want his attention, they want his leadership, they want him to take over the men in trenches repelling the Specials where the river runs into the lough at some place called 'The Waterfoot'.

'I'll never set foot in a trench again.'

'But some of your men are down there.'

'And some of them aren't. How many IRA are in town?'

'Most of your dozen and a couple dozen more.'

'All chased out of the North?'

'A few came up from further down.'

'They're not alone there. What are you doing here, Sean, in your shiny new uniform?'

Molloy lights a smoke and smiles at him.

'I think I look rather dashing.'

'You look like a fanny.'

'The wage is decent; a lot of your boys are crossing over.'

'Why are you here? Local command know what they're doing.'

'I missed you.'

'You missed shooting at people.'

'Well, I couldn't be letting you have all the fun on your own.'

The double doors of the station burst open and a group carry a man to the middle of the room and set him carefully on the hard ground. His name is Frank Deacon, a train driver from Enniskillen. At the depot that afternoon he was slipped some information that couldn't wait. He left work, stole a bicycle from outside the Railway Hotel and took off for the border. Twenty miles later, half dead from the effort and almost shot twice, he comes to and starts to convulse on the stone floor. When he has worked his way through his second mug of tea Frank Deacon spits his story at Molloy.

'The British. They're coming. Now. They've put a column together in Enniskillen and they'll be here in the morning.'

'What exactly's in this column?'

'Armoured cars, Whippet tanks and artillery. There's orders from London. They've had enough of this border shite. They're going to blast you back down to where you came from.'

*

Annie listens as Ireland's armed factions bicker all around her. Francie has sprung to life, barking orders and identifying high ground for defensive positions on a map in a wonderful portrayal of a man who was full of shite when he said he was 'done with all of that'. When she has heard more than enough she rises quietly and walks unnoticed from the train station. Across the street then under a wooden fence and she's sliding down the bank to the water's edge. She slips gratefully from her boots and sits on a large stone, immersing her swollen calves in the cold water. There is a flood receding and the brown dirt from upstream has run off, leaving the water black with white froth in it like a pint of stout. She instinctively looks for the runs and the holes behind stones where the big salmon lie, just like he taught her to all those years before.

She stands and moves forward until the water is nearly at her groin. It takes her breath away and her mind clears somewhat as she assesses the insanity of her situation. How in God's name has it come to this, stranded in a deserted village between the armies of two countries with an alcoholic gunman she used to know? The part of town in the North over the river is built along the base of a hill and its buildings will afford good cover for anyone needing it. She stares across at the empty windows in the houses and wonders if British soldiers already lie hidden beneath the sills.

A sudden urge flows through her to push off and float downstream until the river decides where it wants her to be. If she even got round the next bend she could climb out and take her time walking away while they take their time killing each other. Walk away where, though? Even before Francie's bombshell about the letters she had already doubted whether she could ever go back. She hates what the place has become. Neighbours dependent on each other for generations not speaking any more because of fear and religion. There had hardly been anyone to help with the hay this year as half the young Catholic men had gone on the run across the border for fear of the Specials, whether they were involved in anything or not. Hunted by men she sat beside in school, who helped with their harvest, whose mothers her own goes to church with. She pictures her mother, sat smug and visible somewhere in the front two rows of the congregation. A beacon of virtue. Someone people look up to in the daily battle with their own weakness. Annie plucks the minister from the image and places herself centre stage in his pulpit. When she has finished telling the flock what this woman actually did to her own daughter, she stands back and waits for the shock and revulsion of the crowd to wash over her mother. But it would never come, would it? Many of them would think she had done the right thing. Protected her own from a life of Catholicism. Jesus, why would anyone go back to a place like that when they had the whole world to choose from? Regardless of the situation she now finds herself in and despite whoever Francie Leonard may have become, she has never felt more exhilarated in her life. I don't know where I will end up, Mother, but the first thing I will do when I get there is write you a letter. There won't be much in it, but when you have read it, you will know that I know.

Her boots are a slow pull over wet feet and then she is up and off. She slips halfway up the bank and as she gets off her stomach she starts to laugh involuntarily at the ridiculousness of it. A village with a border running through the middle of it, leaving each half in a completely different country. Surely they can't leave things like that? Why didn't they put the border a few hundred feet further the other way?

She has her fingers around a rung on the fence and her foot raised to climb it when a bullet smashes into the supporting post, not ten feet left of her head. She feels its impact as it reverberates through the wood into her hands but the sound doesn't come until afterwards. She throws herself backwards and tumbles down the riverbank. As she rolls she glimpses black uniforms across the water. When she comes to a stop she is staring at Crozier, who is standing in his stirrups, towering over the shooter.

'Swim for it, Miss Johnston, and we'll pull you out.'

She stares at his long shiny boots framed against the animal's flank as she moves vertebra by vertebra to her feet.

He smiles at her, warm, plausible, then he comes at it from a different angle.

'Don't you want to escape?'

Her mouth doesn't open as she searches his horse for the whip he used to thrash the old man before murdering him.

'What will we tell your mother, Annie? It will be hard to come home later if you're the whore who ran off with Francie Leonard.'

There is a hail of gunfire behind her and she is back in a ball on the ground. Across the river, Crozier's horse rears then bolts as another volley crashes out and then there are rough hands in her armpits and the backs of her legs are scraping the top of the fence as she is manhandled over it to safety.

Francie and Molloy have been joined by another officer from the Free State Army. Annie smokes a cigarette and stares at the man as she composes her thoughts. His uniform looks suspiciously like a regular British army one that's been recently dyed dark green. She wonders if his wife has to look at a big green hairy arse every night when he comes home and gets ready for bed. He is introduced to her as Commandant Harry Coyle. He seems to be the Yank's boss and the man in overall charge. Coyle asks after her well-being then tells Francie and Molloy that there shouldn't be any women this close to the front and heads off about his hairy-green-arsed business. Francie, now with a rifle slung over his shoulder, takes her towards the door at the rear of the station.

'Let's get you into the middle of town away from the shooting.'

'This better not be where you tell me to find more women and prepare food for the men.'

'You sure it was Crozier?'

'And I won't be changing bandages or singing lullabies to dying young fellas either.'

'Annie?'

'Well, let me see now, Francis, he had a big black horse, big black boots and one fuckin arm.'

Molloy crosses the room and steps between them.

'I have a compromise for you. Dig me something like a trench this side of the bridge. No one has to get in the thing, just make it deep enough to stop an armoured car.'

'We're having a private moment, Sean.'

'You're having a public moment, Francie.'

'I'm sorry.'

'Don't you dare apologise to me, miss. Haven't I been on the run with this prick myself? Most nights listening to him talking to you in his sleep. I ain't said hello properly. It's an honour. I feel like I've known you for years.'

'Three years. Three years of listening to your horse shit when I should have been listening to her.'

'Get digging, then the three of us can find somewhere to have a drink. I think that's the least we owe the lady. There are some women left in this dump somewhere, Annie. Could you pull them together and rustle up some food for the troops?'

He turns on his heel and is gone as quickly as he appeared.

'You see, Annie, that's the problem with America: it's full of fuckin Americans.'

They make love in an upstairs bedroom in a large deserted house at the top of the town. In a random act of hospitality, the owners have made the bed up before fleeing in the face of the soldiers. En route to the clean sheets and soft pillows they tore each other naked and fucked on the stairs like the animals they had become amongst the rocks on the mountain.

Afterwards, when they lie together, he can't look her in the eye but it doesn't hurt for she knows that he's frightened of finding her dead brother looking back out at him.

'You never talk about him.'

'Neither do you.'

'Were you there when he died?'

'Twenty foot away.'

'Did he suffer?'

'Not as much as you have.'

He leaves her dozing and collects their clothing from the stairwell. He dresses by the window then puts a fresh clip in the Mauser and tosses it on the bed beside her.

'You know how to use it.'

'I've no intention of shooting anyone.'

'Well, they seem intent on shooting at you, so it's nice to have the option.'

'I'm not staying, Francie.'

'Neither am I.'

'Where will you go?'

'I was hoping you'd decide for me.'

She watches him for a while to see if his words curdle on his lips.

'I leave tomorrow and don't you dare promise me anything.'

'I need to set the boys up right in the morning, I owe them that. Then we vanish.'

When he has gone she wanders through the house naked, enjoying the danger of each new room. In the vast kitchen she boils kettles on the range and fills the tin bath she finds under the oak dining table. The hot water on her skin is sharp and her senses flare then melt in the dull burn that ripples all over her body. She scrubs herself with the harsh kitchen soap she found by the Belfast sink then lies back, letting the suds swallow her. It must be a businessman who owns such a grand house, or a solicitor perhaps. Either way, he's a Protestant. She starts to laugh at her own joke and nearly chokes on a mouthful of foam. As she spits over the side on to the floor she narrowly misses the feet of two older women who stand a few yards away staring at her.

'You Miss Annie?'

'I am.'

'That Yank sent us, there's a hundred men need spuds.'

These women are the ones she's known all her life. Her mother and Francie's mother. Grey hair pulled tight into buns and cardigans tucked under worn aprons. Women who know nothing but looking after men. The one on the left looks pretty stern but her friend beams at Annie, clearly enjoying the very concept of her indulgence.

'What have we got, ladies?'

'Any amount of potatoes and bacon, and I'm sure we could put our hands on a few cabbages.'

'I'll be dressed in five minutes. Where will we cook?'

'Well, here will do; sure the Reverend's house is as good as anywhere.'

CHAPTER SIXTEEN

Thiepval, Somme, France

1 July 1916

Their Mills bombs keep getting chucked back but the German stick grenades explode almost as soon as they land.

'They're setting the fuses short, count two seconds longer before you throw.'

Big Sergeant Cartwright from Coleraine barks at them then takes off at a lick towards the next bend and the wall of sandbags the Germans have thrown up to protect it. He has a rifle with bayonet fixed in his left hand and a length of wood with a lump of metal embedded in it in his right. The club that is tied to his wrist with a leather thong was designed especially for today and constructed from a choice piece of Thiepval wood. His technique is flawless. When a Hun lunges with his butcher bayonet he parries with the rifle then smashes upwards with the stick. Bones smash or testicles crush every time and when the man goes down he shoots him with the rifle. Francie tucks in tight behind and Lieutenant Gallagher and Frank and Jacob Sampson follow suit in a line, along with an assortment of men that the captain has rallied for the push to the Crucifix.

Earlier, as Francie struggled through the barbed wire, Sergeant Crozier was cut down by machine-gun fire beside him. They pull pins and count as they move then release the grenades up and over the sandbags. Jacob Sampson freezes. He is exhausted from hand-to-hand fighting and confused by the new count, his arm and brain still in tune with what came before. They dive out of his way, shouting at him to throw the fucking thing, but it goes off in his hand, mangling the top half of his body. Frank roars and lunges for his brother but Cartwright grabs him around the waist and throws both of them into the sandbag wall, toppling it completely just as the German grenades start sailing over its top.

They rush into the fight, bullets first with blades to follow. Some Germans panic and tumble through the doorway of a dugout where they are caught like rats in a coal hole. Others race along the trench, taking bullets in their backs. The fallen are stalked and finished with blows from clubs and rifle butts to conserve ammunition. Three Mills bombs bounce down the stairs of the bunker and when the detonations have finished but the screaming hasn't, another two follow for good measure.

A Lewis gunner climbs the parapet taking up a defensive position covering the trench as far as the next bend. The system is dug in zigzags cutting it into short sections, which make it easier to defend and lessens casualties from incoming shells. The gunner shouts that he is running low and Gallagher orders Francie back to the wire to look for ammo pans dropped on the way through. More should have arrived with the support troops but the support has never materialised despite the Ulsters pushing through and taking all of their objectives. He retraces their steps carefully, wary of Germans reappearing from the incredibly deep dugouts. Seven days of shelling, yet they were all just sitting down there waiting. He climbs over the bodies of an Ulster man and a Bavarian locked together in death then hops over individual corpses and equipment until he makes the next corner.

It takes fifteen minutes to cover the ground that it took four hours of fighting to capture. He pauses by the first dugout they bombed after jumping into the line and peers back across no man's land. There are shells bursting sporadically but most of the German barrage is now focused behind him on the Schwaben Redoubt, which they are trying desperately to retake from the Ulster men. He slides along through torn wire and chooses a shallow shell hole. Two men from the 9th Battalion lie dead at the bottom but neither of them is a machine-gunner. Onwards through no man's land from body to body until he finds a Lewis-gun team shot to pieces near the beginning of the wire.

The weapon looks intact and it is worth its weight in gold. One of the men has died on top of a sack full of the circular ammunition magazines and it takes some effort and too much movement in the open to get them free. When they are liberated he has a full sack, his rifle and a light machine gun to carry all the way back to the fight.

As he passes the first dugout again movement in its mouth startles him and he drops bag and machine gun and covers the opening with his rifle.

'Come out or I'll shoot.'

No one appears but he knows they are there.

'*Raus, raus*; out to fuck or I'll kill ye!'

The blanket is pulled halfway back and Crozier's face peers sheepishly from the dark. He blinks a few times and stares at Francie as if he doesn't know who he is.

'Sergeant? We thought you were dead.'

He approaches the doorway and pulls it fully open and Crozier shrinks backwards from the daylight.

'Where are you hit?'

As he leans in Crozier pushes past him then throws himself down against the dirt wall.

'Where were you hit?'

Crozier stares at him like he is trying to place him then stands again slowly.

'But I saw you fall?'

'Have you a cigarette?'

'The lieutenant does. Can you carry the Lewis for me?'

Crozier begins to cough then his hands start trembling and he slides down the wall again folding his arms around his knees and rocking back and forward on his haunches.

'I'll wait here and coordinate the support.'

'They're not sending any.'

'I'm staying here.'

Francie grabs him by the tunic and lifts.

'Pick up the Lewis.'

'I'm staying here.'

'You're coming with me.'

'I can't go up there.'

He punches Francie in the stomach and tries to run but he is grabbed around the legs and brought down. From the stench and the state of the back of his uniform, it is clear that Crozier has recently soiled himself and Francie rolls off him in disgust. Crozier pulls his legs into his stomach like a foetus.

'I can't go up there; I won't.'

'You hid.'

'I never did.'

'You fucking hid, you fucking did!'

Crozier sobs rasped gasps then a shell lands much closer than recent impacts and Francie throws himself down beside the sergeant with his arms over his head. When he rolls over and checks the sky for more incoming rounds he finds Crozier standing over him with the Lewis gun pointing in his face.

'On your feet, Private.'

He grabs his rifle as he climbs but he could never pull the barrel round quick enough before he is blown away.

'Can't kill the Hun on your arse, Leonard.'

'No, Sergeant.'

'Lazy Catholic bastard, Leonard.'

'Yes, Sergeant.'

'Shirking round here on your own, Leonard.'

'Lieutenant sent me for ammo, Sergeant.'

He keeps his eyes locked on Crozier's.

'You'll never do anything right, will you, Leonard?'

'No, Sergeant.'

'You know what your fucking problem is, Leonard?'

'You, Sergeant.'

Despite the shell bursts Crozier's laughter is surprisingly deep and loud between the narrow walls of the trench.

'Cheeky Fenian bastard.'

'Always, Sergeant.'

The Lewis gun is lowered from his face to his chest and at that moment he knows that Crozier will shoot him.

'Francie? Francie?'

The call comes from beyond the bend. He holds Crozier's glare as he fires out the reply.

'Over here, Frank; I'm over here.'

Crozier drops the barrel then slowly turns the gun around, offering Francie the stock.

'Luck of the Irish, Leonard.'

CHAPTER SEVENTEEN

Pettigo, County Donegal, Irish Free State

June 1922

With Annie as an official witness, Francie and Molloy had pledged no more than three drinks each. A hangover in the face of superior British firepower was probably best avoided. Francie had offered the vague suggestion of 'two or three' but Annie felt this sounded ambiguous and, knowing Francie, open for interpretation, so the Yank put his foot down and chose the larger number. So, after walking the village perimeter to check on sentries the pair pick Annie up from the Reverend's house and wander to the back of the pub next door to break in.

Molloy smashes a small pane and after an impressive mono-logue of swear words manages to wrench the side door open. As he closes it behind them there is the sound of more glass breaking back out on the main street. They leave Annie in the shadows and sneak back along the alleyway. The front window of the shoe shop has been compromised and the arses of two men are clearly visible in the moonlight as they disappear inside. When they are sure that no one else has been alerted, Francie and the Yank follow the bur-glars through the shattered window. In the middle of the shop two men frantically light match after match as they search shelves and drawers pulling the merchandise down all around them.

'What the fuck are you doing?'

'Finding ones that fit, sir?'

'Flood?'

'Yes, sir.'

Patrick Flood is only eighteen years old and is one of the few men fighting in his home town.

'Who is with you?'

'McCann, sir.'

'You're supposed to be up on that hill with the Lewis gun. Have you left it with one man?'

'Sorry, boss, we'll be quick. I need new boots; these ones are full of holes.'

'Do you have to wreck the bloody shop to find them?'

'We can't find any big enough, sir.'

The Yank stifles a laugh and puts his hand on Francie's shoulder.

'You know what they say about boys with big boots?'

'What?'

'Big socks.'

'Jesus Christ preserve me; get out the back and find a lamp.'

Francie, Flood and McCann examine every pair of boots in the shop while Molloy stands in the centre with his arms raised, a candle in each hand.

'I feel like a Christmas tree.'

'Try these, they must be big enough.'

'But they're tan, sir, I want a black pair.'

'I couldn't give a fuck if they're pink, Flood, we're in Pettigo not Paris now try them on before I march you down to Commandant Coyle and have you put on a charge for looting.'

Back in the boozer bottles of porter are liberated from the shelf beneath the bar, which they sit along in a line on three stools. With their subject trapped in the middle, Annie and Molloy take turns to share their Francie stories, comparing notes on how they first remembered him. The Yank's yarns are full of whiskey and bullet wounds and hiding from the police while Annie's come from a time more innocent and the Yank adores her idyllic memories of their summers in the fields with Archie.

He is never far from the bar. Her stories are so full of him that they might as well have pulled Archie up a stool, but the Yank is a professional bullshit-merchant and the second a memory begins to smell of sorrow he has them pick-pocketing rich traders and drinking stolen booze and outrunning policeman with the assorted cast of his own Bostonian youth. With their pasts exhausted and having no discernible urge to discuss the bleak reality of their present, the Yank brings the evening's proceedings around to the future.

'You can joke all you want about the States, Francie, but where else you gonna go?'

'Call me old-fashioned but I had my heart set on Ireland.'

'You're a gunman on the run if you stay in the North and you're a gunman on the wrong side of the argument if you stay in the South.'

'Maybe the argument's not over. Collins is in London trying to change the agreement as we speak.'

'The treaty's not getting changed. You know it, Michael Collins knows it and the cows in the fucking fields know it. Brits are crafty bastards, Francie. They finally leave, but leave us fighting with ourselves.'

'I didn't get into this to shoot friends.'

'Listen, Francie, I'm not sticking around for no civil war either.'

'Annie and I are leaving tomorrow, Sean.'

'That's the best news I've heard since I punched you in Kerry.'

'If you hadn't started crying I would have punched you back.'

'You can't go home, though; not with your bogeyman.'

'I'm not leaving because of Crozier.'

'No, but he certainly makes it easier to decide.'

'Why does he hate you so much?'

He stares at his beer unable to answer her.

'Is it your fault that he lost his arm?'

'No, he lost that during a bombardment at Messines Ridge in 1917. They sent him home and it was the making of him.'

'Crozier's as mad as a cut snake. You clung to this girl through the trenches and kept me awake moaning her name in your sleep every night because you thought you'd never see her again, and now she's here. Hallelujah, leave tomorrow, a-fucking-men.'

'Leave for where, though?'

'America; it's full of Irish and opportunity.'

'Would you fucking quit with America, it'd be easier to kill him.'

The Yank considers the easy option carefully before replying.

'Before, maybe; but not now. Not in Northern Ireland where he has the entire police force and the Brits at his beck and call. Man, even if you got him they'd never rest until they hanged the coward that killed brave Inspector Crozier, the hero of the Somme.'

Francie lifts his bottle and drains it very slowly. When it's empty he places it on the bar before him and has nowhere left to hide. He can't look at her directly, so he stares across the bar at the whiskey bottles on the back shelf. Staring back at him from the big Bushmills distillery mirror is a greying, bearded, grumpy bastard whom he never said goodbye to. When did they get so alike? That old cunt could never make a decision either.

The legs of Annie's stool scrape the slate floor and she appears between him and his father and places two bottles on the bar.

'You're allowed one more each and that's it. There's a big decision to be made, after all.'

The Yank cheers and Francie slowly drags his eyes up to meet hers.

'You want to go to America?'

'You asking?'

'What about your mother?'

'What about her?'

'You're hurting now, but it will pass.'

'I'll never forgive her and neither will you.'

'If we go to America you won't be seeing her again.'

'She wouldn't come anyway. She'd shun heaven if you were in it.'

'I think I've probably spared her the choice.'

'So?'

'So what?'

'Are you asking me to emigrate with you or not?'

'I already did.'

Molloy stands up on the rungs of his stool and lifts his bottle over his head ceremoniously.

'To America.'

Francie snorts and Annie smiles and raises an imaginary glass.

'To America.'

The Yank takes a gulp from his bottle then hoists it again.

'To Archie.'

Francie raises his half-heartedly and Annie reaches across the bar and squeezes Molloy's arm in appreciation.

'Well, if you're all set for the States, maybe I should skedaddle too and keep the pair of you on the straight and narrow.'

'Not so easy to "skedaddle" when you wear a uniform and draw a wage, Sean.'

'Uniform or not we'll both be deserting our posts.'

'You said you could never go back to Boston?'

'To hell with Boston, it's a big old country. Maybe the three of us could go into business together.'

'Two gunmen and a farmer's daughter, the possibilities are fucking endless.'

He looks at her then explodes, his laughter rattling the glasses under the sink.

'It's the United States of America, Annie; you can be whatever you want to be.'

'I don't want to burst your bubble here, Abraham Lincoln, but how are we going to get there?'

'In a ship, Francis.'

'Paid for with what, Sean?'

The Yank throws his head back and drains his beer. When he puts the bottle on the bar again, he leaves his head where it is and stares at the elaborate Victorian light fitting in the middle of the ceiling.

'That's what I've been wanting to talk to you about. We're going to need another bottle here, Annie. There's one more big decision to make.'

'Which is?'

'Well, we've already robbed the pub, so, maybe we should go ahead and rob the bank.'

Three bottles later and the Yank has admitted it's why he came north in the first place.

'Just think of it as your war pension, Francie. I'm not hanging around to shoot my compatriots.'

'Compatriots? You're American.'

'Fuck you.'

'You couldn't give a shite about Ireland, you're only here because you didn't want to go home and face your brother.'

'Fuck your mother too.'

'If there hadn't been a war here you'd have stopped in the nearest country that had one.'

Annie bangs fresh bottles on the bar and they stop bitching and lift them.

'Three weeks ago in Ballina, a lorry full of armed men pulled up at the bank. They walked in, took ten thousand pounds, announced that as the Bank of Ireland funds the State, and they were the state soldiers, it was simply a down-payment for supplies. A week later a group of armed men pulled the same stunt in Ballyshannon.'

'So now two idiots will go it alone in Pettigo?'

'Piece of cake, Francie. I wouldn't trust anyone else.'

'I'm touched.'

'It's happening all over Ireland. We're in a vacuum until they establish a new Free State police force. Listen, we need to get out of the country and in order to do that we are going to need funds. Three years eating shit and sleeping in ditches to train these assholes to fight the British and now they're going to fight with each other? Bullshit. We deserve to get something out of this.'

'You're overlooking a pretty major hurdle here, Sean.'

'What's that?'

'Pettigo doesn't have a bank.'

'Sure it does, Francie. When I dug around and found out where your column was, that's the first thing I checked out.'

'We've been all over this town and I'm telling you there's no bank.'

'You can't see it.'

'You're going to rob an invisible bank?'

'You can't see it because it's on the other side of the border.'

No one speaks for an age.

'You're off your head mate.'

'Think about it. It's perfect.'

'It's perfectly mad.'

'When the fighting starts the Brits and the Specials are gonna be fully focused on getting across that bridge. We'll sneak behind their lines and simply liberate some funds from the bank.'

'Liberate how?'

'With a big bang that no one will think twice about in the middle of a battle. Especially if the British start showing off with that artillery our friend on the bike told us about. I'm telling you, man, it's perfect.'

'Then we sneak back through their line into the middle of a battle carrying a load of stolen money?'

'That's the easy part. By the time our lot decide they've put on enough of a show for Ireland and pull out, we'll be halfway to the coast. I've even got us some wheels.'

'Sorry, Sean.'

He stares at Annie across the bar.

'Sounds like a lot of fun but I've made a promise and I'm sticking to it. We leave tomorrow.'

'You'll still be leaving tomorrow, only with something to bloody show for it. Where you gonna take her anyway? What you gonna eat? You've got no money and you can't go home. No one wants to help IRA men on the run down south any more. Six years since you saw each other and you're gonna wander round Ireland reading her poems and stealing her some fuckin apples?'

Francie is still staring across at her but he knows that he's losing the battle because Annie is staring back, at the Yank.

'Way I see it, you've got two choices here, Francie. Either you help me rob that bank.'

'Or?'

'I help you rob that bank.'

Francie's collar has been shrinking as the Yank's plan has expanded. He stands quickly, knocking his stool over, and walks into the jacks. When he has mastered his breathing again and emptied his bladder he heads back to the bar to find Annie lifting a whiskey bottle down off the shelf. He picks up his stool and sits on it again without even glancing at Molloy. He watches her eyes as she carefully pours whiskey into three glasses. When she pushes a glass towards him he takes her hand before she can retract it.

'What do you think?'

'Does it matter?'

'It matters.'

She stares at the Yank for a bit then brings her eyes around to Francie when she has decided on her answer.

'I think you've fought for the British in France and the Irish in Ireland and now maybe it's time you did something for yourself. If you don't know how to do that, you could always just do it for me.'

CHAPTER EIGHTEEN

Thiepval, France

1 July 1916

Archie has not spoken for hours. There has been little need as Windy Patterson can talk enough for them both. It started out as a chronological journey through his life in Donegal but as he lost more blood and made less sense his odyssey grew in scale and scope. One minute he was in a Dublin marketplace marvelling at pieces of fruit he'd never even heard the names of and then he was waking on a fishing boat off the Aran Islands as the crew desperately tried to cut a 20-foot basking shark from their nets before it pulled them under.

Archie had listened dutifully all evening, wiping sweat and blood away whenever they threatened to drown the performance. When Windy needed water, Archie crawled over bodies collecting canteens from the dead. He didn't talk to the wounded, though he stopped to attend to everyone who spoke to him. He couldn't bring himself to tell them lies so he settled for telling them nothing instead. Slithering through scores of bodies, his uniform became so sticky it was as if the earth itself was sweating blood.

The constant cries for water were outnumbered only by the desperate calls for maternal intervention. If only they could hear this; the mothers of Ulster have never been so popular. Harris the Welsh miner had taught him never to give water to a man with a stomach wound. 'You think you're helping but you might as well cut his throat.' But for the day that was in it he gave it anyway, whether a leg was hanging off or a stomach hanging out. As far as Archie saw it they were all already dead.

Windy's yarns, as always, are good. The classic components are all there, the girls, the fights, the drinking all night, but as the stars begin to appear his stories change in colour. Family, beloved animals, his fears and inadequacies when working at sea. Archie leans back into the bank and pulls his friend to him, straddling him with his legs and wrapping his arms around his belly. When Windy is as comfortable as a man in a ditch who has had his hand blown off can be, his journey continues and Archie laughs his way with him around the highways and byways of Ireland. The horizon burns furnace orange as it consumes the bodies fed to it along the road and when the sunlight is replaced by a large summer moon Archie makes a startling realisation. The closer Windy Patterson comes to death, the more often he tells the truth.

Twice more they had attempted to make it back to the British line. The first time the bombardment had settled but as they rose, the tap-tap-tapping of the machine gun danced them back down to the bottom again. When later they tried again, the reality of a one-legged man helping a one-armed man who has been bleeding out for hours kept them from even scaling the side.

The stump is neat. A surgeon down the line would struggle to make as smart a job of it as the chunk of German steel that took the hand clean off and cut the rifle neatly in two. Windy explains how his hand was there on the ground still clutching the stock of the weapon and that he had wanted to put it in his pocket in case it could be sewn back on later only he couldn't prise the fingers off the barrel as he only had one fucking hand. They laugh at this for an age and each time they pull themselves together one of them starts the other off all over again. Archie wants to talk but when he opens his mouth nothing comes out and he knows that letting Windy speak is more important, for as long as Windy Patterson is speaking, Windy Patterson is still alive.

The night-time sounds are different. Or maybe they are exactly the same only you can hear them properly as the shelling has stopped. The whine from the flies is as constant as ever but they are so used to being covered in them from head to toe by now that they gave up swatting hours before. The low drone from the chests of the wounded seems to have lessened and Archie wonders if that is down to men falling asleep rather than dying. He doubts it. Death has no rivals. Without the artillery to cloak them the individual cries from the darkness are like needles through his ear drums.

Willy Spence; you can't hide for ever, Willy Spence!
Mother, I'm in the back field if you look for me, Mother.
Willy Spence; don't leave me here to die, Willy Spence.

In the dark Archie fantasises about who the mysterious Willy Spence might be and after two hours of repeatedly hearing the fucker's name he has given Willy a face, an occupation and a slightly overweight wife with two children from a previous marriage. His nerves are so shattered by the voices that he has considered lobbing grenades at them to put the callers out of their misery. When Windy sleeps he lets him in spells. Wrapped together he is in tune with the other man's breathing and when Windy reaches a depth where the heart rate slows considerably he shakes him awake again. Archie won't sleep himself for he knows that when he wakes he will be clutching a dead man.

The earliest birds sing and the sky is greying at the temples when Windy Patterson starts to talk again. He has woken in the arms of his mother and is determined to repent for all the wrongs he has done by her. Archie coos and clucks in his ear when he panics and holds him tight when he kicks. He should never have left Killybegs. He was an ungrateful wretch who would never see the ocean again. Maybe in time his mother and God will forgive him. The

German's mother never will. He killed the man before Easter. Shot him through the stomach when they came into our trench then stood doing nothing while he died. There was a girl in Ardara. Her name was Ciara Jane. 'I could never bring a Catholic home, Ma. I spurned her when the baby came. They shamed her on the streets and I never went back. I wanted to, Ma; I wanted to but I didn't. Charlie Gormley told me the nuns took her and the baby to Galway. It's why I ran to France, Ma.'

Windy takes fits of energy as he fights the inevitable and Archie holds on for dear life to stop him wasting his own on his feet. Each surge is lesser than the last and when he can barely lift his head it rests between Archie's neck and shoulder as he calls out names into the morning.

'Francie Leonard. Archie Johnston. Jack Elliot. Ciara Jane. Ciara Jane. Ciara Jane?'

CHAPTER NINETEEN

Pettigo, County Donegal, Irish Free State

June 1922

The Pettigo branch of the Belfast Banking Company sits on High Street in the Northern Irish side of town. They will have to cross the river and avoid the enemy before taking the bank and blowing the safe. After all of that, they will re-cross the river, hope to make it through their own lines with no questions being asked about them not being at their posts, then get as far away as possible before anyone realises they're gone.

Commandant Coyle has predictably chosen the old Royal Irish Constabulary station as his seat of command despite it having been partially burnt out by the IRA in 1920. Bleary from lack of sleep, Francie and Molloy settle down in the square to smoke cigarettes and look like two old pals in a square just smoking some fucking cigarettes. Annie is in the railway station readying breakfast for a hundred young men who are about to face the might of an Empire. She kissed both of them on the cheek before dawn in the kitchen of the Reverend's house, proffering that she had no doubt their boys would come good and she would certainly feed them well, but all the bacon and eggs in Ireland won't stop high-explosive shells. When she had said her piece they walked her to the door and watched her disappear downhill through the morning mist.

'You don't deserve her.'

'Neither do you.'

The gelignite and detonators are in boxes at the back of the old RIC station. It's the end of a shipment taken from police in an ambush outside Ennistymon in County Clare two years before. If there is any money left in the bank, it is reasoned that it must be in a safe and Molloy fancies that two sticks should more than do the job. The plan is for Molloy to nip through to the back and pocket the necessary while Francie shows Coyle possible escape routes for when the British eventually take the town. Which they will, if they want. The man with the most men always tends to get his way. Their job is to hold them off for as long as they can and take as many of them out as possible while they're at it. Perhaps the powers that be will change their minds if their body count starts rising in a country they are not even supposed to be in.

The Yank knows from the inventory in the barracks that no private cars were left in town. So the only available vehicle is the big open-top Crossley Tender taken from the Specials near Belleek a few days previous. It was hidden up at the railway station between the platforms. While the Yank is filling his pockets with explosives Francie will convince Coyle to move the truck to the church at the top of the town for its own protection. That way they'll have a straight run on to the main road when they make a dash for it. Annie is charged with collecting supplies and any ammunition she can get her hands on and having them ready in the Crossley.

They are nicotine green by the time the sun is high enough in the sky for them to make an appearance at Coyle's command post. In the reception hall of the old police station they're forced to smoke more cigarettes with the commandant and two of his lieutenants as the defence of the town from the Crown is discussed.

In Coyle's office on an Ordnance Survey map, Francie charts possible routes towards Lough Derg and over the mountain beyond. When mugs of tea are produced Molloy announces that he's away for a shite and disappears about his business. Coyle is in full agreement about moving the Crossley Tender and as Francie finishes his geographical observations and starts to give Coyle an assessment of the Prior on the island and where his loyalties might lie, Molloy reappears declaring himself half a stone lighter. When he winks at Francie to confirm that he is, in fact, two sticks of gelignite and some detonators heavier they lament that they must inspect their men again and leave.

Annie clocks them approaching as she dishes out the end of breakfast. As they run husks through the grease in the pan where the bacon used to be, a nod from the Yank confirms that his pockets are full of badness. When they depart to their posts she leaves the other women to clear up the mess left by a swarm of feeding men, and heads off to find sacks big enough for bank robbers.

On the church hill, the Yank Molloy sets his Free State Army troops out in rows: one halfway up the field and the other at its very top. Two lines of rifles covering the approach to the back of town. He can't see the bridge from here but he has eyes on the road approaching it. Below him the arse of the Crossley Tender sticks out from behind the church where Commandant Coyle personally parked it for them.

Francie's IRA men have been shared out among various defensive units throughout the town. Every house along the river holds men with weapons waiting at windows. The train station bristles with gun barrels and on the hill directly above it, Francie sits with young Patrick Flood by the Lewis gun on Drumharriff Hill. Bernard McCann, Flood's partner from the shoe-shop heist, and William Kearney, a smart arse from County Tyrone, lie opposite them in the early-morning sunshine. They look relaxed but the tension is palpable and if so much as a pigeon lands on that bridge the Lewis gun might go off like a burst hose.

'How're your boots, Flood?'

'Grand, sir; cutting my heels a bit.'

'Isn't it well you're sitting up here on your arse, then?'

'The lady, sir, is she your girl?'

'She is, Flood, though she might well tell you different.'

'She's a fine-looking woman.'

'She is that. How you feeling?'

'Grand, sir.'

'You Donegal fellas have the balls for anything.'

'We do, boss.'

'He doesn't even have hair on his balls.'

'Kearney, there's enough hair growing out of your Tyrone hole to cover everyone's balls.'

As their laughter dies they hear the first rumble of engines. McCann is up in a flash with the butt tight between his chin and his shoulder and Flood falls to his knees behind him ready to call in targets and change magazines. They have no tripod and the weapon is belted to a tree for support.

'Right, lads, not a shot till the first lorry hits the bridge. Suck them in nice and easy and when they're lined up like oul women at mass, let them fuckin have it.'

They stare at the furthest bit of road where it disappears over the hill. The noise of engines rattles closer and Francie takes the white towel that Commandant Coyle gave him earlier and climbs the tree the machine gun is tied to. The first lorry appears over the brow of the hill and stops. Even from a distance, he can tell by the distinct blunt snout that it's a Lancia armoured car.

'Have they stopped, boss?'

He can see troops spill out beside the Lancia and the glint of sunlight on the officer's binoculars as he takes in the town up ahead.

'Aye, Bernard, but not for long.'

On cue, the soldiers disappear back into the bowels of the beast and it edges the rest of its body over the brow of the hill and starts down towards the town. Francie waits until he can see three more links in the armoured chain, then he starts to wave the towel frantically at the observers on the train-station roof. When he receives the reply he jumps from the tree and grabs his rifle from the grass.

'Right, lads, I'm off to the bridge; short bursts now, and make them count. If I don't make it back use your heads. If it's looking bad below there's no shame in getting out of here before the town's overrun. Dead volunteers are no good to anyone, all right?'

He runs down the side of the hill like a ten-year-old, letting the weight of his top half drive his legs faster and faster. He can't find Annie in the station. As he moves off towards the lane behind the houses facing the river he starts to panic as he realises that he can't guarantee ever seeing her again. Sprinting towards his post he catches a glimpse of her passing by the end of an alleyway. When he gets there she is halfway up Main Street heading for the church. He calls out and she stops and turns then watches him jog towards her. When they face each there is silence while he catches the breath on which to form the words.

'I'm sorry, Annie.'

'I know.'

She smiles then she is gone again, up the hill, her back stiff with purpose.

In the rear of the armoured Lancia, Lieutenant Parkinson of the South Staffordshire Regiment can no longer feel his legs. His relief at not marching the nineteen miles from Enniskillen to Pettigo soon vanished when his knees locked two miles before his calves began to cramp. When finally they stop and the door opens to let fresh air and sunlight in, he falls gladly out into the morning.

Beside the Lancia, he stares through his binoculars on to the market town below. Pettigo. The strange Irish name still won't form correctly in his mouth. It sounds comical, like a woman's undergarment. For nearly two weeks he has heard little else. The Pettigo and Belleek bloody triangle. Some are even calling it a salient but it is hardly Ypres. An anomaly jutting from one state into another, then out and in again like some child's skipping-rhyme. This song, though, is full of armed rebels and crafty smugglers and general ne'er-do-wells.

Parkinson only arrived in Ireland post-Partition. So his first foray into enemy territory will come during a moment of crisis, when the war is supposedly over and will technically amount to an invasion by British troops of the Irish Free State.

From the age of ten, all he wanted to be was a soldier. He just missed the end of the war in Europe and now, at twenty-one, he will finally taste combat.

Captain Bowles of the Royal Field Artillery joins him, taking in the situation with his own field glasses.

'We're in position. Range is decent. I can zone in on targets at will on those surrounding hills.'

'There are men on the roof of the train station, Captain, and if they have any experience there'll be a machine gun on the hill behind.'

'I'll train guns on those targets immediately. We can drop a curtain of shells behind when they run. Shouldn't be hard to keep them where we want them.'

'Careful not to shell the Specials coming in from behind.'

'Have they crossed the border yet, Lieutenant?'

'Inspector Crozier swore they'd be in place before we got here.'

'Then the town should be encircled by midday.'

'Priority is to not destroy it.'

'Priority is to win.'

'A town that spans two countries. Who'd have thought it, Captain?'

'It won't last.'

'The border, sir?'

'The entire thing is completely nonsensical.'

'Seems madness to be attacking across it.'

'You know what Churchill is like.'

'The Secretary of State for the Colonies does tend to shout until he gets his way, Captain Bowles.'

'I know all about that. I was second wave at Gallipoli.'

Francie Leonard, Charlie Larkin and Seamus Enright sit along the back wall of a bedroom in the house that overlooks the bridge. Francie's mind is calm and clear but his entire body is soaked in sweat. Facing the window but not yet by it for fear of presenting themselves as targets they wait as patiently as their bowels will allow. Timing will be as important as accuracy. They must arrive at the window at the optimum moment in order to maximise surprise. The noise of the approaching column tells him that it's almost upon them. When the rumble of the engines passes through the floorboards up into their buttocks Charlie falls to his stomach and inches forward, dragging his rifle by the strap. When he is safely underneath the windowsill Seamus crawls forward to join him. Tight to the floor, they watch Francie snake halfway across the room then stop dead in its centre. He empties spare clips of .303 rounds from his pockets then all three release their safety catches.

Francie will stand in the heart of the room putting rapid fire through the window over the boys' heads, affording them the cover to pick off targets more precisely. The boys are better shots but no one Francie has run with has ever matched his rate of fire. Good old British army training. He had regularly emptied thirty rounds per minute into the practice ranges in France, though it is never as straightforward in the heat of battle. Ten rounds per magazine. Just keep the bolt working smoothly and try not to let your back seize up completely. He rises on one knee and watches the far end of the bridge. When the Lancia's steel beak edges around the corner on to the bridge he stands and takes aim at the lorry full of troops behind it.

'Now!'

He is startled by the volume of his own cry in the enclosed space as he watches his men take aim at the small square hole in the armour plating that allows the driver to see the road. Charlie and Seamus fire simultaneously and before they have a second round away the lorry changes direction, sharply turning in on itself and bouncing off the wall before toppling on to its right-hand side in the middle of the bridge. Both bullets had found the driver's window. One entered his forehead blowing his brains out on to the men directly behind him and the second bounced off two plated walls before entering Lieutenant Parkinson's groin.

Francie ignores the crippled lorry and puts a full magazine into the one behind it as khaki uniforms spill out on to the verges and run in every direction. A soldier crawls from the back of the crash site and lies stone still in the road. Francie fires at retreating bodies further off but in his peripheral vision he sees the fallen man rise and run. He pivots, breathes, relaxes his shoulder and shoots the man between the shoulder blades as he nears the wall of the bridge. The Tommy stumbles the last few feet then drapes himself over the side where he dies with his arse in the air and his head bouncing above the water.

Two charger clips rammed into the magazine and Francie is picking fresh targets. Breathe and pull, breathe and pull. The machine gun on Drumharriff Hill kicks in, and as its rounds bite into the row of vehicles the houses all around them open fire.

After five minutes of madness calls of 'Ceasefire!' echo along the line from the train station through Francie and out into the buildings in the heart of the village. He counts two bodies below and he knows that the driver must also be dead. There were others dragged off by comrades in the mayhem but there is no way of knowing if those are fatalities. The silence after the cyclone of gunfire is deafening. It won't last, though, as any minute they will reap what they have sown. There is movement at the rear of the capsized Lancia. An arm appears then a dark-haired head and a torso as Lieutenant Parkinson drags himself from the vehicle into the road and slowly starts to inch towards his own line. He has clearly lost the use of his legs and his progress is agonising to watch. Charlie shifts his weight, lowers his rifle and slams the bolt home on a round.

'Leave him, Charlie; he's fucked anyway.'

Charlie looks at Francie then puts his head back to the weapon and Francie hops forward knocking the barrel offline.

The single shot flies off to the left into the river. Charlie stares at him, bemused.

'Gone soft, boss? Chances for killing Brits are running out.'

The walls around them come alive with the smashing of incoming rounds and the three dive to the floor and crawl for the door.

CHAPTER TWENTY

Thiepval, Somme, France

1 July 1916

The miracle of Sergeant Crozier puts wind in their sails. In a day belonging to death, there is nothing like someone cheating it.

'But we saw you go down?'

'Knocked out, Lieutenant, by that blast right in front.'

The men who were there remember no blast but it matters not. Someone has come back from the dead.

They bomb and hack their way to the Crucifix, bend by bloody bend. When they have finally taken it, big Sergeant Cartwright has killed a dozen Germans and his trousers and socks are drenched in their blood. They search desperately for water in dugouts and in the bottles of German dead but there is none to be had anywhere. Their seven-day barrage did little to dent the defences but it destroyed the supply line and now the Ulster men themselves will suffer for it. The shelling behind them means nothing can be brought forward to quench them either. Francie's tongue has swollen, filling his mouth and making it difficult to breathe.

Around him, they collapse, wearing strange yellow war masks from the clouds of cordite released by the explosions. Exhausted, he tries not to find Crozier's eyes, which he knows are watching him. The sergeant will kill him when he has half a chance. Of that, there is no doubt. He must never let Crozier get behind him in the fight. Easy to shoot someone in this confusion. He will have to take matters into his own hands.

Shouts from the way they came and they're on their feet, cornered dogs ready to rip throats out. Major Peacock's name is passed along and Lieutenant Gallagher calls the party forward, convinced the Germans would never have that information. The Major is the battalion's second in command and it is strange for the men to see him here in the middle of the war, carrying a rifle, covered in dirt and looking like he means business. He has seven men left from the ten that took off with him across no man's land. He cuts to the chase and it makes for poor hearing. The Ulsters are being pushed back by fierce counter-attacks all over the Schwaben Redoubt. German reinforcements are streaming forward along support trenches and no man's land is a hurricane of German shells, so the men who reached their objectives are trapped between the enemy's first and fourth lines. Wounded who have made their way back to the wood report as many as four hundred dead in the Sunken Road. There is a shortage of officers on the redoubt so Peacock takes Lieutenant Gallagher and leaves half of his men and Sergeants Cartwright and Crozier in charge. Their orders are to hold the junction beyond the last bullet.

In a lull they clean weapons jammed beyond use and shore up parapets with sandbags and anything else that can be used to barricade. In a dugout thirty steps deep, lines of bunk beds are smashed and the wood and wire ferried back above ground. From the back of the bunker Sergeant Cartwright waves Francie to him and they take turns on a bottle he has found, gagging on the warm flat beer but grateful for the momentary respite from the terrible thirst. The dull thump of grenades detonating has them sprinting upstairs and diving for their weapons. The Germans are many and keen and Francie barely has his Enfield in his hands before a man who looks as old as his father is impaled on its bayonet. He turned into the man's charge and his own speed and weight did the damage. A foot in the groin and a pull but the thing is stuck tight in a rib and he has to drop all and dive out of the way of the next man who lunges for him, catching his upper arm and tearing a long gash in it. When he comes again Francie kicks desperately upwards but the man is shot from behind and Francie is up and snatching the German's rifle and running him through with his own bayonet. When it is over they have lost four men, the Hun seven.

Voices above on the redoubt shouting in English then shattered men appear pushing through the Crucifix in droves. Wild-eyed, some half-naked, barely a weapon between them. Cartwright grabs a corporal from the 10th Derry Volunteers and pins him to the wall for answers. The redoubt is overrun. Germans everywhere. Everyone dead. No support came. 'Where is the fucking support?' He lets the man drop and he hobbles off after the other ghosts.

'You heard the order. No one leaves here until Lieutenant Gallagher returns and says so.'

Frank Sampson mutters, 'For we all know the lieutenant is already dead,' and Cartwright lifts him by the collars and shoves him higher up the wall than the previous fella.

'Beyond the last bullet, Private, you got that?'

They climb out of the trench to await the next attack. In shell holes along its lip, they lie still with grenades lined up in front of their noses. When the howling Germans fill up the trap below they rise and rain bombs among them then leap into the mess to finish the job.

The shadows lengthen along the bottom of the trench as the sun squats in the sky. The pockets of retreating Ulster men become more frequent as the Germans hammer the slopes above and as the impacts creep closer to the Crucifix Frank Sampson begins to unfurl.

'We're the only ones not retreating.'

'That's not retreating, it's running away. Stay at your post.'

'They're heading for the wood.'

'Turn around and keep looking up that hill, Private.'

'I am looking and I'm seeing a full-scale retreat, Sergeant.'

'Get back to your post, soldier.'

'And we're the only men not on it!'

He throws his rifle and pushes through the men towards the southern-facing firing step. Sergeant Cartwright joins Crozier, blocking Sampson's path, and he is forced to stop and review his options. He turns to his right and makes to leave the way they came but Francie steps in and puts a hand on his chest.

'Keep the head, Frank, it'll soon be night.'

'It gets worse after dark.'

'We're all here, it's all right.'

Crozier pulls the Webley he took from a dead officer and points it at Frank.

'Return to your post, Sampson.'

'You're going to die. Just like my brother, you're all going to die!'

'You're a coward, Sampson.'

'And you're a bloody hypocrite, Crozier; you lied!'

Crozier doesn't take his eyes or the muzzle of his gun off Frank.

'He pretended he was hit and you all bloody know it.'

The others watch, doubt creeping in as they look to the miracle who cocks his hammer and steps a foot closer to Sampson. A shiver rolls along Frank's back like someone has walked on his grave and he screams at the top of his voice.

'We're all going to die!'

When he runs Crozier shoots him through the side. When he turns Crozier shoots him in the chest. He drops to his knees and falls to his face and dies at their feet. Crozier calmly places the gun in his belt.

'Cowardice in the Face of the Enemy; you saw him run.'

Francie lunges and manages to rip Crozier's head back by the hair with one hand and punch him in the throat with the other, before Cartwright lifts Francie almost over his head and throws him into the wall. Crozier splutters to his feet, pulling his revolver, but before he can fire every gun in the trench is aimed at his face.

'He struck a superior. You'll face a court martial for this, Leonard, and you're all witnesses.'

Cartwright grabs Crozier's revolver and throws it out into no man's land.

'I saw nothing, Sarge.'

'Me neither, Sarge.'

'Me 'n' all, Sarge.'

Crozier ignores the rifles and steps up to Francie.

'I will see you shot, Leonard.'

'No one saw anything, Sergeant; maybe you imagined it. You must still be dizzy from that blast right in front.'

Voices above and rifles seek new targets as shouts ring out.

'We're coming in.'

Gallagher and the shadows of three men slide into the trench, their eyes wild and their uniforms torn and covered in blood.

'It's done for, lads. I'm sorry but we're pulling out, Cartwright.'

'Apology accepted, Lieutenant; now let's get the fuck out of here.'

CHAPTER TWENTY-ONE

Annie listens to the fighting for over an hour before her imagination wins and she can sit still no longer. The road along the river to the train station is not an option so she heads away from the battle sounds, skirting the town completely until she hits the railway line. Exposed in the natural tunnel it cuts through the landscape; she stays tight to the side and follows the foliage right the way along until she can see the platform ahead where she served breakfast this morning. Inside the main building, chaos is being defined. Men run and shout and bleed. She examines and cleans an arm wound that is no worse than she's seen on the farm and straps up a leg that's had a bullet pass straight through the muscle in the calf.

When she asks about fatalities someone tells her that no one is dead. Then another claims that the bridge is littered with British bodies. Don't they count as the dead, then? Do we dehumanise them so we can kill them? Christ, but men would sicken your shite.

A boy no older than seventeen dribbles his way towards her, his teeth showing through the hole torn in his cheek by a piece of flying glass. She bathes the wound in warm water from a pot on the stove. As she wraps a clown-sized bandage under his jaw and around the top of his head she traces a line across the war map of Europe that has determined the last six years of her life. From Ireland to England to France to Belgium to France to England to

Ireland. The Grand Tour. How many has Francie dehumanised before sending them off to meet their maker?

Nearly ninety minutes after she heard the first shot, the gunfire ceases as suddenly as it began. The men coming down from the roof can barely hold their rifles as the barrels are scalding hot. She works frantically with the other women to get bread and cold potatoes and anything vaguely edible into the hands of those who need it. Two huge barrels for replenishing the steam engines are dragged to the middle of the waiting room and the men queue for a dunk, holding heads under water while they suck until their bellies and lungs can take no more.

The shooting resumes again but further away. A few pops here and there but then an engagement as big as the one at the bridge builds somewhere in the distance. A runner arrives looking for someone senior to report to and Commandant Coyle appears through a crowd. The Specials have crossed the river and are being held outside of town on the Lough Derg side. Annie panics and starts to look for either of them among the melee, then she gives up and moves back to her food station, knowing that if she stands still for long enough in this world of men they will find her.

Half a mile outside town, Captain Bowles absently draws mental lines creating a triangle between the hill with the machine gun, the hill behind the church and the hill that he is sitting on. The real lines have already been drawn, angles and distances calculated, sights set and barrels elevated. The sun is beginning to fade on what was a rare beautiful day for this part of the world but it is still warm so he sits in shirtsleeves watching his gun-teams stack rounds by their 18-pounders.

For over a week these bastards have held out. Firstly from droves of well-armed Specials then today from the British army itself. Bowles is a military man from a long line of military men and he has no time for these Specials. The British army and the police should be more than capable of fighting its own battles without arming the dregs of the Orange lodges, who are driven by hundreds of years of religious hatred. Give an Irishman an axe and he'll find someone to grind it in.

He'd met Inspector Crozier of the B-Specials the week before in Enniskillen and had taken an instant dislike to the man. Too righteous, too certain. A man for whom a missing arm was a validation. There was a discernible sense with these Ulster men that their sacrifice at the Somme justified whatever they needed it to back at home. As far as Bowles could see, these 'Specials' were as unprofessional and out of control as the Black and Tans had been down south. Another of Winston Churchill's many debatable brainchildren and another rabble that Bowles had disapproved of. The very notion of it had appalled him. Nothing he has seen in Ireland over the previous four years has convinced him that his army should be there at all. Crozier is hell-bent on a personal mission to capture an individual named Leonard. He spoke of little else. Later Bowles had heard that Leonard, an IRA man with a hit list as long as your leg, had served with Crozier on the Western Front and that Crozier had taken it upon himself personally to serve justice upon this particular traitor.

He lights a final pipe and internally salutes Pettigo's lightly armed defenders. Commendable, but it will mean little when his field guns have had their say. They'll lay rounds down on both hills and, despite his orders, he'll put a brace in the middle of town and chalk those down to poor gunnery. A few houses coming down around the bastards will spit the message at them quicker than some craters in a farmer's field.

He has had no further reports on the well-being of Lieutenant Parkinson. The last he heard the medics thought the bullet was lodged somewhere in the lower stomach. Bowles tips the contents of his pipe on to the grass then stands and crushes it with his heel. He pulls his watch from his rear trouser pocket and prepares to give the order to fire. Midday. The battle at the bridge this morning was before seven. A bullet in the stomach over five hours ago. Lieutenant Parkinson is surely dead.

Back by the Lewis gun, Francie catches his breath after a rapid climb then orders the belts holding the weapon to be untied. He knows their position will have been plotted as a target and if the boys are to have any chance of holding the strategically vital hill they have to keep moving the weapon.

The crump of distant 18-pounders momentarily transports him to another field in a different country years before. He freezes for a second then the boys are up and moving as the first shell whines overhead, exploding somewhere between them and the station.

They dash behind the brow of the hill and fall flat. Fate will decide whether any shells are lucky enough to find them. Three, four, five explosions then nothing and they are up and back towards the tree, which has been blown completely out by the roots. They put their shoulders behind its thick end and push forward, squaring it off between themselves and the bridge below. A perfect barricade for them to hide behind.

'Stay here and keep the gun out of sight until you hear infantry fire at the bridge.'

He rolls out from behind the tree and watches the road into town. The guns cough again and Francie can see the smoke from their barrels on a low hill along the road out of town. This time the rounds rain on to Molloy's hill and he watches the impacts kick dirt and smoke into the air where he knows the Yank has his boys dug in. He gives his own lads a final yell of encouragement, then as another incoming whine comes towards them he is up and off downhill faster than the shell that comes after him.

*

Molloy counts six impacts before the racket subsides. He pulls himself out of the ditch at the back of the field as a seventh lands too close to the Crossley Tender for comfort. He reissues his orders in a controlled shout. None of them are to retake their positions in the field until they hear sustained rifle fire below. Until the British attack, all they are up here are sitting ducks for the big guns.

'And be ready to leg it for the mountain the second the order's given.'

At the back of the church, he checks the Crossley for damage. Two perfectly round shrapnel holes on the rear-side door let him know which kind of shell it was. There seems to be no damage around the front where the engine lives. The street from the Reverend's house down into town is completely deserted. He is halfway along it when the whine above has him sprinting then tripping sideways and rolling into a doorway.

There is a huge crash as a building across the way takes a direct hit and then a second duller kick that he feels through the ground as his body bounces. When he moves off again the crater from the second shell lies not fifty yards behind him in the middle of the road.

At the bottom of the street, there is commotion at the entrance to the RIC barracks and he is forced to double back in order to avoid Commandant Coyle. Outside town, he crosses fields until he hits the railway line, which he follows all the way up on to the platform. By the benches under the stationmaster's window, he finds Francie and Annie waiting for him. They silently acknowledge that they are actually there, then before anyone can change their mind, Annie is distributing potato sacks for the loot. They tie two each around their midriffs and pull jackets back over the top. The Yank checks they're alone and walks to the hanging baskets by the platform entrance. He pulls one down and tosses flowers and soil out at his feet until he has retrieved the hidden gelignite.

Annie has brought another sack with food, .303 rifle rounds and a box of 9mm for the Mauser. She takes the pistol from her waistband and returns it to Francie. He swaps it for the rifle, which she will take to the car with the provisions. The Yank keeps his rifle and also carries a Webley revolver for anything up close and personal at the bank. They take as much ammunition as they can carry without restricting their movement then Annie shoulders her sack and the three of them head off for the laneway behind the houses by the riverfront. At its end they stop and take stock of one another without a word being spoken then Annie steps out on to the main street and turns left uphill for the church.

CHAPTER TWENTY-TWO

Amiens, France

4 July 1916

The bed sheets are whiter than his mother's Christmas tablecloth yet still he lies trapped in the stench of blood. It is a sweeter smell than when farm animals are slaughtered back at home. It coats his skin and traps itself in tiny pockets around the hairs that his fingers can't reach inside his nose. Each morning on hands and knees Archie searches under all the beds but the ward offers up no hidden bodies.

When nurses pass, he waves and tugs at the sheets but he can't vocalise his issue and they smile their patronising smiles and sing their infantile songs and, Jesus, if they were only fellas he would hop from the bed and punch the fucking nursery rhymes clean out of them.

At night in the dark, the moans lift him from the bed and carry him back through the wood over the top and down on to the Sunken Road. When he finds Windy Patterson's corpse he drags it on top of him and wraps his arms around its chest. It is under here somewhere that he left his voice but each time he comes back to find it he nods off beneath the weight of the big lad then wakes again alone in a hospital unable to speak.

In the daytime when his eyes shut and his brain races he retraces his stretcher journey from there to here. The world is indeed a thing of wonder when viewed horizontally from a moving cradle. Dug from a pile of bodies beside a command post at the front of the wood because someone heard him cough, then thrown flat on his back and bumped and banged for what seems like miles with only a coffin-lid-shaped window through which to view the world above. Trees mostly then gaps made by shells, which reveal more shells exploding in the gaps. Clouds overhead, white on blue, then black rain and yelling as a bearer falls, tipping him sideways into a rancid latrine. Another angel takes the load while the previous calls for a stretcher of his own, then onwards through the holes in the earth they have chosen to live in until he is dropped hard at the front of a dressing station as his bearers can carry him no longer. Limbs piled roughly by the door of a tent and an urge to rise and stack them efficiently so that more arms can fit in the hollows between more thighs. Turfed from his mount while it is used to take serious cases to the section they won't come back from, Archie lies listening to the amputations between the shell bursts. He rarely heard the saw over the screams but the very thought of its work set his teeth chattering and they had rattled for hours, wearing the enamel thin, until the rhythm of the train bringing him to a field hospital in the rear changed something in his brain and his jaw stopped dancing.

She is always there when he comes out of it, mopping the sweat from his chest and throat with a cold cloth. The same nurse with the same smile, a genuine inch wider than the others.

'On your travels again, anywhere nice?'

When he never answers she never minds.

'If you've been to Rome and not told me all about the Colosseum we are finished, Archie Johnston.'

It might be her accent, though it hails from further south than his own, or maybe it's the colour of her hair, but he can always manage one word for her and for her only.

'Annie.'

A doctor pulling a sheet over the face of the man in the next bed hears his word and joins them.

'Must be his girl.'

Archie's laughter throws him out of the bed and when they have tucked him back in again he feels awful when he spots her blush.

'That's that answered, then. Your sister?'

He nods up at the Scottish doctor who winks back down again.

'Good work, Nurse Stack. A smile and a fit of laughter: hell of a lot more than we got out of him.'

When the doctor has left along with the blush on her cheeks she fills his water glass and sits on the bed beside him.

'You must love your sister very much. You talk to her a lot in your sleep.'

He takes hold of the metal rung of the headboard and pulls himself to sitting.

'You know, Archie, if you could manage just a few more words I think they might send you home to see her.'

He allows the tepid water to coat his throat while focusing his mind on his tongue.

'Annie is ...'

'Take your time.'

'Francie's girl.'

'Who is Francie?'

'My friend.'

His uniform was the wrong sartorial choice on several levels. He felt tall and capable walking into the chapel but perched on a pew with the sun beating through the stained glass on to his back the sweat has pooled quickly between his legs and the itch in his scrotum is driving him insane. You can't just sit in the house of God scratching your balls, especially when the God is the other one and his flock are already in shock that a man has walked into the Catholic church in Drumskinny wearing a British army uniform.

The prayers mumble past him in a tone so mono that he can't pick out a single word. The lines are swallowed by the congregation, their very utterance seemingly a thing of shame or perhaps of guilt for another week of failure to take the meaning to heart. There are similarities to his own church across the hill but for the most part, he is lost and he follows the people in front, standing and kneeling when they do, despite the restriction in his leg. The bullet shaved the shin according to the surgeon who patched him up. A chip and a fracture but he'll be right as rain and fighting the Boche again before the leaves come down for autumn.

Annie sits further to the front, on the opposite side, with Francie's sisters and the grieving widow. She turned to him once when he wandered in late and rolled her eyes but it took five minutes and the eyes of the entire congregation before he realised she was referring to his attire.

After communion the priest walks to the centre of the stage and throws away the script.

'Francis Leonard Senior was a hard-working man, a family man, a man of principle.'

Never trust a man who gives his son his own name. Francis Senior, my arse. Francis bastard, more like. Maybe when he gets back to France he'll start calling Francie Francis Junior. The woman beside him gives him a sharp shush and he realises that he has forgotten to keep his laughter to himself.

'Francis worked hard every day in life to provide for the family he loved.'

'Bollocks. The oul goat drank everything he earned and beat the family he loved sideways.'

The woman digs him in the ribs and he realises that he has been muttering out loud. Annie has turned fully in her seat and stares at him with a face like a long walk to school on a cold Monday morning.

Outside he smokes beside men who hang by the door until they all move away from the soldier and he can smoke on his own. Annie is for the graveyard but he has seen enough men buried for one lifetime.

'What the hell are you playing at?'

'Sorry?'

'You're in uniform?'

'Very observant.'

'In the Catholic church.'

'Is that a crime?'

'It's Francie's father's funeral.'

'I gathered.'

'He was a rebel.'

'He was an arsehole.'

'Don't come to the graveyard.'

'Music to my ears.'

He lies over a turf bank dried through by July and scratches his balls as hard as he likes. Francis Senior. A man who told his own son he would burn in hell for joining the British army on the day before he left for training. An armchair rebel. Worse, a bar-stool rebel. A mouth, who pissed his money in jets up the wall at the back of Hegarty's.

Amongst hazel on the roadside verge, Archie trots downhill to the river at the bottom. At the pool below the humped bridge, he turns stones in the water, looking for crayfish. They eat them in France, Windy had told them.

'You're full of shite, you ginger bastard.'

'Same way as they eat snails, I wouldn't tell you a lie.'

'They eat horses, too, Windy; these French headers will eat anything.'

He finds a big male with a raised saddle in the middle of its armour. It's almost black, the same colour as the bottom of the stone it was hiding under. It'll swim off backwards at speed if he dallies so he pinches it in the middle of its back so that it can't get its pincers into him. He watches it squirm and wave its arms angrily then he places it in the palm of his other hand and closes his eyes until its pincers bite into his thumb. He turns his hand upside down letting it hang from him like a tumour then he flicks his wrist and it flies off into the middle of the pool.

The water is cool after the church and the bog so he lets it play over his ankles and take his breath away. The boys swam in the River Ancre near Thiepval the week before the big show. Between re-digging collapsed trenches and carrying endless crates of shells forward into the wood. They'd near fought each other to get their clothes off first and let the water at their filthy bodies.

'Get in, Archie, for fuck's sake!'

'I can't swim, Jack.'

'Get in, ye big girl, ye; we won't let you drown.'

I wish I had, Jack. I wish I had swum with you.

Francie slinked off while they splashed to stalk a quieter pool with an officer from Ballymena who loved to fish. They cut poles and whittled them smooth and improvised hooks for their catgut line. The trout in France love worms too and fried on a mess-tin lid in butter from the officer's mess they had never tasted anything so good.

We'll fish when I return, Francie; we'll fish every day.

'Archie!'

She is standing on the bridge above him.

'My God, Archie.'

He doesn't move, just floats where he is, listening to her feet pound the bridge as she sprints towards him. When she wades in and grabs him under the arms he splashes with his hands and laughs at her.

'I never swam with the boys, Annie; I should have swum with the boys.'

Onshore she slaps his face then starts to cry and he doesn't know what to say and he can't smoke as his cigarettes are all wet.

'Don't ever do that again, Archie.'

'I was too hot.'

'You were in the middle of the river, talking to yourself, with your bloody clothes on!'

He watches her cry then shows her the mark on his thumb where the crayfish got to work.

'Remember we used to collect them in a bucket and count them, then let them go again?'

'Let's go home.'

'Do you remember?'

'Yes, Archie, I remember.'

He watches his father and neighbours ruck hay for an hour before it gets the better of him.

'Sit down, Archie, you're injured.'

'I'm grand in one spot; pull it into me and I'll pitch her up on top.'

The fork feels good in his hands and it takes no time to sweat up a lather. His father works alongside, stripped to the waist, pulling dried grass to him in long strokes with a wide rake. When it's piled knee-deep Archie throws forkfuls up on to the rising ruck then smacks them compact. They work in tandem all morning, moving clockwise around the field yet never sharing a word. The field full of men working in little pockets gradually fills with grass domes as they inch their way towards the gate and their lunch. His leg is a frustration but it's improving by the day and his upper body is hard and tight from the war so he holds his own in the hay and hopes for his father's approval. Archie was never much good on the farm and his father was never any good at communication. At least today one of them is making some progress. Annie and his mother bring the food and tea with the other women. He sits between them, listening to the quirks of their day while staring at his father, who lounges opposite saying nothing to anyone about anything.

Has he asked you what it was like, Archie Johnston?

He has in my hairy hole, Windy Patterson.

Will he take you for a pint after rucking, Arch?

I think I'll be drinking on me own, Jack.

It's his mother that grabs him and throws him sideways on to the hard stubble of the cut grass. The rough stumps push through the cotton shirt into his flesh and he pictures a Victorian strong man on a bed of nails whose mother is about to lie on top of him. When his chest tightens he panics and pushes upwards but the tremors are winners and they know how to drag him back down again.

'It won't stop, Annie.'

The pair hold him on the ground like on the bedroom floor two nights before. Between convulsions and involuntary bursts of screaming, he watches the farmers watch his father frantically rake grass up around them to hide the shameful spectacle of his spastic son.

In the evening in the bedroom, his mother stands guard for fear he'll shake himself into his clothes and out to the pub. The father took his spuds then retired to the barn to pretend to do things and Annie lies by the stove reading *Sister Carrie*, again. Outwaiting his mother's bladder is an easy victory and the moment she heads for the yard he throws his clothes through the window and dives out after them.

There is a general state of meltdown when he materialises in Hegarty's. It's a Saturday night and they're all there and all drunk.

They stare at first, like he's not real, as if his name had appeared halfway down the endless lists they've been reading in the paper. The shock turns to respect before blossoming in various colours of excitement. Hugs and slaps and beer coming at him quicker than machine-gun bullets. A Somme soldier in their midst, by Christ! No better man than Archie Johnston, beating the Germans single-handed and still making the pub before closing time. One of their own who had done his bit. If nothing else he won't put his hand in his pocket tonight.

Wallace the dairy herdsman tells him seven times in a row that he's proud just to shake his hand but then the whiskey twists in him and he demands to know why Archie's not in his uniform. He could try explaining what happened at the funeral but the politics are a minefield with a mixed audience so he opts for a shrug and a smile.

'I asked why you're not in uniform.'

'A question we could all ask of you, Charlie Wallace.'

Wallace doesn't like it but the house does and laughter accompanies Archie to the fireplace where he sits and stares into the empty grate. The pints are going down too well and he doesn't have to move as people keep setting them on the mantelpiece in front of him. It is good to sit as it helps relieve the dull ache in the core of his bad leg. The more drinks that appear the faster they're drunk. They respectfully leave him to his own devices until Jimmy Donegan wanders over and pulls up a stool.

'How's Francie?'

'Grumpy.'

'No change there, then. Was it bad, son?'

'You read the papers, Jimmy.'

'I did but ... '

'But what? You thought none of them was dead and we were just over there eating fuckin cheese?' He gets up and moves to the stained print of the Battle of Waterloo at the end of the bar. As a boy he begged his father a hundred times to stand him on a stool so he could study every detail yet he never saw it for what it was. History washed. The glorious sanitation of death. No blood, no faeces. Beautiful crisp red uniforms impermeable to the mud and the piss.

'What was it like, son?'

Donegan has followed him and stands tight behind, breathing down his collar.

'Nothing like this.'

'Inniskillings held Wellington's line at Waterloo; now you boys have done us proud again.'

He turns to Jimmy and catches a mouthful of stale-beer fumes then steps away to stand directly underneath the painting so he that can study the images properly. Cannons firing in the distance yet no one cut in two or decapitated by the scorching balls of metal. Clean handsome British men dying painlessly in the faces of the swarthy horde.

'Was it bad?'

'For Christ's sake, Jimmy, fuck away off!'

The whole pub stops talking and turns to stare at him.

'He's pissed, Archie, ignore him.'

'Get him the fuck away from me, or I'll put him through that door myself.'

'Leave him bloody be, Jimmy, he's in for a quiet drink.'

Donegan scurries back to his seat by the fireplace and the chat strikes up again, though Archie knows that most faces have one eye on his back as he continues to study the masterpiece. When he reaches up and takes it from the wall he can feel the years of dust and grease on his fingers. When he smashes it over his knee he is surprised as the clean white wood from inside the frame bursts through the smoke-stained exterior like it was only cut from the tree yesterday. It's Wallace who gets to him first. A strong man who has worked outside his whole life but drank himself fat while at it. Archie instinctively smashes the heel of his right hand upwards into the nose and Wallace goes down at his feet, a large quantity of blood updating the pattern on the front of his favourite drinking shirt. Archie lifts a pint from the table under where the picture used to hang and hurls it at the beam above the bar showering them in Guinness and splinters. He knows that he is shouting but he doesn't know what the words are as the fog in his skull descends, blocking his ears from his voice.

'They're shooting prisoners, shooting prisoners, shooting prisoners, shooting prisoners.'

The tremors start lower than before and his legs hop as his engine misfires over and again. He heads for the fireplace but he is not in control of the steering and knocks tables over as he skips and bounces, dribbling and jabbering like a man let loose from an asylum.

'It's okay, Archie; we've got you, son.'

He tries to reach out to Hegarty and take the support of his shoulders but he clips him round the ear by mistake then they are all around him in a circle closing as he reels and jigs like a broken top.

'Ciara Jane, Ciara Jane, Ciara Jane.'

Hegarty rugby-tackles him and Edwards the farrier drops on one knee and punches him hard in the face, twice.

'Barney, get off him, Barney!'

She runs from the doorway smashing into Edwards, knocking him off Archie.

'He went mental, Annie.'

'He's not well; can't you see he's not well?'

Archie twitches on the floor at their feet, the spasms bouncing his body on the flagstones as the blood from his mouth smears across his face.

'Look at him, he's fucking mad.'

Annie kneels then lies across his belly and chest so that the weight of her body slowly squeezes the fit from him.

'Help me lift him.'

'Take him home, Annie.'

'For God's sake, help me lift him!'

'He'll pay me for that painting.'

'You don't know what he's been through.'

'Jimmy, give her a hand to get him out of my sight.'

'You don't know what he's seen.'

CHAPTER TWENTY-THREE

Pettigo, County Donegal, Irish Free State

4 June 1922

The small square is deserted as they walk through it with their story at the ready. As they pass the RIC barracks men run in and out and the situation has clearly spiralled out of control. As they round the next corner Coyle's voice catches them by the seat of the pants.

'Molloy! Molloy, for fuck's sake, come back here when I call you!'

He ushers them hurriedly into the entrance hall.

'Aren't you two supposed to be up on them hills?'

'We have been, sir. We need to know how clear the Lough Derg road is for the withdrawal.'

'The Specials are coming in from Lettercran direction, hundreds of the bastards. We need to get out that road and away before they cut it off completely. Any sign of the Brits coming back down the road for the bridge, Leonard?'

'Nothing moving yet, sir, but I saw their field guns firing from a hill about half a mile off.'

'They shelled two houses on Main Street; fucking ruined them. The second them hoors open up again we're off. Get back to your men and be ready to move.'

Outside they wait until the main doorway is clear then carry on as before. Their assault on the bank must coincide with the one on the bridge so that the British will be distracted from what's going on behind them. As they reach the final houses at the edge of town they slip off the road through a veil of large beech trees and slide through a tangle of roots to the water's edge. The river is narrow but deep so they push on over large rocks and fifty yards further upstream find a shallower stretch they can wade. Francie holds his jacket and weapon over his head and fords the river. The cold water is lush on his knees and thighs and it gets no deeper so he is spared the shock on his balls. On the far bank, he takes up a covering position and waves the Yank across. They climb a steep bank through fern and garlic then stalk a copse completely bedded in bluebells. When they stop to listen the sun warms their necks and bounces at them off the windows of the houses up ahead. A gunshot nearby and they hit their bellies. Two more and they realise they are not the target. Three, four, five from different places along the riverbank and they know the British snipers are softening positions up for the assault.

There are only a handful of houses on High Street and by stomach, they worm their way towards the back of the Belfast Bank, which is perched halfway along. The Yank takes the lead with Francie stopping every few yards to check they won't be taken from behind. Among the tree trunks in the fading evening light, it is hard to separate shadow from fantasy and he stares too long, losing touch with Molloy. He finds him pulled in tight behind a moss-covered stump frantically gesturing at him. Molloy holds two fingers up then points diagonally over his left shoulder. Francie holds both hands apart like he is showing the size of a fish he caught and the Yank opens and closes one hand with splayed fingers four times. Two shooters, twenty yards ahead. Francie gives him the thumbs-up then slowly runs a finger across his throat and the Yank nods. When they are tucked in together Molloy points to himself then his Lee-Enfield. He has the rifle, he will take them both. Francie pulls the Mauser and prepares for the mopping-up. As soon as the two men fire again they rise behind them. He follows Molloy's barrel and finds them kneeling by some rocks up ahead, their Khaki backs square on like coconuts at the shy. The first bullet takes the man on the left clean off his feet, killing him instantly. Francie hears the Yank's rifle bolt slide back and forwards, chambering the second straight after the roar from the first. The second man has time to stand and turn and this movement disturbs Molloy's aim enough so that the bullet enters the man's shoulder instead of his chest. The soldier roars once for help then flounders off towards the river with Francie up and on him like a lurcher to a hare. He kicks the stumbling man's right heel so that it flicks on to his left tripping him on his face.

'If you shout again, I'll kill you.'

The man gasps, his mouth and nose filling with the dirt and the moss.

'Turn around.'

He moans his way on to his back. When he is looking directly upwards Francie lifts the Mauser but his finger won't move when he asks it to and then Molloy is by his side and there is a roar from the Webley and it is over.

'Fuck's wrong with you?'

'Nothing.'

'Bit late for going soft, Francie.'

They wait at the back of the bank as sporadic rifle artists on both sides of the river build themselves into a crescendo. The windows on the sides and back are barred so it's a walk straight through the front door or turn around now and walk away. They are crawling along the solid granite side wall of the building when the artillery kicks in again, the thump of the guns more regular than before. Flood's Lewis gun begins to spit and hum in the distance and they know the Brits are moving along the road towards the bridge. Shouting and running in the street ahead as men leave buildings and move towards the action. Up and forward, pistols drawn, straight down the side of the bank, no crouching nor crawling nor fucking about. Around the corner on to High Street and straight through the big wooden doors of the Pettigo branch of the Belfast Banking Company as if they are fashionably late for a meeting with the regional manager.

The doors swing then bang closed behind them and they stand in a large room with a marble floor and no one in it. At the far end is a mahogany counter with a long grille and on each side under tall church-like windows sit wooden booths for clerks to deal with clients in. There is a door in the middle of the back wall behind the main counter and they move slowly towards it. Halfway along the room the door of a booth on their left bursts open and a soldier leaps out, barring the way.

'Medic: don't shoot, I'm a medic! Don't shoot, I'm a medic!'

Weapons raised they inch towards him, an eye each on the booth he just sprang from. On his left arm, a white armband with a red cross on it but in his right hand a revolver and as the gap between them narrows he panics and shoots from the hip.

Francie and the Yank stand barely a foot apart yet the big heavy slug whips through the air between them, burying itself in the wall of the bank. There is a stunned second as the three look to one another trying to fathom how he could possibly have missed them both, before Francie and Molloy open up, blowing the medic back past the open doorway he appeared from.

Francie takes a diagonal line for the booth as Molloy approaches the body cautiously. As he reaches the feet of the dead man a single shot catches him in the left of his ribcage, sitting him back down on his arse on the floor. Francie empties his magazine into the walls of the booth. He drops to one knee and slaps a fresh strip in the

Mauser before sending half of those off after the others. He sprints the remaining yards to the booth to find a dying man sitting on the floor against its back wall.

Lieutenant Parkinson is stripped naked to the waist bar a cummerbund of blood-soaked bandages whipped tightly around his wound from the bridge. One of Francie's rounds has passed neatly through the middle of his right pectoral muscle. His other bullets have pricked a frantic constellation of holes in the wall all around the lieutenant, which slender fingers of sunlight poke through. He still holds the gun he shot Molloy with in his right hand, though he will clearly never raise it again. All around him on the floor are the props of his personal trauma theatre. Pools of iodine and bile and smashed vials and earlier bandages, which gave their all but failed to hold back the inevitable.

Molloy appears at the doorway raising his Webley for the mercy shot but Francie takes the barrel and points it at the floor.

'Is it bad?'

'Not as bad as his.'

'We shot him earlier on the bridge.'

'You might have fucking shot him properly.'

Francie kneels by Parkinson, takes his gun and throws it from reach.

'What's your name?'

'Lieutenant Parkinson, 12th Battalion, South Staffordshire Regiment.'

'What's your name?'

'Douglas.'

'Can I get you anything, Douglas?'

'My wife, maybe some champagne?'

'Where you from?'

'Rye, Sussex.'

'Nice place; I was stationed in Seaford before France.'

'The 36th?'

'The very one.'

'We cycled the whole way to watch you disembark. It was over before I was old enough.'

'Lucky you.'

Parkinson slides to his left, exposing the Van Gogh his exit wound has donated to the wall of the bank. Francie pulls his legs out straight and lays him on the ground on his side, rolling the officer's own tunic into a bloody pillow.

'They'll be back for you.'

'Have we taken the town?'

'Yes, we're on the run.'

'That's something then, isn't it?'

'Indeed it is. It's something.'

In the back room, the big black safe sits cockily on the side wall like a challenge. Molloy is in no mood for arrogant engineering, though, and as Francie keeps an eye on the street he ties the two sticks of nitro and the detonators to the back of a Windsor chair. A stick on a spindle each with a gap in the middle. When the chair is pushed up against the safe on its back legs the locking mechanism has a bomb on either side of it.

The sounds of battle on the bridge below have scaled even the fury of this morning. When another salvo of shells wails overhead Molloy blows the safe halfway across the room.

Bank drafts, debtors' letters, wills, keys, property deeds and money. Lots of money. Crisp white English pounds. Fucking lots of crisp white Bank of England pounds. The contents of the safe now populate the entire room and as they scramble around separating cash from family feuds Molloy's movement is noticeably restricted.

'You okay?'

'So so.'

'Fuck does that mean?'

'It's not going to kill me but it's nearly as big a pain in the ass as you.'

'How much?'

'Thousands, just grab as much as you can and let's get out of here.'

They are peering around the front door at the street, a potato sack full of money under an arm each, when Francie swears, tosses his to the Yank and runs back inside.

In the booth full of bullet holes he finds Lieutenant Parkinson's corpse counting cracks in the ceiling. Francie stares at the boy for a while then kneels beside him and shuts his eyes. He finds the lieutenant's ripped shirt on the floor under the desk, shakes the dust from it and spreads it over his face and chest like a blood-soaked shroud.

'Too young for France, Douglas, but there will always be Ireland.'

They slink back through the trees to where they crossed the river but Molloy's Free State Army lads have come down from the hill and are gathering on the road opposite to begin the retreat to Lough Derg. Further downstream the gunfire around the bridge is still heavy. There is a Vickers gun somewhere across from them firing sustained bursts over their heads towards the British. Francie can hear at least two British machine guns returning fire but the artillery at least has stopped for now. Molloy is moving much more slowly than before and by the time they pick a spot for crossing he is completely out of breath.

'You all right?'

'Never better; let's get going.'

'Can you hold both hands above your head with a sack in them?'

'No.'

'Well, you're not fucking all right then, are you?'

In the deepest part of the crossing, the water comes up to Francie's throat. He makes four journeys. One each with a sack full of money over his head and one with the Mauser, the rifle and the Webley revolver all tightly rolled up in his jacket. It's hard work fighting the weight of his waterlogged boots and clothes as they conspire to pull him under. The fourth time he swims on his back with Molloy's head and shoulders pulled up on to his chest and an arm around his throat for support. Exhausted, they lie between rocks just under the lip of the road. The market square is only fifty yards away. Hit that and turn right up Main Street and they'll be in the car with Annie in no time. The problem is one of exposure. There is no way of getting from here to the church without someone asking them what they are doing and what the fuck is in the sacks. When most of the water has run out of his woollen trousers, Francie pulls his jacket on and crawls off along the edge of the road until he is directly behind the old police barracks. There is a gap in the buildings to allow women from the houses access to the river to wash clothes and he moves through it until he can see the street out front. Dozens of armed men are marching past on their way out of town. Directly in front of the barracks, Commandant Coyle and two officers watch the retreat, sucking desperately on cigarettes. Coyle has one finished and another lit off the end of it by the time it takes Francie to reach him.

'Leonard, why aren't you up on that hill?'

'Came down to find out what was happening, sir.'

'That's all of our men back up from the Waterfoot. There's Brits everywhere to the south and the east and sure we know fuck all about the west so it's north we go, cross-country to Donegal town. First time they've used artillery since the Rising. No shame in pulling out now.'

'Definitely not, sir.'

'I've sent a runner to the hill with your orders. Your machine-gun post and some men below at the station are to cover the retreat. Just keep as many of the bastards from crossing that bridge for as long as possible.'

He collects the Yank then they return to the gap in the wall by the barracks. They wait with their backs against the stone building for the last of their comrades' hobnails to spark by out of town. Molloy is shivering in his wet clothes and Francie watches the colour drain from his face. He lights a cigarette and jams it in the Yank's mouth then closes his eyes to let his ears read the battle. Rifle fire from the station is building again. He can clearly distinguish Flood's Lewis gun up above as it spits more regularly now. They are moving for the bridge again.

'Come on, we need to get through the square before it's full of Brits.'

Molloy looks confused for a moment then takes a few deep breaths, awakening a surge, then they rise with their sacks and edge through the gap. The street out front is deserted. Francie takes the rifle from his shoulder and they set off at a trot. As they pass through the far side of the square a shout comes from the bottom towards the bridge. Francie urges Molloy onwards then turns and drops to his knees then his stomach. The Englishman reveals himself, rifle tight to his shoulder as he edges into enemy territory. Francie allows him and the man behind to come on and when there is ten feet behind them and the nearest covering wall he starts to unload. The first man turns and runs but the second falls and won't be getting up again.

At the top of the town, Annie has given them up for dead. She climbed the hill earlier and sat with Molloy's men watching the incoming artillery rounds land around town until one fell too close and she scrambled to the bottom again. Twice she has searched the train station to no avail and she knows that she must make her way through the British line and find the bank. She starts to make her way back through the town to the river but is stopped almost immediately by heavy shooting not far in front of her. Shouting now, coming towards her, and she ducks into the front porch of the Reverend's house. Boots pounding and another volley, then the Yank Molloy appears coming up the street, a sack gripped in one hand, the other covered in blood clutching his side. As he makes the distance, gasping for breath, her own stops momentarily as she realises that Francie is not with him but then he appears sprinting over the brow of the hill shouting at her.

'Head for the car, run for the fucking car!'

At the front of the Crossley Francie locates the crank handle under the hood and begins to work on the engine, which quickly explodes to life. They throw the bags of money into the back with the supplies then stand looking at each other.

'How is it?'

'Stopped bleeding.'

'You fit to drive?'

'I'm fit to, but I don't know how to.'

'What do you mean?'

'I mean, I've never driven a car.'

'It's more of a lorry.'

'I've never driven an anything.'

'Well, neither have I.'

'You're joking?'

'I was infantry.'

'You were a farmer?'

'With a fuckin donkey.'

'I can drive.'

They stare at her, confused.

'Sonny Atcheson let me drive the churn lorry to town all the time; can't be that bloody different.'

Francie turns the corner on a smile, takes the Mauser from his belt and throws it to her. She catches it, shoves it in her waistband and climbs up behind the big steering wheel.

The road hugs the north shore of Lough Erne, crossing the border several times before bringing them directly through the village of Belleek. The Yank announces that he is seventy-five per cent sure that it's still occupied by Irish troops, even though it shouldn't be as it's in the North. When Annie points out that twenty-five per cent of him therefore still thinks they will have to shoot their way through the British army to get to Ballyshannon in the South, the Yank roars with laughter.

'The North, the South, the British, the Specials, the Free State Army, the IRA. It's a right fuckin mess up here, Annie.'

The wheel fights against her and she needs all her strength to keep the vehicle moving in the line she wants it to. There is a long straight section from the church to the top of the hill to begin with, and as she nears the end of it and gets ready for her first corner two British soldiers climb over the fence to her left just in time for her to wave at them before she takes the curve and disappears.

The Yank has it all mapped out. Once through Ballyshannon they will pass Finner Camp, where Francie and Archie first crossed swords with Crozier, then on through Bundoran and south along the coast to Sligo town. Here they will ditch the Crossley and pay someone to take them by boat to Queenstown port in County Cork and from there they can sail for America.

*

As they pull out of town fresh artillery rounds thud into the hill-sides and Francie swivels in the passenger seat and stares towards his boys on Drumharriff Hill.

'We're running away, Sean.'

'We've held that town for a week.'

'It's not right.'

'You've never run from anything in your life.'

'Well, I'm running now.'

Molloy sits in the rear with his back pulled into the board behind Francie and his legs stretched out in the open-top flatbed of the truck. As the Crossley bounces on the rough road his feet clock from side to side, waving the town goodbye. He watches the shells biting into the hill where Francie's men are. There is a whine over-head and a shell bursts in the field to the left of the truck. He sees the orange rip as the high explosive takes and when the roar comes he throws himself sideways instinctively. He stays down as Annie pulls the Crossley round a sharp corner and when he sits up straight again Pettigo is gone.

CHAPTER TWENTY-FOUR

Ploegsteert, Belgium

August 1916

The day after the battle the silence that greeted the unanswered names lasted well beyond the roll-call. The following morning they sorted through dead men's kit, labelling items for future owners and identifying personal details that could be sent home to grieving families. When the silence hadn't lifted three days later they were ordered into their packs and out on the march. From Hédauville to Herissart on to Conteville and Setques for seven nights via Racquinghem then on to Bollezeele through Quelmes, Moulle and Watten. Up and down the French and Belgian border they tramped as though sweating the horror from their pores was the very medicine prescribed by the brass.

They have settled back into the mundanity of reserve life, interspersed with spells in the trenches near another village by another wood. Plug Street, they call it. Ploegsteert being a bit too much of a mouthful. Here in Belgium, like France, there is pleasure in making the territory sound more like the home it can never feel like. Eight miles south of Ypres, or Wipers as the Tommies have dubbed it. The work parties are much the same but the trenches are different. Dug much shallower due to the high water table, they must be constantly heightened and bolstered with sandbags filled with dense wet clay. The area is dark and gloomy and given to flooding and there is a constant threat from Germans tunnelling beneath and sending them all sky high.

Finally in one place, Francie allows the tedium of graft to numb his brain in tandem with his body. When a sandbag is placed before him he fills it, when a drink takes its place he drinks it. Drink not to think. As long as he asks no questions he will get no trouble from his reaction to the answers. Dig and lift, eat and shit, drink and drink. Make no new friends who can become new corpses and stay the fuck out of Crozier's way.

The battalion swells quickly with new recruits from back home then some from England when the length of the Ulster death lists keeps volunteers safe on the farms. The fresh meat wants to learn from the veterans of Thiepval but Francie doesn't want to know and he doesn't want them to know either. He passes the necessary with the men he knew before, mainly McClintock and Williamson from Enniskillen town, and he keeps himself to himself.

In their first week in Belgium, Crozier tried to put Francie on a charge for subordination relating to an incident from before the Somme but it backfired when Gallagher, newly promoted to captain, reprimanded Crozier within earshot of the men, telling him that they had enough to deal with never mind his petty feuds. Crozier went on leave for three days after that and when he returned Francie barely saw him until the night in the bar.

They had just come out of the line after holding it for eight nights. A London double-decker bus was waiting to bring them seven miles back across the French border to the market town of Bailleul for some recreation. Before they climbed on board they formed lines and Crozier and Gallagher walked among them while Crozier droned on about the evils of drink and pox-ridden foreign women and God and Ulster and your poor mothers back at home. When he was done they laughed like wee boys as they beat lumps from one another, fighting for the best seats on the open-top deck.

In town, Williamson and McClintock pulled him aside to share a secret address for the procurement of French tarts but Francie declined their offer, telling them the lice were bad enough without an itchy chap. In a small, almost empty *estaminet* he drank himself sideways. In a larger one full of soldiers he took a table in a corner and ordered steak and potatoes and a bottle of red wine. He had the bottle finished and another en route when he spotted Crozier at a table by himself near the front. Crozier wasn't drinking tea either. The Lord Protector of the Protestant faith sat framed by a pair of empty wine bottles staring at a glass of green-coloured liquid which he held about a foot from his face. His lips moved intermittently and after a minute or so Francie wondered if Crozier was actually in conversation with his drink. Eventually he tipped his head back and downed it and was shouting for another before the empty glass hit the table. The waitress arrived with an odd-looking contraption and placed it in front of the sergeant. It looked like a large silver teapot but with multiple little spouts all the way around it. She placed another glass with a measure of the green liquid in it under one of the spouts then put a spoon with holes in it on top of the glass and carefully placed a sugar lump in the middle of the spoon. A key was turned and what Francie assumed was water began to drip through the sugar from a spout. Crozier watched mesmerised as the sugar slowly dissolved into his absinthe. When the waitress had left and taken her paraphernalia with her Crozier lifted his new drink and began to mutter to himself all over again.

When his own waitress returned with his food, Francie smiled and indicated another table to his left that he would like to move to. From here he could still watch the show but the sergeant didn't have as good a line through the other soldiers to him. By the time Francie had finished his spuds Crozier had taken to shouting at the wine bottles and the waitress and the ceiling and at anyone else who would listen. When a French soldier stepped in to protect the girl, Crozier squared up to him then the overweight owner appeared and Crozier told the man that his premises were as lousy as his poxy fucking country and stormed out through the front door. Francie left money on his plate and followed him out into the night.

He gave Crozier a decent start as even a drunk man might instinctively feel himself being followed. The sergeant stumbled back towards where they had scrambled off the bus and as he passed the junction where Francie left McClintock and Williamson he turned a sharp left. Surely not? Not Crozier? The scratchy-cocked, hypocritical, Protestant bastard.

In the darkness of a doorway opposite the brothel, Francie formed a plan. When Crozier left he would call him over and beat him black and blue. When he was finished he would drag the unconscious fucker back into the brothel and alert the military police. Crozier's disgrace would stain eternal. Even if he saw or heard who his attacker was he could never prove it, and Francie would run back to his dinner and pay the waitress to claim he had never left. Captain Gallagher would vouch that the accusation was another random attack on a soldier Crozier had a history of picking on. He walked to the railway bridge at the end of the street and slid on his arse down the bank beside it until he found a suitable weapon: a section of the railing, which he broke over his knee to create a piece easy enough to handle and which would do plenty of damage when swung hard enough. And oh how hard he would swing.

On the way back to the doorway he practised his blows, systematically working his way along Crozier's body as he smashed a limb or punctured a kidney for each of his dead friends.

If only you were here, Archie; I could hold him cosy while you kicked his teeth in.

Back in the doorway, it became apparent that the sergeant liked to get his money's worth and as the wine's anger turned sleepy Francie gave in to it.

Crozier's exit from the brothel woke him and he watched as a girl appeared and argued with the groggy sergeant, clearly unhappy with his tip. Crozier stumbled off up the street and Francie fumbled on the ground for the piece of wood then stood up, but when he played with its weight his arm and hand were numb from where he'd been sleeping on them. His mouth was coated with a black glar from the cheap wine and as he tried to swallow it over a throat like sand he retched violently. His arm shook from the shoulder and when he dropped the wood on the ground it sounded like a gunshot going off on the quiet street.

Crozier stopped dead in his tracks and swivelled, staring into the shadows. Francie coughed in the darkness and Crozier's head shifted an inch and then he started at speed for the doorway. Neither man was armed, though Crozier could have had a knife on him, and now Francie had lost his length of wood. As Crozier bounded across the final few yards Francie lit two cigarettes and left one in the corner of his mouth. When Crozier stopped in front of him he held the other out to the sergeant.

'Leonard?'

'Smoke?'

'Smoke, "Sergeant".'

Crozier took the cigarette and cautiously pulled on it.

'What you doing lurking around here on your own, Leonard?'

'Could ask you the same question, Sergeant.'

'You know, I've just about had enough of you, Leonard.'

Francie stepped in close to Crozier, dragged on his Woodbine and blew a slow steady stream of smoke into his bloodshot eyes.

'What was her name, Sergeant? Was she younger than your wife?'

Crozier said nothing as rage and shame fought for control of his tongue. Francie watched him for a minute then stubbed out his smoke with his toe and walked off up the street, waiting for the blow to land on the back of his head. It never came.

On the bus back to the front the next morning Crozier was his usual self, firing orders and disdain in equal measure, though he found time for a laugh with some of the men and Francie knew that cards were being kept tight to the chest. They made no eye contact, though Francie searched for it through the waves of his hangover and he accepted then that the next round must be lethal.

Back at the front when they disembarked they were informed of a mail delivery waiting for them in their billets and Francie sprinted off, expecting at least one letter from Annie. What he didn't expect to find on his blanket was her brother, curled up around a shiny new rifle, snoring like a pig.

CHAPTER TWENTY-FIVE

County Fermanagh, Northern Ireland

4 June 1922

Annie struggles at first to move the gears through the numbers as she pumps hard on the heavy pedals. The force of the road on the machine is conducted along the gear stick into her arm then absorbed by her left shoulder. As her confidence builds the machine moulds around her and she becomes part of it. She backs herself, putting her foot down, and when she spots Francie's knuckles white on the edge of his seat she laughs and presses the accelerator even harder.

The railway line and road hug each other closely and she imagines herself racing a steam train, its windows full of Donegal day-trippers whistling and waving at the crazy girl on wheels. She loses sight of them as the road enters a long tree tunnel where the sun only seeps through in green and gold mottled patches. As the light recedes she cuts her speed until the end appears then she races for the last of the daylight.

As they zoom between fields bordered by whitethorn she knows it's not only the battle that is disappearing behind her. It is a life of crippling mundanity. Endless seasons knowing that as each of them changes the inevitable becomes even more unbearable. She looks across at the man she has waited for. How many, Francie? How many people have you killed with the gun that is digging into my back against the driver's seat? For four nights she has lain and wondered. For four years. Since the stories began to filter north from the counties where the killing was happening. When his name was first whispered she knew half of it would be pub nonsense. It's easy to sit drunk, pinning murder to the name of the only IRA man you've ever met, but the more she heard and the longer he stayed away, the more she knew that some of it had to be true. He was there, after all. What else was he doing in Kerry, digging potatoes?

In Pettigo she saw fragments of the boy from before. When they made love there was a window into him but she couldn't hold it open long enough for more of him to crawl back through. Maybe she will fall in love again with the man he has yet to become, in another place, when the killing is behind him? Or maybe she won't. Whether Francis Leonard is part of her future or not, she knows she will never go back.

The road forks ahead with a dirt track shooting off to the right and as she slows Francie signals to stay left. He watches her work her way down through the gears and when she looks sternly back at him his boy laugh bursts on his face and she fires him a filthy then laughs it all right back at him. He turns around to check behind them and then he is tugging on her sleeve and shouting at her to stop and she knows that there is something wrong with Molloy.

Francie opens a wooden gate and she steers her mount through, leaving it tight by the hedge so that it can't be seen from the road. The field runs down to the wooded shoreline of Lough Erne and the trees hide them from any water traffic. The Yank has passed out and when they slide him from the back and wake him in the field he denies having left them at all.

'Who wouldn't doze off if you lay them in this long grass, Annie?'

'You're lucky it's here; it'll be cut for hay any day.'

'Jesus, one farmer was bad enough.'

'We need to look, can I help you undress?'

'The Francie fella will get jealous.'

Francie holds Molloy in a sitting position so that Annie can release his tunic over his shoulders. His entire shirt is almost black with blood and when she has freed him from it they watch it bubble as it pumps through the neat hole at the top of his stomach. When they ease him on to his side and Francie finds no exit wound, he knows his friend is already dead.

He sends Annie off through the trees to fetch water in a petrol can that was attached to the back of the Crossley.

'It's still in there.'

'I'm not meant to leave Ireland, Francie.'

'Fuck Ireland.'

'You don't mean that.'

'I definitely do.'

'Two's company, three's a crowd.'

'There'll be a doctor in Belleek. We're nearly there; we'll get the bullet out and you can bore us rigid about it all the way across the Atlantic.'

'It's the same wound.'

'As what?'

'The boy in the bank.'

'So?'

'So, he managed to shoot me in exactly the same place he'd been shot himself and "so" he was fucking dead anyway before you shot him.'

'Coincidence.'

'One less on your conscience.'

'One is not enough.'

'He killed me.'

'I will if you don't shut the fuck up.'

'I am meant to die today, Francie.'

'No one else is dying today.'

Annie returns and they lie the Yank flat on his back and rinse his torso. When the water is all gone the blood still springs from the bullet hole, pooling in his navel before flooding the pale valleys of his ribcage in an intricate system of small red rivers.

Captain Bowles exits the RIC barracks and wanders into the square where he joins Major Rogers of the South Staffordshires for a smoke. British troops pour through town in every direction as they go about the business of occupying it.

'Congratulations, your artillery made the difference.'

'Having the biggest guns usually helps.'

'The rounds you put into the machine-gun post allowed us to get behind it. There's at least one of them dead up there.'

'They found Parkinson in the bank. They finished him off then blew the safe.'

The sound of horses' hooves on stone, and a mounted Crozier appears around the corner from the direction of the Lough Derg road. He dismounts and walks his horse towards his fellow officers.

'Captain Bowles, great work.'

'Same to you, Inspector Crozier. You got your men across the border in time?'

'Indeed. Though they still managed to get though the circle.'

'Yes, they've retreated, across the hills.'

'And you will follow and finish them off?'

'There are no such orders as far as I am aware. This is Major Rogers of the South Staffs.'

'Infantry have no orders to pursue, Inspector. We believe from the direction they took that they're all headed for Donegal town. I say all, but my advance party saw a Crossley Tender leave towards Belleek.'

'We have the unit that was cut off near Belleek, we could intercept.'

'I wouldn't waste your time, Inspector; there were only two men in it. Funny thing is, though, Corporal Bingham swears blind it was being driven by a girl.'

His words are barely air before Crozier is galloping up Main Street past the church.

Bowles danders through the detritus of the railway station, his feet tinkling on the carpet of spent cartridges. On the platform at the back, he plots a route over the fence, through the bushes beyond and up the side of Drumharriff Hill. He knows exactly where the machine-gun post was as he called it in himself with his observer. One tree still stands and he makes for it as the sun waves goodbye over the hill to the west. Leaning against it he looks down on to the village below. Troops move on the hill beyond the church and there are men on the roof of the railway station taking down the Irish Tricolour that flies there. When the Union Jack starts to snake its way inch by inch back up the pole each tug on the rope is greeted with a loud cheer from the victorious soldiers beneath it. Maybe later he will point out to someone further up the chain that they have invaded another country and perhaps shouldn't, therefore, be raising their flag in it. Or maybe he will just let them get on with it. No one seems to listen to anything akin to common sense where this border is involved.

He checks his pocket-watch and learns that it is half past eight in the evening. Only two hours to take the town, so well they might cheer. Though he knows full well they'd still be fighting if the enemy hadn't decided to pull out.

On the other side of the tree, he stares on to the majesty of Lough Erne before walking the few paces to where he knows the body will be. He finds the remains of the Lewis gun first. The barrel bent out of sorts, the wooden stock shattered and its distinctive round magazine lying flattened a few feet off to the left. The ground has been churned by his shells and he sees no sign of a body. He stares at the fresh earth and large sods topped with grass until he finds the clue. A lighter shade of brown over to the right, thirty feet beyond the shattered gun. It takes a moment as he walks towards the almost orange detail on the brown-and-green canvas, but as he gets closer the penny drops. A rather new-looking pair of tan leather boots are poking out from the soil and he knows that he has found his man.

CHAPTER TWENTY-SIX

Ploegsteert, Belgium

August 1916

The work and drill routine help with the shakes. When Archie digs and marches his arms and legs are steady and strong. By the end of his six weeks in Ireland, the tremors had almost left him. They seemed to heal on a par with his leg but the closer he got to the front again the less sure he became about who was in control. The day they sailed wasn't rough but there was a steady swell through the hull of the ship. Most of his travelling companions vomited over the side while he sat with his back pressed into the wall of the gangway watching his feet hammer a sporadic rhythm over the constant one of the sea.

In St Omer during their final night before returning to their units the sounds of the big guns drove him from the mess tent with most of his meal all over his uniform. In a shallow depression near the latrine ditch, he lay flat until an hour after the bombardment when his body was his own again.

Francie is the only medicine that works. In reserve, the day after Archie's return, a gun-team got to work and Francie watched the effect it had on his friend. He dipped his shoulder under an arm and had him off to himself before anyone else had time to notice. He sat with his legs wide and pulled Archie between them, clasping his arms around his belly.

'It's great to see you, Big Ears, but I wish they'd kept you at home.'

'I'm not meant to be there any more.'

'Come on, it's just like your chest, calm your mind and your body will follow.'

'They don't want us at home any more.'

'Home is home.'

'We'll be back soon for the wedding.'

'What wedding?'

'Your wedding. If you don't write and ask her soon I'll shoot you myself.'

He wrote that night. Even dropping a floral seed or two into the stodgy soil of his prose. *Darling, you know we're as one. Nothing else mattered from the moment our eyes met.*

Archie made him read the entire letter out loud twice. He managed to keep a straight face the first time and nearly shat himself laughing the second.

'Imagine her in with the pigs, up to her knees in dung reading that shite!'

'Shut up.'

'Reading your poetry to the cows so they can all have a good fuckin laugh at you.'

'I mean it, Arch.'

'Paddy de Bergerac.'

'Fuck you.'

When he eventually tore the letter up, promising to master it before the next mail collection, they drank a bottle of apple brandy that Francie had stolen from the officers' mess. They laughed about home and what had happened in Hegarty's pub and planned what they would do with Francie's farm once he and Annie were living on it. Francie asked Archie if it was true that he'd been found under

Windy's corpse and Archie told him about seeing Jack cut down by machine-gun bullets and Windy's stump, then Francie told Archie about Crozier hiding and Jacob Sampson blowing up and Crozier shooting his brother Frank and when the bottle was empty Archie told Francie about Ciara Jane and they wept.

Two days after the brandy wears off they are sent back into the line. There is to be a large-scale raid the following night. Four parties divided into small groups. Rifles, bayonets, knobkerries, ten bombs each, and scaling-ladders, wire-cutters and grapnels. Top brass wants intelligence to determine whether gas is installed, which German units hold the front and the positions of their machine guns. It is the first time any of them will have gone over the top since 1 July. Francie makes a request to Gallagher and he and Archie are selected in the same squad.

On his first day back in a fighting trench, Archie is able to lay low. He plays cards for the afternoon with McClintock and Williamson, despite Francie insisting that the wily Enniskillen men will clean him out. Four hours later and most of his money lighter, he is sent back with Williamson to carry the hot ration forward. When they have eaten and smoked their final cigarettes of the day, they draw lots for the watch. McClintock is up first followed by Archie, who will wake Francie when he is done. Archie lies back into one of the man-size scrapes in the wall and pulls his knees in off the thoroughfare. The 10th Worcesters, who they relieved this afternoon, have only recently dug out the bottom of the trench, laying brand-new duckboards, but the water is already rising through them again and before long he can feel it soaking through the seat of his trousers and up into the back of his tunic.

The evening is bright and long and it is nearly ten o'clock before it is dark enough for him to catch his first shooting star over no man's land. Half an hour after that and he shivers as he watches the night's first flare arc between the trenches. Francie snores solidly in the scrape opposite and he feels jealous knowing that his watch will come round all too soon. He twists and turns in the wet muddy hole until his mind wanders up and over the parapet and he is back retracing every inch of his first raid months before. He closes his eyes but it only focuses the mind and the sounds of that night play crystal clear until the thud of the club in the prisoner's head makes him jump up and walk up and down to break the spell.

Back in his hole in the mud, the cold creeps into his bones and the shivers threaten to turn to tremors. There is movement off to his right and a scuffling sound then McClintock's face appears before him.

'Not sleeping, son?'

'Can't.'

'Keep it that way; Sergeant's on the prowl.'

He puts a round up the spout and climbs on to the fire step just before the next junction in the trench. There is the usual loophole covered by an empty sandbag and he knows the drill like he knows Francie's snores. Don't look unless you have to. Let your ears do the seeing. Never look when the sky lights up. Jerry's watching. He knows you're here. He crouches into the wall of sandbags, making himself as comfortable as he can, and props his rifle where he can call on it immediately. He is sliding his ear as close to the loop as he dares without losing it to a Mauser round when he is grabbed roughly from the front and pulled into Crozier's face. The sergeant's eyes have an intensity to them that is impressive even by his high standards and the smell of whiskey off him is like a slap in the face.

'Sleeping, Johnston?'

'Never, Sarge.'

'Fucking better not be.'

He shoves Archie roughly back into the wall and is gone as quickly as he appeared, the smell of his breath lasting longer than his visit. Must have started drinking hard after the Somme.

Murdering bastard. He's capable of anything and if he's on the booze Francie really needs to watch his back.

Back tight into the compacted bags of earth he stares at the sky and lets his mind wander over the open space between him and the enemy. He sees his second and third shooting stars and wonders what they would have meant a thousand years ago to an ancient Gaul or a Roman legionary staring up at the very same sky. A noise brings him back down from the clouds. Gone now but there again. Voices. Laughter from the German line. The fuckers laugh. Of course they do, you idiot, they're people just like us. Just because you've only seen them dead or dying doesn't mean you couldn't have had the craic together before the war. I wonder where these ones are from. Bavaria? Württemberg? Saxony? The laughter intensifies then dies away again then reaches out occasionally in bursts. He tries to picture the men enjoying the joke. A song now, maybe they're singing themselves to sleep.

He tries to remember German faces to compare Irish ones with but all he finds is the line of prisoners outside Thiepval Wood with their hands raised as they were gunned down. Tomorrow night he might see some. If they take prisoners. Tomorrow night he might kill one. With one of his ten Mills bombs or his rifle. Maybe he will run one through with his bayonet. His back spasms and he gets the familiar pain from his groin down through his left leg and into his ankle. Could he do it? He tries to imagine the full weight of a man on his bayonet, a man still trying to reach him to gouge his eyes out. He jumps up too quickly, forgetting where he is. The shot rings out after the dull punch of the bullet in the sandbag and he is down again on his knees in the mud. They always know where you are, boy. Sniper's bullet missed me by half a yard. This time he does puke and then he lies in it thinking about how close he just came to death. Wiped out in a muddy field by a stranger from five hundred yards.

Nearly came to you see you there, Windy. Give poor Jack's ears a rest, eh? At least you had lived a bit. Even if you never met the baby, at least you left something behind. I've never even been with a woman, mate. Wish I'd listened to you in England. Wish I'd got it over with before we came.

The smell of vomit forces him up on to his knees and he crawls from it to the other side of the loophole. Not been sick in a long time, Archie. Even with all that brandy. Booze stays down now. Not like before. Estelle's *estaminet*. Outside in the bombardment. That was when. What a fool. What a night! Those Aussie boys were top drawer. I wonder are they dead now? Estelle. Silent Estelle. Beautiful Estelle. *I don't want to kill a German tomorrow, Estelle. Or the day after that. I don't want to kill anyone. I want to talk to you. Even if we don't understand what we are saying. I want to kiss you. I should never have come back here, Estelle. I should have come for you.*

When Crozier kicks Francie awake he rolls into the middle of the trench and hops on to his feet with his rifle at the ready. When his eyes adjust to the moonlight he finds Captain Gallagher behind his target and quickly lowers the rifle from the sergeant's chest. Crozier steps towards him and pulls the gun from his hands.

'Sleeping on watch, Leonard.'

'Not mine, Sergeant.'

'It is by my watch, Private.'

McClintock and Williamson wake and bolt to attention behind Francie.

'What time is it, Williamson?'

'02.30, Sergeant.'

'Who should be mid-watch at 02.30?'

'No one woke me.'

'Who was supposed to?'

Francie looks desperately around for Archie but he is nowhere to be seen.

'Private Johnston.'

'And where might lover boy be?'

'I don't know, Sergeant.'

Crozier moves to the scrape where Archie made his home. The rest of his kit is no longer there.

'Well, neither do we, Leonard. It appears that Private Boyfriend has run away.'

CHAPTER TWENTY-SEVEN

County Fermanagh, Northern Ireland

June 1922

With Molloy dying in the back Annie could never drive fast enough. The bumps that brought laughter before are punches to her kidneys as she pictures his body bouncing around on the floor just behind her. The green fields disappear into another plantation, though this time the trees are tall dark conifers. To her left, she still catches glimpses of the railway as it makes its way along the edge of the forestry and then, did she see that or not? Grey stone battlements flashing by, from a fairy story in one of her old books. She panics and lashes out for the memory. A newspaper story somewhere before. A railway bridge that is also the gatehouse to a castle near Belleek. Where the pottery barons lived until it fell into ruin. They must be close, then. Only twelve miles between the two towns, Francie had said, so they must be bloody close.

Beyond the pine trees, the lough is still there but considerably further away. On her other side sits the base of a shallow hill covered in bogland and heather. She looks for her imaginary train with its holidaymakers to spur her on to greater speeds but it is no more. She turns to her right for inspiration and behind the low hedge sits a man on a horse and he is matching her machine yard for yard. Her instinct is to wave at this fine rider but she has both hands firmly on the wheel so she smiles across at the man who smiles right back at her. He holds his reins cockily with one hand and when he doesn't wave with the other it dawns on her that he has only one arm. She manages to shout 'Crozier' once before the first volley of bullets from the roadblock ahead smashes into the front of the truck.

She roars at her ankles, her head thrust between her knees, her chest full of the wet leather stench of her own boots. She counts to five in an effort to seize control of herself then she is up and thumping the clutch through the floorboards as she rips at the gear stick and they careen blindly backwards along the road.

In reverse she has no idea where they are until the conifers cloak them again then she locks the wheel so that the arse of the truck screeches through forty-five degrees then they are stalling and shuddering and roaring forwards with bullets dancing along the road all around them.

When the castle gatehouse looms she slows instinctively and pulls through its middle. The Crossley is framed momentarily by large iron-grilled windows on each side with the railway bridge above and then they are through on to the estate. The forest thickens as the highway disappears behind them, the large indigenous trees superseded by ever denser rows of the new pine. A few hundred yards in, the road splits with the right prong breaking cover and shooting away through open farmland. Francie waves her right then fifty yards later shouts at her to stop. Annie pulls the wheels off the road into the ditch and they ease Molloy down off the flatbed and double back on themselves. She has a sack of money in each hand and the rifle strapped across her back while Francie stoops and takes the weight of the American. Every few yards Molloy joins the flight, his feet taking a fraction of his weight as they skip along for a handful of steps then he is gone again with Francie taking the brunt of the load. The open road is no option and when Annie points to a structure in the distance through the trees they leave it and enter the forest. Squares of intricate rusted railings surround huge ornate headstones and the church beyond them sits slouched from the blow an oak tree gave it as it came in through the roof. Molloy is out cold and it takes both of them to drag his dead weight through the broken marble slabs that litter the forest floor, exposing the holes where the rich folk spent fortunes to bury their dead.

When they have laid him at the back of the church and retrieved the money bags Annie tries to read the ornamental stone set into the wall above him. She manages the dates and the name of the deceased before the strange Olde English confuses her to the point of quitting. She wanders under an archway into the shell of the old church. No altar, no stained glass, no seats for the people. Back outside beyond the graveyard, there is a steep drop through the trees to the water's edge.

'We're trapped.'

'We'll slip around when they come.'

'They're too many, Francie.'

'Just a squad, ten or twelve. Is he alive?'

She slaps Molloy conscious and when he has finished coughing blood they haul him to his feet and move further out on to the peninsula. Hidden by clumps of tall straight hazel and bunches of barbed briar they spurt along the shoreline. A large stone wall blocks their path and they move uphill until they find its beginning. Beyond it, the remains of the castle stare down at them through melancholy arched Gothic windows. Medieval in parts, Georgian in others, it is an out-of-place monstrosity being slowly reclaimed by nature. Trees grow through windows and ivy strangles chimney stacks. Beams, slates, glass and bricks lie scattered everywhere. It is built into a hill on two levels with tunnels from the front allowing access to the inside and rear. As they stand and stare up at its faded grandeur Crozier's voice echoes through the subterranean passages, calling out to them from behind the house.

'There's no way out of here, Private Leonard.'

They take the boundary wall towards the water. At its bottom, a boathouse paddles in the lough, half of its roof gone and the rudimentary pier out front almost completely submerged.

Crozier's voice comes again, bouncing through the ruins of the castle.

'You will die here today, Francie. At least bring the girl in or she will die too.'

Inside they find no boats, just splintered wood and coils of rotten rope. They sit the Yank in a corner, his back wedged in the angle where the walls meet. He has woken again and watches them.

'I'll go out and draw him away.'

'They'll shoot you on sight, Francie.'

'Crozier has galloped ahead. The rest were on foot, there's no way they're here yet. I'll take him now then we slip through the others back at the road.'

'We should stay together.'

'I'll be back before I'm gone, Annie. Anyone approaches, shoot. If they surround you, leave Sean the Mauser and swim for it.'

He locks eyes with the Yank who summons a grin.

'Goodbye, Francis, it's been emotional.'

'I'm going nowhere and stop calling me Francis.'

'You're going to Hell.'

'Well, you can keep the bed warm.'

He lifts the rifle and disappears up the hill towards the castle.

Beside Molloy, with her back against the wall, Annie places the Mauser between her knees.

'You know how to shoot it?'

'He showed me.'

'You and half of Ireland. You shot anyone?'

'Of course not.'

'Might be better if you don't; plays havoc with the sleep.'

When the blood comes to his lips there is less of it than before.

'I'm dying, Annie.'

'I know, Sean.'

'I'd really like some water.'

She wipes his mouth on the sleeve of her blouse then rips it off. At the front of the boathouse, she saturates it before bringing it back to his mouth.

'Odds aren't good, Annie, even for him.'

'I gathered.'

'If we hear more than a handful of shots forget about me and get going.'

He hands her two battered letters from inside his tunic.

'My family. If you make it to Boston they will look after you.'

'I will tell your mother all about you.'

'Tell her nothing, she'll use it against me when she dies. Please tell my brother that I was sorry.'

Annie takes his face in her hands and kisses him on both eyes.

'What were your family told about Archie?'

'That he was killed in action; a letter came, and the penny.'

'You still don't know the truth, do you?'

'Do I want to?'

'It would help you to understand what happened to Francie.'

She picks up the Mauser and slowly runs her finger around the red number nine on the pistol grip.

'Then I guess you'd better tell me.'

CHAPTER TWENTY-EIGHT

Forceville, France

August 1916

Archie waits for morning sprawled in a copse of silver birch on the edge of Plug Street village. As the day breaks he dusts himself down and steps out into it. At the junction the English call Hyde Park Corner, he joins the back of a queue waiting for the double-decker bus to Bailleul. His new companions from Belfast are still drunk from the night before when they came out of the line and released the pressure valve. They are happy to have a Fermanagh muck-savage in their midst to take the piss out of. Five friends have been lost in six days to sniping and mortars and they're excited about getting into town and blacking out. On board, he sits downstairs in a corner and closes his eyes and no one looks at him twice.

In town, he scouts the rail platforms until he has their number. He picks a carriage filled with wounded men mostly from Ulster and Dublin and sits on the floor between two stretchers. As they pull away he regales his horizontal cohorts with tales of his recent trip home and the butter-soaked potato bread and pints of porter they have to look forward to. One of the wounded soldiers' entire head and torso are swathed in bandages and Archie doesn't know if he can hear him at all, but the other lad smiles away as he talks about Annie and Francie and how he's going marry Estelle if it is the last thing he does and even if he can't speak a word of French.

He figures this leg of his journey is the most precarious as he's heading towards the coast. The coast means ships and ships mean home and home means deserters and the military police. He has no interest in that route, though, and around midday when they pull into a busy junction in the middle of a vast expanse of flat country-side he climbs from the medical train, asks the necessary questions of an appropriately officious man with a shiny whistle hanging proudly from a black lanyard and steps on to a train full of Somme reinforcements bound for Amiens. There are fewer questions to be asked of a lone soldier in full kit with a rifle travelling back towards the fighting. He has the Movement Orders from his recent return but they would cause more trouble than they're worth as they clearly state that he is supposed to be in Belgium. When the train stops and four hundred men jump down to piss on France he scrunches them up and throws them under the train. Back in the wagon he sits on the floor and squints through tobacco smoke at the stark white inscription painted above his head as every bump and jar from the tracks bite through the floor into his arse.

40 HOMMES OU 8 CHEVAUX

He executes a basic equation in an effort to square the usefulness of each species with the capacity they require in a standard French railway transport. Five men to a horse, he feels, tallies perfectly with the labour output of both on their farm back in Fermanagh. This brings him on to the death of Sirius the stallion three years earlier. The horse and the boy had been inseparable from the day his father brought the foal home from market. He relives the moment the gunshot ripped through the animal. Only now, crammed into this stinking carriage full of strangers, does he real-ise that it wasn't him who had angered his father that day but the twist of fate that had twisted the horse's leg. His father's tears were not of rage because the boy shouldn't have been riding the horse, but those of a man who had loved the horse as much as the boy but who didn't have the means to allow anyone to see that.

During leave, his father's coldness had cut deep. The disgust he felt at his son's weakness was palpable. As soon as he finished a meal he left the house whether he needed to or not and Archie became so aware of his father's desire to be rid of him that he spent most of his leave trapped in his room in a vicious cycle of shock. It wasn't until he was having his leg checked in the hospital in Belfast before embarkation that he heard a nurse give it a name. She wasn't referring to him. He was only there for a bullet wound and was momentarily freed from the fits since leaving the farm. The corridor they were passing through was full of other men. Men shouting involuntarily at no one and pointing at imaginary shells as they came through the ceiling. Men bouncing in circles like they were mocking him in Hegarty's bar. Men staring point-blank at walls or crying and laughing and carrying on everyday conversations while their bodies twisted and wracked into shapes that bodies should never pull.

He sees MPs twice on his way through the streets of Amiens but they take no notice of him. His uniform and a confident stride are the perfect disguise. The second pair he passes have a drunken soldier between them. With no helmet or tunic and his braces round his knees, it is easy to guess from which type of establishment he's been lifted. When Archie steps to the side to let them by, the drunk man takes in the number on Archie's shoulder and as he is dragged onwards his cockney accent is as clear as the Bow Bells.

'Gizza fackin 'and will ya, Paddy?'

When Archie turns for another look one of the policemen is staring after him and he panics, realising that the '36' on his uniform will give him up to anyone keen enough to remember that his division is in another country. At a busy junction on the edge of the town, he ignores the main road to Albert and takes a smaller one to the left of it that heads north-east towards Hédauville. Tired and exposed he stops a farmer with a starving horse and repeats his destination slowly three times before climbing into the man's cart and lying flat. The farmer wakes him sometime later and he climbs down into the familiar surroundings of the village where they billeted when they first went into the line. The front has shifted many times and there is no sign of reserve troops or supplies but nothing structural looks vastly different and he finds the schoolhouse easily. The gas-testing trench has not been filled in and he slides into the darkness beneath the corrugated roof to wait for evening when he can walk the last mile to the hamlet and Madame Bussiere's *estaminet*.

He is halfway there when a wave of exhaustion washes over him. He has barely eaten for a day. He hasn't washed for three. My God, what must I smell like? What must I look like? Will she even remember me? There've been a lot of soldiers through here in the last nine months. What if she is already spoken for?

It is the silence as he approaches the hamlet that tells him something is wrong. There are field guns firing sporadically further ahead but between volleys, there is nothing but birdsong. As he reaches the end of the track the size of the shell holes and their increase in number tell their own story. In the courtyard he had run into after Windy embarrassed him with Estelle, he climbs on to a pile of rubble and tries to work out the geography. When he finds the hole down into the cellar where the French family once sheltered he calculates where the pub itself used to be. Amongst that pile of stone and dust, he finds bottles and stools and parts of the wooden bar top. The bases of the doorposts are still in place and when he digs around behind where the bar stood he finds smashed crockery, the old till and the photograph of Monsieur Bussiere still in its dark frame with the glass miraculously intact. Next door at their house the roof is completely gone and the top floor has collapsed on to the one below. Some clothes are piled in a corner and he finds a blouse that he thinks he recognises then he wanders out through the back door into the vegetable garden and finds the crosses.

The gunfire from the front intensifies and he sits out the roaring by the pile of clothes in the ruined house. In the silence that follows he hears voices approaching from the way he came and he sprints through the lengthening shadows for the cellar, dragging the ancient door back over the hole for some privacy. There's a single shaft of dying evening light coming through a hole down into the back of the cellar and he sits on the floor beside it. Madame Bussiere, her three beautiful daughters and her sullen son. Five in the family yet only four crosses. He hopes against hope that it was Estelle who escaped, though he knows that the numbers of corpses actually recovered means nothing. Behind him, the wall is lined with wooden crates and he works his way along them until he finds a bottle that is not empty. He smashes the neck and there is no mistaking the smell of wine. He sets it in the shrinking beam of light then stands up and starts to undress. When he is down to his socks and underwear he pauses then he rips those off too, determined to rid himself of all traces of the army. He sits down as naked as the day he was born and takes his time over the first half of the wine. When he stands again he puts on Estelle's brother's clothes, which he has taken from the pile in the house. The trousers, shirt and jumper are a decent fit and tomorrow at the last minute before heading for the coast he will pull his boots back on to his feet. As the beam of light through the hole above finally disappears, he lifts the bottle.

CHAPTER TWENTY-NINE

County Fermanagh, Northern Ireland

4 June 1922

At the end of the boundary wall, Francie turns from the castle and moves back the way they came. He needs to get behind Crozier to have the advantage of surprise. The Crossley at the junction wouldn't fool him. He probably saw the tracks where the Yank had to be dragged off the road into the graveyard. He pins a mental map of where he knows the voice came from then moves through the trees five at a time. He changes the pattern and zigzags between the trunks at odd angles, though still moving gradually towards the opposite side of the castle. When it rises in front of him again he lies in a rain ditch cut through the trees in a straight line. There has been no shouting since he left the boathouse. He slides the rifle off his back. Peter Crozier is a veteran of three wars on two continents. He is a shrewd operator but a greedy one. He shouldn't have ridden in here alone. A man with one arm can't handle a rifle.

It's the horse that gives him up. It snorts to the right of the building and Francie is off on his belly towards it. He lies with his face in the pine needles and begins to regulate his breathing. The first shot is vital. When he rises he must be calm. He must not shake. The horse coughs again and he knows it is not fifty yards off. He rolls sideways until he is tight into the facing wall of the ditch. When the time comes he rises slowly to his knees and peers over the lip.

The boundary wall continues on this side of the castle and tethered halfway along it is Crozier's horse. He drops again, counts to ten, then moves a few feet further along so that his head doesn't reappear at the same spot. He stays above ground slightly longer, then down again and ten feet further and when he rises for the third time he is directly in line with the animal. He keeps his head where it is until he finds what he is looking for. A momentary glimpse at first through a ground-floor window then the black uniform hovers at a second opening higher up. When the voice comes again from the tops of the trees Francie knows that Crozier has climbed to the roof of the building.

'Francie, we can talk. Come on in, Francie, we haven't had a chat for years.'

In the trench, beneath the pine trees, Francie lies still, snippets of their historical conversations ripping through his head like gunfire. Screamed mostly, one-sided always. He memory-maps the sergeant's boots as they move along his belly and back. So many mornings hammered awake. Pissing blood at Messines Ridge from the blows he took to the kidneys. Kick the rat to sleep, kick the rat awake. The Catholic rat, more dangerous than any Hun. He fights an urge to call out. He has something he has long wanted to tell him, something that would hurt Peter Crozier more than any bullet. They have more in common with each other than with anyone else. Crozier could never be British enough for the British and Francie would never be Irish enough for the Irish. We're the same, Peter Crozier. We're just a pair of arseholes that no one wants from the northern end of Ireland.

He rises on one knee to form a stronger platform. He flicks the catch on the Lee-Enfield then pulls the bolt back and pushes it forward as quietly as possible. There is an arched doorway in the wall to the left of the horse and he finds the point just over halfway up and slightly to the right where Crozier's heart will appear. He must let Crozier come on a few feet so that he can't crawl back through when he's hit. His head fills with birdsong from the trees above but then the moment takes him fully and the music is gone, leaving nothing but the rasp of his own shallow breathing. In his peripheral vision, the horse flicks its tail now and then but nothing else on the planet moves. Crozier's head peeps around, lingering in the doorway, then it is pulled back as if he has remembered himself. When he comes again he stops dead in the centre and is silhouetted perfectly in the archway, the big revolver out in front clutched firmly in his only hand. Francie holds his breath and pulls the stock into his shoulder but his timing is off and the roar comes too early and as he hits the ground he realises that the sound has come from further away and he knows that he has been shot.

The searing burn between his jawbone and shoulder tells him he's been hit near the collarbone. As he drags himself along the ditch his breathing is not his own and he starts to choke on blood that he knows is filling his lung. Their voices come clearly as they stalk the place where he disappeared.

'You get him?'

'Right in the neck, Inspector.'

Crozier has picked a man up from the road block on the back of his horse. Of course he has. You got arrogant. You got stupid. It has been a long fucking day, Francie. His path is blocked by a tangle of roots so he checks that both arms are still willing to help then hauls himself upward. The constable has just made the point where Francie fell but there is no sign of Crozier. Francie levels the barrel and yells and the man turns as the bullet catches him, blowing him into the ditch. The bolt is pulled and rammed and Francie faces front but Crozier is already on him from the other side and the rifle is too long and the Webley is being smashed into the side of his head then levelled and fired point-blank through the middle of his chest.

CHAPTER THIRTY

Ploegsteert, Belgium

August 1916

The morning rum ration is doubled for those who have made it back from the midnight raid. It helps dilute the news of five men dead and three unaccounted for. Dead men are hard to take but when they are lost on a raid it feels self-inflicted. Soldiers hate nothing more than bored brass planning pointless daring raids for other people to die on.

There's a nest of wasps over there, Private; why don't you wander over and stick the old chap in it?

Many are full drunk and half asleep when news filters through that Captain Gallagher is one of the dead. One prisoner was taken and no gas was found. The German machine-gun positions were exactly where everyone assumed they were beforehand, given the lay of the land. The raid is announced a success. They are taken out of the line that evening. In the morning they are assembled to be told that notification has been received of Captain Gallagher being awarded the Distinguished Service Order for his actions on 1 July. For conspicuous gallantry in action. The announcement by Lieutenant Lafferty from A Company is met with total silence. There is nothing conspicuous about him now. Apart from his fucking absence.

Back in billet, Francie refuses when Williamson and McClintock tear into the wine. He wants a clear head so that he can work out what to do about Archie. It is the third morning since he disappeared. How far has he got? Where is he going? Every cell in Francie's body is urging him to take off running until he finds him but how can he? Where would he even start? Then the pair of them would have deserted their posts and what good would he be to Archie? Both of them would face a court martial and Crozier will testify that Francie leaving later to meet Archie was clearly part of the plan. He sits alone all day, desperately poring over every eventuality but all roads lead back to the same terrible conclusion. Finding him is the last thing he needs. Archie must remain very much unfound. What he has done won't be forgiven by the army even if he wanders in now of his own accord saying he is sorry and offering to clean all the pots on the Western Front.

When the plonk is all gone Williamson rounds up a posse and they head off to drink what they can find. The rest of the platoon gladly settles in for sleep, relieved to be under a stable roof again.

He takes Annie's last letter out and reads it twice by candlelight. When he closes his eyes she takes him by the hand and leads him under the bridge at the bottom of the brae. They swim naked in the deep dark pool under the archway safe from the rest of the world. She glides towards him, resting her hands on his shoulders before laughing and forcing his head under the water. When he resurfaces she silences him with her mouth on his as she slides her legs around his waist.

You'll look after him. You always do. Just swear to me you won't come back without him.

He gasps upright into the blackness. Breath won't come with no heartbeat and he panics and stumbles further out into space. He trips over something then lands on someone else who swears and bucks until he rolls off and bounces to his feet. He searches desperately for a reference point of light that will tell him that he isn't dead. A shout to his right and a lantern, thank Christ, then another behind it and he can just make out the figures sneaking back to their beds through the ranks of sleeping men. Four come towards him carrying something between them, the horizontal passenger twisting and shouting until the sniggers take them and they dump him on the floor.

Williamson is very drunk and now that he's been dropped on his head he might as well be very angry while he's at it. When he starts to shout his cohort give up and dive for their kits. When he begins naming generals and majors then renaming them bastards and cunts and the scum of the earth, blankets are pulled over faces and no one dares even breathe. Francie joins McClintock in the middle of the stable and they leap on their mate in a bid to shut him up but he is having none of it and when he punches Francie in the balls and tells McClintock what he is going to do to his wife when they get home they have no choice but to leave him to it.

He manages two entire songs before the cavalry arrives to shut him up. A raging rendition of 'The Inniskilling Dragoon' followed by a heartbreaking lament to a girl from County Down, which has them all wide awake and the hairs standing on the backs of their necks. By the time a captain and a corporal from the Dublin Fusiliers burst into the stable half of the platoon is belting out the final chorus while the other half sit weeping for home.

Williamson stands in the middle of the rows of seated men calmly conducting his choir, which has broken naturally into a commendable three-part harmony, and only when the song is finished does he address the captain.

'We have lost our captain, sir. The bravest, fairest man you could ever meet. I am sure you gents have no problem with us singing him an oul song, sir.'

The captain offers his condolences for Gallagher, who he heard was a fine officer loved by all, then spins on his heel and leaves them to it.

As they eat breakfast reminiscing about the stable being transformed into a music hall the night before, the conversation turns to Crozier and why he never intervened. No one has put eyes on him since yesterday just after they were pulled from the front. Francie knows that Gallagher was his last line of defence. Crozier won't rest now until the war between them is over and he will have no intention of losing. No doubt the new lieutenant will be poisoned against Private Francis Leonard the minute his feet touch Belgian mud.

'Any word on Gallagher's replacement?'

'Bit early; should hear something by tomorrow, though.'

'Not a lot of spare officers knocking about.'

'Maybe that is where Crozier is, off getting himself a promotion.'

The thought panics Francie. Surely not? With his record?

They have been filling sandbags with clay for two hours and breakfast, poor as it was, is a distant memory when the rumours start to filter through. A man in custody. Brought in on a supply train by Crozier and an English major. Locked in a shed behind the ammunition dump for the 18-pounders. Lifted yesterday down south somewhere wearing civilian clothes.

The sun is turning by the time Crozier is seen again. It has fairly well set when he calls on the company to form up immediately in full kit outside the stable block. When the mad scramble is finished he puts them through their paces with some basic drill for half an hour to remind everyone who is pulling the strings. When he has them suitably wet with sweat and back to attention he walks the three long lines of men until he finds Francie and stops directly in front of him. He watches Francie for a minute then he moves on to the end of the row and turns to face them all. He lifts his chin so that his voice will elevate before addressing his men at a shout.

'Yesterday morning, Private Archibald Johnston was arrested at a train station in Amiens. He was found in civilian clothing having discarded his rifle, his ammunition and his uniform. Private Johnston has deserted his duty in the face of the enemy. He will remain under arrest until his field general court martial. Cowardice is a disease. It spreads. When found guilty he will be executed as an example, to stiffen resolve and to help maintain some discipline in this battalion.'

He lights a cigarette as he lets the severity of his words work their way from the brains to the shoulders then down into the bowels of his men. He walks back along the middle row until he stands facing Francie again. He takes a deep pull on his cigarette then blows a steady stream of smoke into the younger face just as Francie had done to him outside the whorehouse in Bailleul. When he has stubbed his cigarette with his toe he keeps his eyes locked on Francie's and drops his voice to deliver his final line personally to him.

'There is no place in the British army for cowards.'

CHAPTER THIRTY-ONE

County Fermanagh, Northern Ireland

4 June 1922

Crozier grabs the rifle and hurls it into the trees then scrambles from the ditch. He levels his gun at the body again, refusing to believe that the man he has wanted for so many years is actually dead. The hole in the chest is ringed black from a powder burn as the shot came from so close. The first wound higher up in the shoulder looks fatal in its own right and he smiles at the thought that they killed Francie Leonard twice today. The eyes stare up at him like he has just been woken from sleep but hasn't quite remembered who he is yet, and then there is a low sigh and the chest heaves slightly and Crozier jumps backwards. When he steps forward again he hops down and kicks a leg just to make sure.

'I told you I'd kill you, Leonard, and here you are in a ditch.'

He follows the drain to the fallen constable. The man is still alive but only just. His eyes are half closed and his blood is pooling on the ground all around him. Crozier reasons that they are in the middle of nowhere and that the man will die anyway long before he can receive proper medical attention, and then shoots him in the head. He will send a party in to retrieve the body later with instructions to leave Leonard for the magpies and crows.

Back at his horse he holsters his weapon and has his foot in the stirrup and his hand on the saddle before he sees the girl. She is halfway between him and the gateway to the gardens and she has a Mauser automatic pointed at him. He wagers that he could pull and shoot before she could ever hit him but as he lets go of the saddle and reaches for his holster she puts a round into the ground by his feet and the horse goes berserk. By the time it has calmed and he can drop the rein she is standing not ten yards off with the piece in his face.

'Throw your gun away.'

'He's gone, Annie; we can bring you in now.'

'Throw it.'

'He's dead, Annie. I'm offering you a reprieve so don't be stupid.'

The weapon starts to shake in her hand and she lowers it slowly as her shoulders lift and drop and when the sounds come he knows that she doesn't have it in her.

'It's all going to be grand, Annie. We'll ride back in and let your mother know you're safe.'

He steps forward.

'Shh now, Annie. There's a good girl.'

She raises her eyes and he registers the moment the anguish starts to turn towards something else then she shoots him through the middle of the left foot.

On the ground, he gets his gun into his hand but she is quick and stands over him with her barrel pointing at his forehead.

'I said throw it.'

He tosses it underneath the horse and she walks to it then hurls it over the wall.

'I'm a policeman; they'll hang you for this.'

She stands looking down on him, the gun by her side.

'You're a murderer.'

'Francie had it coming.'

'And Archie?'

'I didn't kill your brother.'

'You killed them both on the same morning.'

When she raises the Mauser he panics and digs his heels into the ground, desperately cycling himself backwards. She stalks him slowly as the fear turns into a frenzy, exhausting him in the dirt at her feet.

'You can't kill me for your brother.'

She raises the gun and points it at his chest.

'Francie was a murderer; you can't kill me for him.'

'Oh, I am not going to kill you for Francie. And I won't kill you for Archie either. I am going to kill you for the old man you whipped and murdered up on the mountain.'

Crozier looks confused and his breathing starts to quicken again.

'You didn't search very hard. We were under his house.'

'I'm an inspector in the police; my men will all be here soon.'

'Not soon enough, Inspector.'

'They'll find you. They know where your mother lives; they'll burn her out and she'll starve in the fields.'

'Burn a loyal woman's house down who sacrificed her son at the Somme? Wouldn't go down too well now, would it, Mr Crozier? And sure nothing in war is more important than propaganda.'

His breath gets trapped amongst his ribs and when he forces it out again it is released in a long dull groan.

'Beg me.'

'I beg you. I beg you, please don't kill me!'

'What has it been like, living for years with one arm?'

He stares at her, confused, his mouth opening and closing like a banked trout.

'Been a bit unbalanced, has it? One side stronger than the other?'

'I am begging you, Annie. Please!'

'I heard you the first time.'

She drops the gun from his chest and shoots him through the middle of the right kneecap. His howls come in waves and she waits patiently for them to settle into a whimper.

'That should even things up a bit for you.'

She untethers the horse and whispers to it while she watches Crozier writhe in agony on the forest floor. When she mounts the animal it relaxes and they trot to him as he drags himself agonisingly towards the drainage ditch.

'Going to be hard to catch me, once I disappear over the border on this beautiful big horse of yours, Inspector Crozier.'

When she reaches Francie's body she dismounts and crouches beside him. He looks no different. His eyes have the same faraway look she saw in them in the early hours when they lay naked together in the Reverend's house.

'Six years, Francie Leonard.'

She rubs her hand across his face, gently closing his eyes.

'But you came.'

She bends down and kisses his lips.

'Thank you for setting me free.'

At the boathouse, she takes lengths of rope and ties the two sacks of money across the horse's flanks. She says goodbye to the dead American then rides through the pine trees towards the main road. From inside the old church she listens to Crozier's howls of rage and agony and watches his men race past her then she mounts up between the contents of the Belfast Banking Company safe and trots out through the castle gatehouse.

On the main road, she stops to make sure that the Specials are all behind her. She will buy luggage to hide the money in when she gets to Ballyshannon. At the port in Sligo, she will sell Crozier's fine horse for good money. Not that she is short of that. Sweat runs off her back and along her thighs and she wipes her eyes with her remaining filthy sleeve. She will be buying new clothes while she's at it. She stares along the road towards Pettigo and beyond to the Rotten Mountain where her mother lives, then she turns the horse around and gallops towards the coast.

CHAPTER THIRTY-TWO

Ploegsteert, Belgium

August 1916

The night after the court martial Private McVitty from D Company, who was one of Archie's guards, came looking for his section. He told them that Archie had been standing in a room at the back of a chateau in front of a Major Crenshaw from the Royal Irish Rifles, Captain Moore from the Inniskilling Fusiliers, Lieutenant Blackwood also from the Inniskillings and an English brigadier-general with a big moustache and more medals than the Catholic Church. Three witnesses were brought forward one after the other: Crozier, who had discovered that Archie wasn't at his post; the corporal who Crozier first raised the alarm to and a Scouse fella from the Coldstream Guards who had apprehended Archie in Amiens. After each gave their evidence Archie declined when offered the chance to cross-examine them. He never opened his mouth until he was cross-examined himself. When asked why he left the trenches he said that he didn't know, that he hadn't been himself. When asked where he was heading when he was arrested he said simply, 'To see the sea.'

Crozier was brought back in towards the end as he had something to add that he felt was relevant. He told the court that Archie had just found out the day he disappeared that he would be taking part in a large-scale action the following night. Crozier felt it was no coincidence that the private had absconded so close to the raid.

The brigadier-general concluded that it was one of the most serious cases of Dereliction of Duty he had ever come across. The death sentence was passed very quickly.

The platoon are kept extra busy the following day for fear of unrest. In the morning they are marched in packs and full kit for ten miles for no reason and on their return sent to stack shells for a detachment of Royal Artillery a mile behind the line. In the evening when they have eaten, Crozier materialises at the stables with Major McIlroy and their new lieutenant, a man called Best from Ballymena, who has been transferred from the Royal Irish Rifles. Lieutenant Best introduces himself in a timid fashion before Major McIlroy addresses the men with a sombre tone. What a difficult time, what an unfortunate crime. Discipline was your only man, discipline was all they had. Private Johnston has shamed himself but also shamed the battalion. It has been decided by fellow officers of the 36th that out of sympathy, and with an eye on keeping morale up back home, Johnston's family do not need to share in his shame. They will be spared the truth of his cause of death. It is also felt that to restore order and to learn the necessary lessons from the betrayal, the firing squad tomorrow morning shall be made up from men from the deserter's own platoon. The selection process will be left in the very capable hands of Sergeant Crozier, who will pick a squad for the task after the evening rum ration has been dispensed.

When the major has departed Lieutenant Best orders the rum ration to be doubled that evening, in some absurd attempt at softening the blow. Always the showman, Crozier waits until the men are drinking the rum before reading the names on his list out one by one in a dramatic fashion. They all know Francie's name is on there, even though Crozier leaves it to the very end for cheap effect. McClintock steps from the line and shouts at the sergeant and lieutenant that you can't fucking send a man out to shoot his best

244

friend, and Crozier scrubs the first name from the list and adds McClintock's instead. Lieutenant Best mumbles something about a ghastly business but it all being for the best and slinks away from the ghastly business.

There is no point in arguing. There is no point in protest. There is no point.

Private McVitty stops by again with his pal Corrigan en route to their night shift guarding Archie. They have a full jar of rum with them and orders to get the prisoner as drunk as a skunk and keep him that way until morning.

'We'll sit up with him all right; don't you worry about that. He's a good kid, he likes to chat.'

'Can you get us in to see him?'

'If it was just us we'd swing it, but there's English fellas on the main door outside. They rotate them all the time so no one gets bought.'

While McVitty and Corrigan get Archie drunk in his makeshift cell, Williamson and McClintock do Francie the same favour in an old dummy training trench under the stars. There is wine, and apple brandy, and something made from pears bought from a farmer that would blow the balls off an elephant. They drink and rant but they know that there is no answer to the equation. Archie is caught fast in the web. The system will not be defeated. Williamson announces that they will all fire wide but Francie explains that if they miss him or wound him, the officer in charge puts one through his head anyway. McClintock agrees that they can never stop the army from killing him once the bastards are hell-bent on doing so, and the most humane thing to do is to shoot their friend properly.

When Francie explodes from the dummy trench just after midnight, bayonet in one hand, spade in the other, McClintock gets hold of his boot just before he can slide off into the blackness. Before Williamson can get to the other leg, though, Francie kicks himself free and is off towards the section of stables where Crozier and the other NCOs are sleeping. They chase after him through the dark, blind, but never lost, as his roars are crisp and easy to follow. They find him lit up in the courtyard baying for Crozier in front of a gathering crowd.

'Come out and fight, you yellow bastard!'

Crozier appears half-dressed and steps forward from the crowd. Francie points at his foe with the short-handled shovel while brandishing the bayonet like a man determined to use it.

'I saw him, hiding in a dugout while the rest of us fought for our fuckin lives.'

Williamson and McClintock launch themselves on Francie from behind, disarming him, then hold him on the cobblestones. Others come forward to arrest him but Crozier gets between them and the men tangled on the ground.

'Leonard's drunk and emotional. I think under the circumstances we can turn a blind eye.'

He stares down at Francie, who struggles with every fibre to get at the man he knows is only showing leniency so that he won't be cheated of tomorrow.

'Get him out of my sight and get him sober. He has a big job to do in the morning.'

Williamson and McClintock lie on top of Francie until the anger has finally died inside him. As they take an arm each and drag him away Crozier turns to address his crowd.

'It is a terrible thing that we must do tomorrow but this is war and war is a terrible thing.'

The dozen rifles are propped along a wooden fence at the edge of the orchard. Williamson and McClintock place themselves each side of Francie. They drank in silence until 03.00 when there was nothing left to drink then they passed out. It is nearly 06.00 now and like most of the men who make up the rest of the firing squad they are still drunk.

Thirty yards across from them stands a solitary post. It has a crude hook protruding from either side at shoulder height. There is a murmuring behind them as those there to watch the execution take their places, blocking the escape route of those there to carry it out.

Francie could barely see when he was woken by a smiling sergeant he didn't recognise. He drained an offered canteen but the water couldn't wet his tongue nor douse the scald in every cell of his being as they took off on the short march. He stumbled often and was aided always by the friendly sergeant with the Belfast accent. The man shouted no orders, just gently made sure that they got to where they needed to be. When they arrived the man produced a hip-flask and wouldn't leave until Francie had drunk its contents.

There are flitters of movement ahead through the apple trees. Lieutenant Best, who will command the firing party, coughs nervously as he walks along the line behind them. Francie can make out the prisoner now, small and hunched between two guards who appear to be holding him up. The chaplain and the medical orderly appear behind them and all five move out from the edge of the trees through the ankle-deep mist. Archie's knees buckle and they have to drag him the final few yards to the post. Someone in the line sobs quietly then another retches. As the guards try to hang Archie on the hooks he breaks in the middle again and Francie's world blackens and he starts to fall but McClintock is there and the rifle is here and he breathes deep and grips its solid construction between his fingers.

When his vision returns he finds Archie, blindfolded and alone, with a piece of white cloth pinned to his heart for them to aim at. Inside his head the dull roar of a river in full flood builds to an unbearable crescendo then it stops suddenly, leaving a total silence that swells in him, forcing his eyes forward out of their sockets, and just as his teeth will surely pop from his jaw he opens his mouth and gasps air and the pressure bursts, leaving space in his head for their voices.

Annie first, laughing as she calls out their names over the din of a waterfall, then Archie spluttering as he tries to stop laughing in order to stop drowning, then his own voice as he crosses the pool and grabs hold of the smaller boy.

I've got you, kid; calm your mind and your body will follow.

Another voice, louder, outside his head and off to the right. The training kicks in and he lifts the rifle to his shoulder.

Archie raises his chin from his chest and tries to spy the sky from under his blindfold. He opens his mouth and yells a single word into the morning.

'Francie?'

Lieutenant Best shouts the final order.

Calm your mind and your body will follow.

He shuts his eyes and pulls the trigger.

AUTHOR'S NOTE

At the Battle of the Somme on 1 July 1916, the 36th Ulster division was the only division of X corps (United Kingdom) to achieve its objectives. The reinforcements planned to bolster them when they had taken the notorious Schwaben Redoubt were never sent forward and by the end of the day, like everyone else, they were routed and back where they started.

In two days of fighting the division suffered nearly six thousand men killed injured or missing. Of the nine Victoria Crosses awarded in the Battle, four were awarded to men from the 36th Ulster division.

Three hundred and six British and Commonwealth soldiers were executed for cowardice or desertion between 1914 and 1918. In several cases, like that of a seventeen-year-old boy from Belfast, the family were not told the truth, perhaps to protect the reputation of the division or of the officers involved.

In 2006 all three hundred and six men were finally pardoned by the British Government.

During the Irish War of Independence many Irish men who had fought for Britain during World War One joined the IRA and fought against their former employers.

The Battle of Pettigo and Belleek was the only occasion in the conflict where Irish and British forces fought each other across defined battle lines. It was also the only time the British army used artillery against Irish forces. It is viewed as the last significant action in the War of Independence.

The border still runs through the village of Pettigo. People live on one side and work on the other without any constraints.

For now . . .

ACKNOWLEDGEMENTS

My sincerest thanks to Elizabeth Foley at Harvill Secker for publishing this book, and to my agent James Gill at United for putting it in front of her. Thanks also to Mikaela Pedlow for her priceless input in the edit. I am eternally grateful to Lieutenant General Sir Philip Trousdell, battlefield-guide extraordinaire, and to my father Dermot for their help and enthusiasm on our research mission to France and Belgium.

There are too many extraordinary sources to acknowledge them all here. However special mention must go to Philip Orr's invaluable *The Road to the Somme: Men of the Ulster Division Tell Their Story*, to the regimental Great War Diary of the 11th Battalion Royal Inniskilling Fusiliers, and to Ernie O'Malley's *The Men Will Talk to Me* interviews with veterans of the IRA.

Of great help also were *bureauofmilitaryhistory.ie*, and the incredible collection of veterans' recordings held by the Imperial War Museum. As were my grandfather Denis Gormley's memories and anecdotes from the battle of Pettigo, in which he fought.

penguin.co.uk/vintage